THE IMMORTAL

A NOVEL

ILOW ROQUE

Publishers Since 1798

THOMAS NELSON PUBLISHERS
Nashville

Published in Nashville, Tennessee, by Thomas Nelson, Inc., Publishers, and distributed in Canada by Word Communications, Ltd., Richmond, British Columbia.

Scripture quotations are from the NEW KING JAMES VERSION of the Bible. Copyright © 1979, 1980, 1982, Thomas Nelson, Inc., Publishers.

Library of Congress Cataloging-in-Publication Data

Roque, Ilow.
   The immortal / Ilow Roque.
      p.   cm
   ISBN 0-8407-6895-8 (pbk.)
   I. Title.
PS3568.0694W4
813'.54—dc20   93-18406
                                                        CIP

Printed in the United States of America

1 2 3 4 5 6 7 – 98 97 96 95 94 93

▼

It is right that this, my first novel, a labor of love, be dedicated to my beautiful wife Sheri, who by the grace of God and to my own great good fortune is as perfect in love as any soul could hope to be this side of paradise.

ACKNOWLEDGMENTS

My first thanks go to my parents, Polly and Rocky, for their love and support, with special thanks to my father for his encouragement early on. Thanks also to my good friend Reb Forté for his early enthusiasm and priceless sense of humor. A heartfelt thank-you to my dear friend, author Marcy Heidish, whose generosity with her time and gifts both inspired and transformed me. Thanks also to my agent Leslie Breed for her care and thorough professionalism, my editors and friends at Nelson for their early and enthusiastic interest in my work. God bless and keep you all.

PART ONE

Jesu, Juva

Then the LORD God said, "Behold, the man has become like one of Us, to know good and evil. And now, lest he put out his hand and take also of the tree of life, and eat, and live forever"—

Therefore the LORD God sent him out of the garden of Eden to till the ground from which he was taken.

So He drove out the man; and He placed cherubim at the east of the garden of Eden, and a flaming sword which turned every way, to guard the way to the tree of life.

Genesis 3:22–24

CHAPTER

1

Montreal, Quebec
October 2, 2065

Dr. Lanning Balcourt stared at his reflection in the mirrored ceiling. From the span of vertical blinds at his side, lines of red light and shadows crossed the bed where he rested partially inclined, his head a tangled mass of dark hair. The light from the adjacent laboratory distorted his high cheekbones, exaggerating the loose folds of skin at the corners of his thin, frowning lips. His face seemed angular, gaunt, emaciated.

Lane studied the eerie play of light and shadows over the prominent ridge of his brow. For a moment, he flashed back to the anxiety he had felt as a young boy, long before the onset of his paralysis, whenever he had glimpsed a mirror in a darkened room. He saw himself now as that same terrified child he had once been; alone in the dark, trembling in his bed, watching the mirror glinting on the wall.

The mirror, it seems to beckon, he cannot look away; the glass holds his gaze like a flame. Outside, the wind moves a tangle of branches against the windowpane. A jaundiced street lamp glow scatters and enlarges leafy shadows on the wall; the looking glass takes on an ominous, liquid sheen like mercury. The child watches a lambent, shapeless vapor unfold like pale smoke at the center of the glass; he sees a child like himself, draped in graveclothes. No, not a child: a changeling—ghoulish, inhuman. Abruptly, he feels the dread weight of the incubus press down on him like a dead corpse from the tomb, silent, sinister, sustained on bat-like wings. The child squeezes his eyes shut, holds his breath. His throat tightens. His heart pounds wildly inside his chest. He feels the very light of his soul being eaten away by a vast darkness he cannot comprehend. He fears this presence, in the mirror, in the room, lingering over his bed . . .

Now, just beyond . . . a sound. Distant. Dissonant. Predatory.

Lane shifted his gaze to the vertical blinds along the wall and eyed carefully the gauzy half-lit interstices. Slowly, his childhood night terrors whitened and faded. With unsure, mobile eyes he searched for movement, for shadows, straining to hear.

Silence.

Lane closed his eyes and made a quick mental search of the laboratory, the dimly lit room just outside his door. The superoptic computer would be idle now, its dark glassy control surfaces—illuminated from within by a dense network of flickering synaptic lights—glimmering faintly like a small, whirling galaxy of fireflies. At this late hour, no anatomical schematics would be hovering like wiredrawn specters over the work stations, no medical/surgical holograms, only a vacant cluster of engineering work stations recessed like hollow craters into the raised drop-tile floor at the center of an all-quiet room.

Something, he had heard something. For a moment the silence had seemed to breathe, shuffle—soft and soft, whispery—low, faint, fleeting. Once more, he strained to hear . . .

Silence.

At once, a vivid picture of the laboratory gathered and clarified in his mind. The WEDGE had been named for its architecture, thirty thousand square feet of sleek black obsidian thrust deep into the grassy soil at one end and strung along a split-level, L-shaped plan. The medical engineers and genetics researchers who had dedicated their lives to the work being done within these walls had teased each other about the way this new building had practically consumed them. The drab, monolithic architecture looked more like a primordial beast than an advanced medical research facility, the very image of Leviathan, they had said, rising from the dark and dolorous realm. In his mind, Lane was seeing the facility's animal research lab clearly now, as if he were gazing through the diagonal glass wall that kept the beasts quarantined from the computers. He studied the dimly lit enclave that stretched out before him like the elongated nave of an ancient cathedral. *Leviathan:*

> *He beholds everything that is high:*
> *He is king over all proud beasts . . .*

A wide, polished stone ramp descended into the lab through the double doors at the far right of the glass partition. The vaulted pale oak ceiling, with exposed joists, gave the highly ordered work area a high-tech, yet Byzantine, feel. Animal cages were stacked like penitentiary cells from floor to ceiling along the facing walls and around the semi-circular apse at the far end of the lab. Along the room's central spine, the tubular ivory lights that hung from the ceiling like an enormous pan flute would be extinguished at this late hour. A colonnade of ruby laser lights, rising from the floor between the cages in slender tapered shafts, bathed the entire area in a languid red glow. Shadows would cover the parallel rows of white rubber-topped lab benches that split the room at its center. The benches would be cleared, the place still; no activity, no work being done, no bustle. Except for the night sounds of animals stirring in their sleep, the great room would be silent.

In her office, Dr. Sandy Benson attended to some of the more mundane requirements of her job as Senior Administrator of the WEDGE: project management, surgical scheduling, the financial and management tar-babies she and her partners loathed, but which she had reluctantly agreed to handle.

From her desk lamp, a cone of yellow light highlighted the straight geometric lines of her short blonde hair, giving it an almost platinum hue. Sandy took pride in her appearance, her trim physique, Nordic good looks. When she was younger, she had given some thought to having her nose fixed, straightened a bit at the bridge, but somehow she just never seemed to find the time. It had taken her forty years before she was finally happy with herself. Now she was content, even with the slight space between her two front teeth. She liked the way it complemented her nose and broke up the symmetry of her face, the "earthy" quality her friends had said it added to the wide warm smile that frequently curled her ample, unadorned lips.

Sandy stretched, stifled a yawn, and pushed herself away from the computer screen. Leaning back in her chair, she clasped her hands behind her neck for a moment's rest, peace.

A sudden burst of shattering glass startled her from her reverie like the blunt shock from a concussion grenade. In an instant, she was up from her desk and out the door. Her heart pounding dread and adrenaline, she instinctively headed for Lane's room, running through the darkened computer lab, her blouse, long white skirt, and sneakers all glowing fluorescently as she passed work stations, keyboards, scopes, monitors, and holographic projection rings; a familiar clutter of idle research equipment and odd-shaped shadows over the vacant tables nearest the wall.

Sandy opened Lane's door and leaned in, "You okay?" she panted. Behind her now came the not quite muffled sound of a jungle in tumult.

"The animals . . . something—" Lane stopped to clear his throat.

Wheeling around, Sandy caught the glimpse of a shadow, like an animal, darting across the floor, disappearing in darkness. *What on earth?* she wondered.

Sandy turned again to her bedridden colleague, "I'll be right back," she said, then stepped out once again into the lab. She slapped the outer light panel with the heel of her palm.

Nothing.

Not good, she thought, moving cautiously toward the ramp, the great iron and glass gate backlit by a fiery night-light glow. She waited for the enormous double doors to rumble open. The great glass barrier disappeared into the wall with a low, labored groan. Instantly, a furious, primal shriek rose into the air, bouncing off glass and tile and metal. One voice, then another, then a third, even more excited, shrill, then more voices, more screeching—the animals' screams rose like a floodwater surge. Sandy froze at the foot of the ramp, immobilized by the bedlam. The madhouse tumult clawed at her ears, growing louder and louder, consuming her in a frenzied howl of animal panic.

She scanned nervously the shadows at the central spine of the lab, the long benchtop cluttered with polymer litter: artificial animal limbs and organoids, synthetic tissue, bone and cartilage prototypes, rows of vivisected animal limbs floating within tubes of dimly lit sanguinous gelatin substrate. Some were exposed to the air, impaled on chrome steel support brackets of various shapes and sizes; others were covered with bell-shaped glass; many were connected by wire leads that sprawled out over the cluttered benchtop like tendril feelers. The entire surface of the benchtop was littered with brightly colored wire and manmade anatomical debris.

Again, a shadow streaked across the floor. This time, it moved away from the bench, disappearing rat-like, under a darkened recess at the foot of the nearest cage. *How many?* Sandy wondered, anxiously checking the floor around her feet. She lifted her head. Awestruck, petrified, her gaze snapped to the movement along the wall. A desperate, uncoordinated motion of forelimbs and shadowy black hands jutted through the cage bars like Gorgon snakes, like overgrowth; seeing this invidious primate jungle born of panic and madness filled her with an ineffable sadness and terror.

Sandy jerked the laser prod off the hook at the end of the bench. Quickly, she twisted the grip to the stun position and stepped cautiously toward the back of the lab. The clamor of metal banging against metal added to the din. Keeping back from the cages, she searched each cell. Eyes. Eyes. More eyes. The beasts' eyes glinted in the light like candled rubies. Heads shaved and deformed by deep neurological implants, the animals' skulls—stitched and scarred—appeared horned and terrible, mottled by grotesque bolt-shaped ceramic plugs. The apes clawed the air as if possessed by demons, screaming madly, as if desperate to escape some unseen inferno.

Sandy felt stale breath rush against her face as she moved deeper into the dank lab. The room seemed to shrink. She stood halfway in, unable to move farther; the lab seemed to close in on her. She struggled to draw a breath.

Another shadow darted across the floor toward her feet. Something snagged the hem of her skirt. She jumped away from the cages and froze. *Get a grip, girl!* she finally admonished herself, her heart pounding in common with the frantic swirl of sound.

Just inside the apse, beyond the last slender column of light in front of her, up high on the wall, she suddenly saw a bulge, a form, something. She stepped closer, straining to make out the figure in the movement and shadows. Around her, the screaming intensified. As she reached the wall, the form swiftly clarified. An ape coiled on the outside of its cage, a huge brutish silhouette, angry, snorting, howling, foam at its mouth, fur standing on end. Sandy felt her own hair rise as she stepped back, keeping her eyes on the contorted, snub-nosed, ebony face. His nostrils flared, lips curled back, long pointed teeth glistened like mottled amber in the red light.

The ape let out a loud guttural cry and abruptly dropped from the cage. Sandy felt her knees buckle. The animal's full weight struck her chest-high and slammed her to the floor. The force of the blow knocked the laser prod out of her hand and sent it spinning toward the bench. Stunned, Sandy was only dimly aware of the sound of the metal prod as it clanged to the floor and of the animal's wild, demonic screams that followed. She tried to get up, but sank back, woozy, the strength gone from her limbs. Motionless, head pounding, ears abuzz, she watched as a large, black simian hand gripped the metal prod. The animal lurched, flailing the titanium bars with its newfound club. The screams, the bell-like noise from the cage, everything seemed distorted, a distant buzzing cacophony echoing in her head. Unable to move, her cheek still pressed to the floor, Sandy watched helplessly as the ape hurled the prod against the wall in yet another wild, violent convulsion.

A shrill, tortured sound rose from the nethermost depth inside the beast and for a long time seemed to hang chillingly in the air. Abruptly, the animal lunged past her, once again snatching up the prod from the floor and swinging it maniacally over its head. The beast's screams seemed to fill the room with demonic malevolence; defiant, lustful, ravenous. Sandy was unable to move; the lab blurred before her eyes. Then, there was darkness. . . .

Lane listened, as if locked within a dream, to the far-off hammering of steel against benchtops, the sound of shattering glass and toppling equipment, and then, briefly, silence. Then there was the sudden raking noise against the cages, approaching in a rapid, metallic arpeggio, like a child's stick against an iron fence. At the door, then, a sudden, loud jolt. A moment later, with a second, sharp *crack!* the heavy door burst open. The red night-light seemed to swirl like smoke behind the dark, man-shaped silhouette now beating its chest in the doorway. The ape lifted the prod high over its head and screamed.

"Code! Code! Code!" Lane gasped, setting off a high-pitched alarm that penetrated the entire facility. The sound seemed to touch off an even more violent rage in the beast. In a flash, the animal leaped onto the bed, swinging the metal prod in a brutal, uncontrollable fury. Lane felt himself fall as the ape loomed over him, the prod red-glinting in the night-light. He watched the metal bar swing down, thought he heard the muffled blows beneath the din, striking his paralyzed, unfeeling body like a sandbag—*Thump! Thump!*—again, then again, the blows coming in a hysterical frenzy.

Something thick and acrid backed up into Lane's throat. Gulping for air, he choked, vomited, spitting blood and bile. He felt nailed to his bed; the ape seemed to swell as it arched its back above him and brought the bar down to crush the side of his skull.

A psychedelic burst of light filled Lane's sight. Countless luminous sparks, bubbling, effervescing, as bright and blue at the edges as magnesium fire, appearing and disappearing, rushed by him like an electric fountain spew. Far below him, a black star's corona swept his vision like the spokes of a vast spinning wheel, drawing him toward its dismal axis with a great swooping blur of sound and color, louder and louder, pressing him, piercing him, transforming him into raw aural nerve until he lost all sense of time, of space, and only the distorted sound itself remained.

▼

The telephone startled Dr. Henri Nakasone from a deep sleep. He fumbled with the alarm clock, slipped on his wire-rimmed glasses, and checked the digital display: Friday, 2:00 A.M.

He recognized the voice on the other end at once. Sandy sounded urgent despite the labored speech, under tight control. Henri found himself standing when he hung up the phone.

A man of medium height with a habit of standing on the balls of his feet, Henri projected the image of a taller man. Now he opened the closet, his long fingers moving deftly over the meticulous arrangement of clothing.

His daughter appeared at the door. The hall light added a sheen to her long, blue-black hair. "Dad, what is it?"

Henri slipped into his shoes.

"Daddy . . . What's wrong?"

"It's Lane," Henri grabbed his keys and stepped away from the closet. His face looked stern, too big for his wire-rimmed glasses. "There's been an accident," he said, as he stepped around his daughter.

"What happened? Is he all right?" Masako moved out of the way and followed her father to the door. Down the stairs they walked in silence, through the darkened house, into the garage.

"One of the animals escaped. I don't know if Lane's going to make it." Henri opened the garage door and continued toward the van without breaking stride, leaving Masako barefoot at the steps. In one motion, he opened the side door, stepped up into the driver's seat, and started the ignition. The van started with a muffled hum.

"WEDGE." He spoke curtly as the seat belts fastened automatically around him. "Emergency."

The headlamps flipped up and flooded the garage with white halogen light. A feeling of odd vulnerability washed through him as Masako stepped gingerly onto the concrete, her hand raised to shield her eyes as she tried to stare past the high beams. He watched his daughter recede as the van backed out of the garage. Against the pitted pavement, the tires made a gravelly, crunching sound that seemed to coil Henri's stomach, as if he were listening to something vital being crushed inside himself. He remembered the last time he felt his guts twist like this; he remembered his wife's funeral almost two years ago.

Henri had always prided himself on being a robust man, oak solid, planted and steady like a mighty tree. Although he was quiet, to his colleagues and especially to his family, strength, control, and power always seemed to radiate through his soft-spoken manner. But that day was different. Remembering it now, he felt himself recede, shrinking into an old man all over again.

He watches the wind tousle his daughter's hair as her mother's coffin is lowered into the vault. She seems so strong and dignified as she tosses her long, raven hair out of her way with a motion as graceful and unaffected as a falling leaf. Seeing his child's strength, he notices a sudden frailty in himself. She leans forward, opens her fist and lets sift slowly through her fingers a handful of sepia dirt. Henri watches the dirt drop into his wife's grave. When the cascade stops, his daughter turns, teary-eyed, from the grave and seems to look at him as if he were a stranger.

For the first time he can remember, there appears a visible space between them, a vast gulf, separating father and child. He feels pulled away from everything and everyone he loves, so far away he can recognize neither his daughter nor the strange, hunched-over old man he feels he has just now become in her eyes. A heaviness presses in on him as he mourns his wife. When he realizes he is also mourning for himself, his eyes fill again. Yet another test of faith, he knows. He tries to pray, but his heart is heavy. He cannot find the words, only Amen. So be it.

▼

Tires squealing, Henri arrived at the WEDGE. He pulled to an abrupt stop at the emergency entrance, scrambled out of the van and into the medical unit, tossing his keys to the guard at the door as he jogged past.

The O.R. doors swept open. *Thank God, she seems to be okay,* Henri thought, catching his first glimpse of Sandy as she issued orders to a team of nurses around Lane's bed. *Lord, grant me balance,* he prayed, as he approached the bedside.

Briefly, Sandy looked up from Lane. A bloodstained gauze bandage sat askew on her head.

"Henri—" the lump in her throat cut her words short. Her eyes filled.

Henri kept silent, gently pushing his way to Lane's bedside. He locked his jaw and drew in a deep breath, studying his colleague's battered and bloodied face. Lane's wild crown of graying black hair was flattened against his head, matted with crusty clumps of blood over his left ear and forehead. A loose flap of skin lay open from the bottom edge of his left eye to his upper lip, leaking a slow, pulsing wash of blood across his cheek. Bone fragments, like tiny shards of glass, pierced the flattened bridge of his nose; the nose itself, no longer in the center of his face, occluded nearly half of the right eye.

Taking the penlight from Sandy's pocket, Henri lowered the side rail and gently pried open Lane's swollen eyelids. First the right, then the left. Lane's pale smoke-blue eyes, normally bright and curious, were now strangely dull and unreactive. Henri straightened himself and handed the penlight back to Sandy, then raised the side rail.

Sandy murmured as she turned to Henri, "Beaten with a laser prod—" again her words stopped short. Her lips were dry. She returned her glance to Lane and drew in a breath to steady herself, hold her ground. "Flail chest, cracked ribs, compound fractures in both femurs, concussion—"

"Internal injuries?"

She nodded. "You can bet he's bleeding somewhere in there."

"I see." Henri looked down at Lane, an ET tube taped to his mouth, the rhythmic drone of his ventilator the only sound audible. "EKG?"

"V-FIB when we got him here. I started him on Lidocaine," Sandy's voice shook. "I don't think we can hold him."

Henri shook his head, "I see. . . . All right, let's start a Pavulon drip. I want to keep him in a coma. We need time to think."

"What do you have in mind?"

"I want to speak with Azeem."

"Henri!" Sandy's voice cracked. She wiped her face twice, frantically, with her hand. "You can't be serious. That procedure is years away!"

"Maybe not." Henri pulled away from Lane's gurney.

Years away, the words echoed in Sandy's mind, taking her back in time; fourteen years ago, back to the early part of the second year of the Balcourt/Nakasone collaboration, back to the very first lab.

She can see it clearly now. She's walking toward it—the early lab—before the move to the WEDGE, before the formation of Lucien Machine Corporation. There's a rustic feel to it, almost like going home. Lane lives inside the laboratory compound, a modest, three-story, ivy-covered stone building located on a small hillock on the perimeter of the McGill campus.

She looks up at the massive crystal sundial, reaching thirty feet into the air, jutting toward the sky from the center of the lawn in front of the lab.

The students call it Gentle Ben after Big Ben in London—gentle because it remains silent with the passing of each hour. It's composed of a special crystal composite which, while being both stronger and more transparent than glass, nonetheless refracts a multicolored shadow that continually sweeps the grounds, illuminating the lawn with a clockwork rainbow.

A smile creases her face as she passes through the shadow and then stands at the door of the lab, the inner sanctum.

The door opens and she surveys the cluttered room, filled with computers, medical equipment, and research animals, a wondrous mix of sterile machines and caged fauna. Someone has knocked over a Styrofoam cup and spilled coffee over the surface of one of the black rubber-topped lab benches. The coffee puddles on the tile floor. Around her, the bookshelves seem to sag from the weight of too many ideas. She looks at the chalkboards, the abandoned jackets on the swivel chair backs, and the editorial cartoons, teasingly altered by the team to poke fun at its various members, pinned on the bulletin boards.

She shares her love for this old lab with the man in the wheelchair at the center of the room. As usual, he's surrounded by his team. Most are sitting on the floor at his feet, like acolytes, their faces raised to him in various expressions of awe and wonder. One stands beside him, frantically transcribing some painfully subtle mathematical nuance onto the dusty chalkboard. There's a lively discussion. She understands how much Lane enjoys his own quarters. This rustic old lab gives him at least the illusion of independence. She's convinced the abstract concept of personal space has lost its abstraction for Lane. Territory becomes so much more important to a man who cannot feel his own body.

Lane. She sees him slumped in his high-backed wheelchair like a child at his father's desk; everything around him seems to dwarf him. Still, his mind is unbelievably clear, focused with an almost superhuman intensity. They had said Dr. Balcourt's was the most gifted sublunary mind the world had ever known. A cosmic intelligence, a man whose intellect, they said, probably far surpassed that of Newton, Goethe, and Einstein. Sandy watches him work and she believes. She feels exhausted just trying to keep his pace, despite Lane's terrible physical challenge. To him, the simplest tasks pose insurmountable obstacles.

The fact that he is a quadriplegic puts a burden on everyone—willingly taken. Lane's ALS is a baptism, Henri tells her. Amyotrophic lateral sclerosis—Lou Gehrig's disease—a motor neuron disorder that gradually destroys all muscular control. A baptism of fire, she tells herself. Over the years she watches the stress bring the team closer together.

Like the sorcerer's apprentice, Sandy struggles to keep up while Lane continues to rise higher and higher, reaching into an abstruse ether of intellect that only he truly understands, soaring far above the enormous constraints placed on him by his disability. She sees his extraordinary commitment to the work, the long grueling hours he spends in the lab. His life affects her. Like *everyone else, she can't help loving this man who presses on doggedly, day after day, year after year, in the face of his disabilities, unable to move even the smallest finger on his hand.*

She's standing right beside him in that old lab when Lane makes his first experimental observation of this session. He calls it The Genesis Experiment. In one of his early papers, "COPS: the Dynamics of Complex Organic Process Synthesis," Lane anticipates that the Krebs Cycle can be reproduced using inanimate compounds that had been molecularly altered. His COPS paper predicts that specially irradiated polymers can be shown to break down complex sugars, releasing energy to do productive work. In the Genesis case, the process mimics the contraction and expansion of living muscle fibers.

She's there, unable to move, transfixed. She's aware, for the first time in her life, that she is part of an extraordinary, historic moment. Wide-eyed, she watches as an inanimate, molecularly altered plastic mass responds to a weak electrochemical pulse as if it were a living organism.

The team forms Lucien Machine Corporation. Tactile prosthetics follow soon after. A silent partner in Geneva provides the vast capital and computer resources required to make Lane's dreams a reality. The press fastens onto the work, the story is hard currency in the advertising game. In the States, Madison Avenue plays it for all it's worth: THE LAME WALK! THE BLIND SEE!

Soon even the members of the team talk in terms of "medical miracles." It's infectious; everybody expects the miraculous.

Miracles. Lane had been working exclusively on the final phase: the transfer procedure. Maybe one miracle too many . . .

The transfer. She remembered first hearing about it from Lane. The transfer was his all-consuming passion.

"Take the ear, for example," he says during their very first meeting. His labored speech makes Sandy uneasy. His tone is pained, hoarse; the words come in strained gulps as he fights for breath. "There are three sets of instructions required to produce the human ear—"

"Genetic instructions?"

"Of course," he croaks, obviously annoyed with the undergraduate interruption. "Anyway, the first set creates the ear and describes gross morphological structure. The second set establishes the physiology and describes the functional characteristics of the ear. What does an ear do exactly? The third set describes the support biology necessary to sustain the ear within the biological system."

Sandy nods. "I'm with you. What does it look like? What does it do? How is it supported?"

Lane rasps excitedly: "Listen! Now imagine the entire human system defined in this way—all the way down to the submolecular level. Much of the genetic instruction code can be completely bypassed since the synthesis doesn't require a living system to create it through normal reproductive means, or a living system to sustain it through normal metabolic means. The *synthesized system isn't subject to biological decay since it's not alive. It looks alive—behaves exactly as it would if it were alive—but it's completely synthetic." Lane's eyes seem afire. His chest heaves as he works to catch his breath. "That's my dream. The future. The final phase."*

Sandy remembered it all. It had been a strange ride these last fifteen years. Now, she looked into Henri's dark, resolute eyes set under wide, bushy eyebrows inverted like quarter moons. "It's your call, Henri. You know you've got my cooperation . . . no matter what your final decision is." She wanted to say something else, something vaguely tugging at her just beneath the surface.

"Good." Henri turned and started for the door. "Stay with him," he said over his shoulder, "I'm going to get Azeem on the horn."

Unable to put her feelings into words, Sandy watched in silence as Henri left the unit.

Henri entered his office and collapsed in the chair behind his desk, rubbing his face wearily. He wiped his eyes clear and touched the COM panel. "Patel."

The phone rang twice before a groggy voice answered the line. "Hello?"

"Azeem," Henri began hurriedly, "Henri Nakasone. There's been an accident. Dr. Balcourt's been hurt. I need you to get down here right away."

"But, Dr. Nakasone—"

"Azeem, we need you here immediately."

"I understand." Azeem cleared his throat.

"I'll be in the medical unit." Henri ended the call without further explanation. He pushed himself away from the desk and paused, turning his chair to face the illuminated grounds. Slowly, he stood and leaned against the window, gazing out at the exquisite rock garden below, a tribute to his Japanese heritage. *Nihonjin.* Henri looked down at the rows and rows of perfectly straight lines, meticulously raked across the sand, defining the vacant intervals between filled spaces—wide, empty spaces around the few moss-covered stones and boulders emerging from the striated sand like an archipelago from a placid sea.

"*Wa,*" he whispered to himself in his native tongue, searching his heart for the harmony he'd just pronounced. He tried to silence the voices warring inside his head by putting himself in the presence of the Lord. He waited for his prayers to emerge from the confusion like the stones from the sand, but ever since Martha's death, his heart-thoughts had seemed blocked somehow, unable to take their form in words. His mood had been too elegiacal, his mind too dark, forlorn, crowded more with fear and apology than with true Christian supplication. There was a difference between prayerful meditation and just plain talking to yourself, he knew.

Most unwanted, he thought, finally, his mind resigned to the decision he now felt forced to make. He drew in a deep breath and stepped out from behind his desk to return to the medical unit.

Amen, Henri'san. Amen.

The unit's automatic doors opened with a quiet sweep. Inside, Henri spotted Sandy speaking with one of the nursing team in the glassed-in observation room. Except for Lane's unconscious body and the electronic life-support equipment, the room seemed strangely stark. The rhythmic drone of a ventilator was the only sound in the O.R. Henri stepped into the observation room and gave Sandy an inquiring glance.

She shook her head, "We've got him stabilized, that's about all I can say."

"If you'll excuse us for a moment," Henri said to the male nurse standing at Sandy's side. He waited for the big man to leave and then closed the door behind him. Henri looked at Sandy soberly. "Azeem's on his way."

Sandy kept silent.

Henri checked his watch: 3:00 A.M. "If you could get the surgical team ready . . ."

She nodded.

"And the body shop," Henri added, thinking out loud. "I don't want to keep him under electronic capture any longer than I have to."

Body shop . . . capture, Henri considered what he was up against. So many people involved, overwhelming opportunities for error: surgical error during disengagement; design error from the technologists in the prosthetics lab—the body shop—responsible for manufacturing the world's first neural synthetic humanoid; computer error from the engineers responsible for capturing and then maintaining Lane's consciousness as a disembodied electronic spirit within the vast memory of the Sony Solar 2000, the 1.7 billion dollar superoptic computer that would now carry this team to staggering heights on a living pulse of coherent laser light.

Sandy reached for the phone directly behind her. "Okay," she spoke over her shoulder, "I'll get the techs on the set-up right away. I'll do the prep myself," she turned and repeated the instructions to the O.R. technologist then headed for the observation room door.

Passing through the O.R., Sandy approached Lane's bedside, her gaze drawn to the jagged pattern scrolling on the cardiac monitor. An unwelcome weight seemed to press down on her shoulders. She turned from the bed and headed out of the room.

Leaving, Sandy bumped into a familiar bearded face: the man the team had affectionately dubbed the "Karachi kid." Azeem Patel froze in the doorway for a moment, his hair pulled back in a ponytail, dark puffy circles under his eyes, his face uncharacteristically pale. "I'm scared," he said finally, a thin layer of sweat filmed his brow.

Henri stepped under the bright lights in the surgical amphitheater exactly as he had countless times before: elbows bent as if he were balancing his orange-yellow stained hands, careful to keep them sterile. The surgical nurse met him at the door and after a ritual toweling off, nimbly stretched two sets of clear elastic gloves over his hands.

Routine, Azeem lied to himself, fighting the nausea that now tormented him in waves. He followed Henri and Sandy into the O.R., taking his place at the computer's V-shaped control console. Azeem nervously adjusted his seat, his heart fretting the two surgeons' determined approach toward the motion platform that kept Lane's body strapped in and completely immobilized, his neck elevated at an odd forty-five degree angle and locked securely in place.

The laser microsaber stood poised at the ready, hovering over Lane's shaved head like an electronic praying mantis. Lane's shaved body, stained orange with Betadine and completely encased within a sterile, clear, plastic film, looked frail and vulnerable, like a pithed frog suspended within the sparkling steel gimbal rings of the immense operating table.

Azeem swallowed hard, waiting for the computer to confirm his last instruction. The computer responded: GLOBAL NEUROSYNTHESIS PROCEDURE: SURGICAL CAPTURE ROUTINE. SYSTEM READY.

"We're ready," Azeem announced.

"Go ahead and calibrate," Henri nodded toward Sandy.

Azeem watched as three ruby-red laser beams extended like brilliant rapiers from what looked like the snout of the microsaber. Slowly, three separate dull spots appeared on Lane's scalp, merging into one much brighter red dot as the microsaber traced its intended incision path over the surface of Lane's shaven head, leaving a ghostly negative outline on Azeem's retina as he watched. He blinked his eyes and tried to refocus on the computer monitor in front of him.

Sandy read the alpha-numerics text displayed on her own surgical screen: MAGNETIC RESONANCE IMAGING SYSTEM ACTIVATED.

"We're good," she said with a nod.

"Azeem?" Henri asked.

Azeem's voice cracked. "We're set, sir."

"Let's get the image up," Henri said.

"Ready the ring." Sandy spoke her instructions maneuvering the doughnut-shaped MRI ring into position like a giant constricting iris around Lane's head. The ring twisted closed to within a distance of three and a half feet around his skull, leaving ample space for the microsaber to pass unimpeded.

Instantly, an enormous hologram of a human brain appeared in the empty space over the operating table, rotating slowly, magnified seven times its actual size. "I'm going to administer the serum," Sandy said, injecting a chemical contrast medium into Lane's carotid artery.

Just as suddenly as it had appeared, the holographic image vanished, replaced by a brilliant panoply of primary colors that translated the metabolic workings of Lane's mind. The abstract outline of the brain seemed to bloom with vivid, shapeless colors gathering and fading within its boundaries, at times glowing red like smoldering coals.

Henri paused for a moment, studying the hologram before him. "Give me a Cartesian overlay." He watched as a three-dimensional reticulated grid surrounded the image of the brain. "Okay," he turned to Azeem, "set the origin and recalibrate."

The image of the disembodied organ rotated slowly until its central *sulcus*, the seam that split the cortex into two distinct hemispheres, was positioned in a direct line relative to Henri.

"Good." He nodded, his breathing tightening. Henri stepped away from the table and looked around the O.R. at the nurses and surgical technologists, at Sandy and Azeem, their faces betraying the tension and concern for the man strapped down, so helpless before them. "Okay, before we begin, I want you all to know that no matter how this turns out, the decision to go ahead with this—" he paused and drew in a deep breath, "this experimental procedure is mine and mine alone. We are all family here. We are here to give Lane the very best we can give him."

He paused again, searching the expectant faces of his surgical team. He felt a strange complex of emotions weigh down on him like a heavy tangled web: concern for his battered colleague, for *their* work, for the superhuman efforts made by these same men and women around him now, for all the time and labor invested, the intensive hours, the years they all had spent to get to just this point.

Henri felt different somehow. He had built his entire career caring for the sick and disabled, inspired by a vision of God in the people for whom he had cared. But this time everything was different. His actions now seemed to grow out of a new and peculiar self-interest. This time he had a personal stake. Without even realizing it, he wanted this transfer to work not just for Lane, but for him. Rising to motivate his troops, Henri omitted absently his customary pre-op invocation. Now, instead of focusing on his commitment to God, as was his custom, his mind turned only on his commitment to his work.

"We've got a job to do—*girl.* We do what we must. Let's get it done." Henri turned abruptly to the troubled anesthesiologist. "Doctor?"

"Ready on this end." The anesthesiologist snapped back into focus and read the pulsing digital screen before him, "B.P. is ninety-six over fifty-six, pulse holding steady at eighty-eight."

"We start," Henri said, his mouth dry as he stepped closer to the table. "Drills." His voice tensed as he worked on one side of Lane's head while Sandy operated on the other. The high-pitched whine of the two bone drills rang out through the room.

Henri returned the bone drill to the tray. "Screws." The scrub nurse unrolled a sterile cloth containing seventeen chromium steel screw bits and placed it on Lane's chest.

"Let's get these in place," he said, pausing as Sandy selected the first screw bit and twisted it into the right frontal section of Lane's skull. Both surgeons repeated the procedure until six screws protruded from the top and sides of Lane's denuded skull.

Henri turned and gave Azeem a reassuring nod. "Let's take his top down." Again Henri drew in a deep breath. *Akirame,* he reminded himself—*cut off all feeling, surrender . . .*

Azeem spoke some orders into his star-set and instantly a single brilliant blue-white laser beam appeared, a flaming sword between the three ruby-red calibrating beams, and began to cut into Lane's scalp, searing the incision as it cut.

The laser scalpel made a faint sizzling sound as it cut through the flesh and bone, disturbed only by the rhythmic sounds of the ventilator and the low-pitched moan of the microsaber's power supply. Azeem tried desperately to control his nervous stomach as the sweet-sick smell of burning flesh filled his nostrils like smoke from an ancient and unholy immolation.

Slowly the microsaber made five precise incisions into Lane's head. Sandy called out each incision as it was completed. "One circumferential incision, transversing both left and right parietal and frontal regions. . . ."

Henri studied the incision. He felt his hands sweat underneath his elastic gloves, his heart pounding. A tremor he'd not known since medical school shook his hands. He felt dizzy, his mind flashing from English to Japanese. This time the Japanese word for "endurance" held his thoughts. *Gaman,* pronounced the quiet voice within. He tried to clear his mind, checked meticulously the work before him, searching the seared wounds through the magnifying lenses that hung over his eyes like a welder's goggles.

Azeem looked over at the table, watching in horror as Henri and Sandy both pawed and probed Lane's blood-drenched skull, first with light-pens, then with cautious exploring fingers. Lane's shaven head, completely stained with blood and Betadine, now showed the black, slow-bleeding laser cuts through flesh and cranium. His head had been sliced roundabout the hatband and then neatly quartered to a space completely through the back of the head, and in front, straight through the center of his nose and filtrum to a spot just above the top of his lower jaw. A single incision running down the center of his skull split the top of his head into two hemispheres. Azeem struggled to steady himself. His own head began to teeter.

"Okay, I'll remove the bone," Henri said, startling Azeem, who snapped his attention back frantically to his console, fighting a new wave of nausea.

Azeem entered the control instructions, too ill to return his gaze to the gruesome surgical procedure taking place less than three feet from his right shoulder.

Henri held his hand out. "Grips."

The scrub nurse slapped a tool that resembled chrome silver vise-grips into his hand. He attached the grips to the forwardmost bit at the top of Lane's head and gave it a sharp, violent tug. The left top of Lane's skull came off with a loud sucking *pop,* exposing the milky covering of the *dura mater.* He dropped the bloody bone fragment onto the surgical tray and repeated the procedure with a new set of grips, first exposing both hemispheres of Lane's *cerebral cortex,* then the *medulla oblongata,* and finally, after snipping the optic nerves with scissors and removing both eyes from their bony orbits, the forebrain.

Henri stepped back away from the surgical table and exchanged somber glances with Sandy. He turned back and stared at the network of blood vessels throbbing beneath the gray-white *dura mater* that enveloped Lane's brain in a milky sac now glistening with blood and fluid. The thin membrane revealed the folded *sulci* of Lane's brain just beneath its transparent surface.

Henri stepped forward. "Scalpel." Pinching the dura at the top center of the brain with one hand, Henri used the scalpel to make an incision the length of the organ, front to back. The *dura* spread open like a ripe cocoon, revealing the glistening surface of the brain.

Sandy leaned in, slid both hands between the dura and the brain and peeled the tough elastic membrane down around the cortex, her hands making sucking sounds as she exposed the folded, blue-gray organ. She stepped back and peeled off one set of gloves.

"Are we ready to begin the capture?" Henri asked,

Azeem swallowed dryly then croaked, "Ready."

"Sandy, give me a cellular MRI," Henri said, wiping his forehead with the back of his forearm.

She turned to her console and switched the scale from seven times magnification to that of one micron to the inch. "You've got the frontal lobe," she said with her head down, staring at the surgical monitor.

The hologram of Lane's brain flickered and then changed shape from the recognizable outline of his brain to a strange, twisted topography that resembled an alien moonscape: strange elongated peaks and valleys, a dense, distorted, brush-like, sawtooth geometry.

Sandy raised her head and watched as Henri leaned in through the constricting iris of the MRI and studied the exposed organ. "Set the grid," she instructed Azeem, as Henri withdrew from the iris and nodded. Immediately, an array of fine lines covered the phantom image that floated over the table.

Henri turned to Azeem. "Can we watch the capture matrix?"

"Overhead," Azeem answered, nodding toward the hologram. He spoke a few instructions before an array of test numbers flickered into focus and began to scroll like a ticker tape just above the hologram.

"Is everything ready?" Henri asked, surveying the room. He counted an affirmative nod from everyone present before he gave the word. "Let it begin."

Azeem adjusted himself in his seat and activated the laser microsaber. The neck of the electronic scalpel telescoped to a position over the region where Lane's forehead had once been. Its exact location in the three-dimensional space over Lane's brain was traced precisely on the grid over the magnified image with a flashing white cursor.

"Cue the laser," Henri prompted.

Instantly a razor-thin beam of light projected from the snout of the laser and slowly changed colors from red to blue to green. The light sequence persisted, recycling back and forth as the microsaber shifted its position imperceptibly, the flashing white cursor moving slowly over the peaks and troughs of the hologram the only evidence of its movement.

Henri raised his eyes to the matrix of numbers that would ultimately form the life map of Lane's consciousness. The array scrolled furiously across the screen overhead.

"Well?" he asked. "What's going on?"

Azeem cleared his throat. "So far, so good, sir," he said without taking his eyes from the monitor in front of him.

▼

Twelve hours into the operation, Henri scanned the masked faces in the room, waiting for the final word from Azeem. Doctors, nurses, technologists, everyone looked tense, anxious. Stress had turned the O.R. into a sweatbox, and perspiration beaded and filmed their foreheads.

Again, he let his gaze fall on Lane's bloody corpse. Henri felt his own jaw lock, his pained, involuntary grimace magnifying the taut, tortured expressions of those who now surrounded him. He stepped away from the operating table and looked over at Azeem.

Azeem's brow furrowed in intense concentration, deep, dark circles hanging like swollen bags under his dark, bloodshot eyes. He jumped as the microsaber switched off with a loud crack, recoiling into a resting position several feet away from Lane's neck. Everyone held their breath.

"Okay, the capture's ... the capture is complete," Azeem announced finally without looking up. "Twelve hours, twenty-seven minutes!"

"The map?" Henri asked nervously without taking his eyes from Lane's neck.

Azeem paused a moment while he studied his monitor. "Yes," he said finally, "we got the map. It's good, sir, the map is good. No glitches. The data's clean. I think we've got a capture here." Azeem beamed as everyone in the room broke into a loud cheer.

Azeem stepped out from behind his console. His eyes went to Lane's decapitated body at the center of the room, the brain stem picked completely clean from the spine's glistening tip. Faint blue coils of smoke and steam rose from the body and vanished into the air. Again, Azeem's nose filled with the acrid smell of charred flesh. The body seemed to waver before him. The room receded and began to spin.

Quickly Henri reached out, catching the young computer engineer as he swayed helplessly toward the spar-like point that jutted from the flayed, bloodstained vestige of what had only hours ago been Dr. Lanning Balcourt's neck. There was a long, anxious pause before anyone spoke.

"It begins," Henri said quietly.

Chapter

2

"You're wondering why on earth you ever let me talk you into doing this, aren't you?" The archbishop's voice behind her made Carla MacGregor turn. He read the anxiety on her face. "I wish I could say something more to make you understand how important this is."

"I think you've said enough already, Alejandro," Carla answered quietly, her eyes drawn to the white tab of his clerical collar. *Opposite ends of the earth,* she reminded herself—he, from the Catholic clergy; she, a Protestant with a Ph.D. in the biomedical sciences. But, then again, she had grown enough in her own faith to know that even the most opposite of ends must find their connection somewhere. Their connection was the Cross. Although, exactly how the archbishop had managed to balance the worldly affairs required of his high office with the heavenly affairs of the heart, required of the lowly religious desiring to live the devout life, remained a mystery to Carla.

Mysteries, complexities, enigmas—the sum and substance of the Catholic faith as far as she was concerned. And her friend Torrez was no exception. Carla had always perceived that here was a man made of enigmatic stuff. She rose to her feet and impatiently raked back her short dark hair. The archbishop quietly closed the door and went to his desk.

Torrez was her longtime friend. More than ten years had passed since Carla's husband first introduced her to his strange new friend, this earthy old archbishop. Working as Senior Environmental Biologist for the Metro Water District in Mexico City before the big quake, her husband had frequent contact with the politically active Torrez. They had worked closely together to establish a potable water supply for the network of base communities that the archbishop was busy spreading all over Central and South America. It had proved timely work. The earthquake had prompted riots and unrest and a mass exodus from the major population centers to the countryside. The pandemonium had spread worldwide. All over the globe, the cities were dying.

A deep and lasting friendship had blossomed among the three of them in those early days. The archbishop's companionship and caring had helped Carla through her most difficult hours. He was the one who had brought her here to this tiny base community in Pachuca, to the children's hospital.

She thought about it now. So much time had passed since her arrival in this open ecumenical community of believers that at times it was difficult for Carla to tell who was helping whom. Yes, they both acknowledged an abiding affection, a deep familial respect for each other, a compassion informed by a mutual love of God that transcended mere denominational differences. But this "favor" was changing all that. Recently Carla had felt put upon. An unexpected and unwanted burden of responsibility was now the cause of a new and totally unforeseen strain on their friendship.

Carla knew the archbishop well; she knew every shading of his voice. His words could not quite mask his own frustration and concern. Lately, he seemed preoccupied. The scarlet piping on his black robe was the only trace of color on this white-haired old man whose face was normally florid from the sun. Today, his face seemed drained. The long lashes of his dark-rimmed eyes, like her own, seemed unusually heavy at the corners. He sat down, gathering his robe, and pulled his chair twice closer to his unadorned pale oak desk.

"The papal legate spoke of a secret consistory. Would you please tell me what's going on here, Alejandro?" Carla's tone had an uncharacteristic edge—hard, skeptical. She sat down in the stuffed armchair at the front of his desk and waited for the archbishop's response, absently reaching for the abraded leather armrest, but then resisting the temptation to finger the chair's fraying upholstery. She sat back and folded her hands impatiently on her lap.

Torrez slid his reading glasses down his nose. His eyes went from the rolled papal bull she held in her clasped hand to the open folio of papers on his desk. "The consistorium, my dear, is . . . *how* it's done."

He seemed to go out of focus momentarily as he leaned back in his chair; slowly, he brought his fingertips together in a steeple at his chin. The archbishop paused for a moment, then said, "Look at it as you would any other contract for hire. The Vatican has merely contracted with you to do some research in an area in which they have some interest and you have some expertise," he thumbed through the papers on his desk and nodded. "Don't get caught up in the formality of the papal edict. It's boilerplate, really."

"In case you've forgotten, Alejandro, I am a Protestant. I'm not at all comfortable with all the Catholic . . ." Carla struggled to find the word.

"Our ways seem strange, I know." Torrez smiled apologetically. "Of course you're uncomfortable, but then again, I'm not really sure the Holy Father—the pope—is all that comfortable with the formality either.

Carla's shoulders seemed to sag. She moved to the edge of her chair. Her own words echoed in her mind. *I'm not at all comfortable.*

Torrez continued, "Try to remember, Carla, my colleagues in Rome are only interested in your scientific credentials. Obvious as it seems to an old catechist like me, I sometimes forget that our ways may at times appear somewhat mysterious to those who don't share our faith. Perhaps it would relieve you to know that at least at the organization level there's nothing really so extraordinary about this consultancy of yours. Think about it; if the Vatican relied only on Catholics to keep it apprised of new developments in the sciences, we'd soon find ourselves in rather slim company. Unfortunately, there are not many world-class Catholic scientists left. I mean," the archbishop chuckled, "Galileo's been dead a long time."

"Not that he would care to speak on behalf of Vatican benevolence," Carla added wryly.

"Be fair, that was a long time ago, Carla. God's will, we've all grown since then. We have nothing but the highest respect for the dignity of the human sciences." Torrez returned the papers and his glasses to the desk. His gaze wandered to the faded, fourteenth-century replica wood panel of the Crucifixion hanging on the wall next to his bookshelf.

"I say this Balcourt thing's got them worried," Carla said.

Abruptly, the archbishop turned his gaze on her. "No doubt. But keep your eyes and ears open. I've told you about my dealings with Verrechio before. He's a notoriously political animal. He keeps his agenda—" the archbishop finished his sentence by folding an imaginary hand of cards close to his breast. His eyebrows lifted, seeking her understanding. Content with having made his point, he pushed himself back away from his desk.

"But why me?"

"Let's just say I've not been altogether silent when it comes to voicing my pleasure with your voluntary dedication to our community here. I might have said something about your background—"

"You mean you sent them my *curriculum vitae*," Carla snapped mildly.

The archbishop laughed, "Ha! You see, we're all political animals." Sliding his leathery hands into his soutane, he continued, "Yes, Carla, I must confess, I may have done a *bit* of lobbying for you when I found out about this particular opportunity."

Carla unrolled the document and read: "Vatican . . . Counsel . . . for . . . Scientific . . . Affairs," she translated with some difficulty the Latin of the papal bull.

Again Torrez lifted his eyebrows, nodding his head in pleasant surprise, watching, preoccupied, the red papal imprint disappear as Carla re-rolled the document and once again laid it across her lap. She shook her head. "I don't like this, Alejandro."

Torrez drew in a deep breath, "It is a great honor and, may I remind you, no small amount of money."

"This is not why—"

"Nonetheless," he cut in with a gesture of his hand, "it *is* a prestigious offer," he said. His frown was mildly impatient.

"And if I refuse?"

Slowly, he rocked back in his chair. Again, he brought his fingertips together. This time the steeple crossed his lips. He waited a moment before he spoke. "I would have to counsel my dearest friend against making such a hasty decision." He held her gaze. "We may be able to work this assignment of yours to our advantage."

Carla thought she saw a harsh gleam appear for the first time in his eyes. "But this is not why I came here. I came here to be with the children."

"Perhaps that's no longer where you are needed, my dear. Especially now. Politically speaking, Rome may be the best place for you." He watched her stand and walk to the window.

After a moment's pause, she turned around to face the archbishop. "If I go, I go for you. I could not care less for your politics or anybody else's."

"Ha!" Torrez smiled wide. He put his hands on his knees and spoke as he stood. "You do me more honor than I deserve."

Carla glanced back at the window. "Rome—the pomp, the circumstance—"

"How could it compare to this?" Torrez' arm rested on the glass, a starched white cuff peeked out from the dark sleeve of his soutane.

Carla looked beyond his well-tanned fist, out through the second-story glass wall. Her heart filled, as if anguished by a sad, almost musical compassion welling up within her, taking form like a tragic orchestral overture.

Sacred music. Above, clouds moved slowly. Overhead, the sky seemed to tighten, changing hues from a diffuse white to pewter and then to the odd green that comes just before a storm. She glanced out over the land and let out a long, lingering sigh.

To the east, at the junction of three vast, manicured lawns, a cluster of modest terra alba adobes wedged into a dense stand of tropical trees and floral gardens. Several villagers had gathered around an electric flatbed cart stopped on the narrow, stone-paved crossroads. A floppy straw sombrero nearly concealed the old cart driver's face. His long gray hair streamed in the breeze. His hands punctuated an animated flow of words. As Carla watched, the old man removed his hat, placed it over his large belly, and rocked back and forth in laughter. She smiled. That was the thing about this place. She loved the wise simplicity here that seemed always to give her more than she could ever hope to give back. The base community was a place for spiritual renewal and faith. Here people were family; they were kinfolk. And this was her place, with them. *How can I leave?*

The archbishop followed her gaze. "These little villages—for you, for me, they *are* our mission."

"Yes." Carla turned to him again. "Always—*yes.*"

The archbishop nodded his head, his voice quiet, reassuring, "Even so, you honor us all by offering your help, Carla."

"These people are my *heart*," she looked back out the window and touched her breast. "Offering my help—you make it sound like this is something I'm doing because I want to when the truth is I'm very upset with you, Alejandro. You know how . . . how *ambivalent* I am about leaving all this. You're asking me to go back to something I left behind long ago. I know, you say it's only for a short while, but it feels like I'm being ripped away from every—" her voice caught, she coughed to clear her throat; her eyes filled. Her thoughts went to her husband. (Ten years since their friend Torrez had come to her with the fateful news.)

> *The archbishop stands at her door; his tone is elegiacal, "I'm afraid I've come with bad news. Terrible news, Carla."*
>
> *She opens the screen door and, in a daze, steps out onto the porch. Somehow she hears his words before he speaks them. "It's Jay."*
>
> *A wave of anxiety crashes over her, through her, she cannot speak, she cannot cry. After a long, stunned moment, she finally dislodges the word from her throat, "How?"*
>
> *The archbishop's eyes are wet with compassion, "Three of them . . . all Metro Water District people . . . evidently out checking fill levels . . . a remote mountain reservoir . . . something happened . . . the plane went down. I'm so sorry, Carla. If there's anything—"*
>
> *Carla cannot hold his gaze. In an instant she feels she'll never be able to look another living person in the eye. "Precious in the sight of the LORD is the death of His saints," she mutters, giggling inappropriately.*
>
> *The archbishop gathers her into his arms. She looks at him questioningly. When she tries to speak again, she begins to cry.*

"Once we as Christians know, as you most certainly do, my child, we go where we're needed. And yes, the joy is sometimes long in coming, our service not always as cheerful, perhaps, as we would hope. But . . . we have our comfort: we do know. We *know*."

"The work must be done. Let it be me who does it," Carla intoned in something less than cynical agreement.

"An inspired motto for us humble Christian soldiers, don't you think?"

▼

Lord, help me to know . . . Carla prayed. The irony of herself, a Protestant, serving as Vatican Counsel for Scientific Affairs. It would mean leaving Mexico and its people. And its solace.

She cleared her mind and slid beneath a hill of bath foam. The warm bubbling water filled the room with fragrance. White noise soothed her; jets of water massaged her back. She wiped her brow, then reached behind her neck and squeezed the dampness from her hair. Turning her head, Carla gazed across the oak-plank floor to the lush blue-greens of a miniature rain forest at the far end of the room. The foliage shimmered, magical and moist, the color of olives and jade and ocean—the colors, for her, of Mexico.

Jay. . . . She closed her eyes and drew in the steamy redolent air, *Mexico and Jay.* She had teased her husband—he'd spent so much time in the bath, she'd told him he must be half water buffalo. Hard to believe so many years had passed since his death. *He was a water buffalo.*

She smiled. She could see him clearly, as if he were in the tub with her. Jay MacGregor, his golden brown hair, curly just above his forehead. His dark eyes, often thoughtful, sometimes sad, his firm chin and square jaw—those dimples when he smiled.

The water jets stopped abruptly.

Still, eyes closed, she lingered. The water teased her. *Jay. . . .* Slowly, the tingling of her skin faded.

"If only I could have had your child. . . ."

Now she sees the children, Hispanic children, back at the base community, her home these last years. She imagines herself a young Hispanic mother, imagines the plush feel of her own infant son's skin against her palm as she immerses the tiny child in the water. His mouth soft and square, his lashless gray eyes incredulous. She hears the archbishop's voice replay in her mind.

"Eduardo Francisco Cabal, I baptize you with water in the name of the Father and of the Son and of the Holy Spirit." *The archbishop makes the sign of the cross on the child's forehead with Holy Chrism.* "Eduardo Francisco Cabal, you are sealed with the Holy Spirit and marked as Christ's own forever." *The child seems to laugh as the old man anoints him with his thumb.*

Carla lifted her hand out of the warm bath and let a plump drop of water break and trickle down her own forehead. She reached for the towel, patted her face dry, and stepped out of the bath.

She looked at herself in the mirror above the sink. Her skin, flushed from the bath, was still tight, still youthful across her ribs and abdomen. Short dark hair framed her face, accentuated by high cheekbones, full lips, and wide-set almond eyes.

Innocent of her own beauty, her look was informed by the dignity of one vitally alive, vitally human. Over her shoulder, reflected in the glass, her plain cotton blouse and Mexican work skirt hung on the door—the accoutrements of the simple life she had gladly accepted as her fate in order to continue her work within this inspired community. Her eyes moved from the fiesta-colored skirt back to her own image in the glass. She drew in a breath, reached for another towel, nodding almost imperceptibly at herself.

Forty-two years old already. She smiled, pleased that she could think those words without feeling a sense of loss. That thought was a gift, something Jay had taught her long ago. Jay had never been one to confuse *having* with *being*, she remembered. He was a man whose wealth came from an almost transcendent grasp of the authentic meaning of life.

It was Jay who had introduced her to Torrez. Thinking about it now, she could smell the sweet lingering aroma from the rosewood Celtic cross Jay had carved for her one summer while they were doing research together in Greece. She hung that cross on her office wall, right alongside Jay's holographic fine art poster of the King of kings, Jesus Christ, standing upon a cloud in the full glory of the heavens, clusters of galaxies spinning in every direction at his back, a boundless army of seraphim at his feet, His left hand raised in silent benediction. *I and My Father are one.* Carla's thought-prayers had repeated those precious words countless times. *Precious in the sight of the Lord is the death of His saints.* The light logo along the poster's bottom edge and above those simple words the Greek caption: ΑΓΑΠΗ ΟΥ ΖΗΤΕΙ ΤΑ ΕΑΥΤΗΣ "Charity seeketh not her own."

What would Jay think? she wondered, patting herself dry and slipping into her clothes. She reached for her toothbrush. It was all becoming clear. Seizing on her interest in following the medical developments coming from the WEDGE in Montreal, Torrez had pushed her into a position that would enable her to keep an eye on political developments coming from Rome. His insensitivity, uncharacteristic as it was, had made her feel like he was selling something.

It was an honor. Yes, she had traveled to Stockholm. She was there in the audience when Lanning Balcourt and Henri Nakasone had received the Nobel Prize for medicine. Since then, she'd kept up with their work, always with an eye toward the children's hospital. And yet, she thought now of reversing herself, declining the offer. She ached to stay *here*, in Pachuca, with the children.

Leaning over the wash basin, Carla returned the toothbrush to the sink and splashed cold water in her mouth. Water dripped from her nose as she grabbed a towel. *Go for us.* She patted her face dry then ran her damp fingers through her hair. *Go. . . .*

She drew a deep breath and refolded the towel, lingering over the flickering scented candle. She felt something flicker inside herself, unsettled, disturbed as if by an unseen wind. She shook her head, draped the folded towel over the brass wall rack behind her, and then returned her gaze to the basin. More drops of water fell on it—her tears. She tasted salt. She wiped her face again.

Inevitable, she thought, straightening her skirt before reaching for the door. She stepped into the corridor, thinking about her conversation with Archbishop Torrez, her new responsibilities in Rome. For a moment, she could see herself ten years before, standing shy and hesitant in this same washroom. She had not thought she would ever again feel like that outsider she'd once been.

Ten years working with the archbishop. He was there when she needed him. She had come to value his friendship and his judgment since her first days in Mexico City with her husband. *Ten years,* had it been that long? So much had happened . . . so much had been accomplished since then. The archbishop was a remarkable man. It had been easy to admire his work expanding these base communities, which were now everywhere throughout Latin America. They had become the model for economic growth in Latin America, Africa, Eastern Europe. They had attracted millions of new followers and a new fire, a new life to the Christian faith. These were working charitable communities; believers sharing a deeply rooted spiritual fellowship similar to that enjoyed by the early Christians. It was as if these people had one heart, one soul. They had gathered together in these simple villages from all denominations, all walks of life, like the winds from the four corners of the earth: many grains lovingly blended and kneaded together to make but one loaf. Manna, the archbishop liked to say.

Working day after day with the village people and at the children's hospital, Carla had felt a deepening of her own faith, another gift from God, she knew. Lately, she wondered if Torrez had not begun to lose touch with his religious convictions. Yes, she knew the archbishop had come under fire recently. These widespread, autonomous villages, originally established as predominantly Catholic communities, had become a sore spot within the Vatican. The powers in Rome had expressed a growing uneasiness as many within the villages had turned to a more "fundamental" means of expressing their faith.

"Well, Alejandro, 'We must never forget the impossibility of assimilating the earthly city to the heavenly city,'" Carla had goaded him, retorting with the words of his own St. Augustine in *City of God.* She had teased him, trying to get his mind off the pressure. It was difficult. Torrez was a man under many pressures. Regionally there were the wars and rumors of wars, the usual Latin American political exigencies with which a man of his position and responsibilities must contend.

It saddened Carla. She watched her friend as he had seemed to harden in the face of a senseless escalation in social tensions outside the community. These base communities were his life's work. It tormented him to see them threatened. Or maybe he tormented himself, Carla thought. It was as if he had begun to internalize the conflicts raging around him, as if all the political intrigue and instability had somehow poisoned the well of living water within.

Torrez had his own explanation for the turmoil. Characteristically, the archbishop's words had a decidedly "political" spin. The collectivist movement had died long ago, he insisted, before the turn of the century. Those in power wanted to make sure it stayed dead. Fearing the worst—a resurgence of communism within their struggling democracies—they refused to see these special communities for what they were: free villages, organized on strong legal, ethical, and religious grounds. The government perceived only a threat to liberty. All politics and rhetoric, as far as Carla was concerned.

Yet, despite the archbishop's current political crisis, Carla knew she would go on trying to model herself after the side of Torrez she had grown to love—the humble man of heart; his dedication to the poor; his willingness to see Christ in his fellow human beings. The old man's compassion for others had spread to whole communities. The people had learned to empower one another, to truly love one another. Carla knew why she had turned to Torrez in anguish and despair after her husband died. She remembered the feel of Torrez' robe against her cheek as he held her in his arms those first days following the plane crash. Those first days. Hard days. Graced days. They opened like doors before her again.

She is following Torrez into the large kitchen in his modest terra alba adobe. The gentle fragrance of bayberry and apple beeswax candles is evident just beneath the scent of fresh baked bread rising from the oven against the far wall. Torrez' home seems alive, the exposed blond timbers of the ceiling joists, the coarse plain-woven jute curtains dyed ochre and streaming in the breeze at the open window above the sink.

Carla marvels at how the old archbishop seems to float above the rough cut stone brick floor, moving back and forth between the great bench style oak table and the professional size Wolf range, harvesting the miracle of the loaves out of the gaping mouth of the oven, replacing the steaming bread with still more risen dough. She watches the ritual and feels that she belongs, she feels this is the family she never had. Before long she is on her feet, helping with the hot loaves of seven-grain bread, gingerly tapping them out of their copper bread molds and dropping them onto the terra cotta dishes that cover every available square inch of the oak tabletop. Soon, she is stacking the loaves in steaming pyramids one on top of the other. The sweet smell of oven-fresh bread brings startled tears to her eyes.

They finish the baking late in the night, both collapsing on the oak bench nearest the kitchen door, a cool breeze wafting through the house from the living room reminding Carla that her face is damp with sweat. The archbishop reaches out, selects a still-steaming loaf of bread, breaks it in half, and hands it to Carla. Without speaking a word, he stands and walks over by the refrigerator, picks up an uncorked bottle of local wine from the counter, and reaches into the cupboard, stepping back toward the table with two clay goblets. Carla watches the wine pour into the goblets. She can smell the liquid rose bouquet of the wine and the bread laced with scented candles, now transparent pools of wax in their shallow candle plates, sending slow, dancing *shadows across the walls. She bites into the steamy bread and drinks from her full goblet. There is no need to speak for a long time. This is peace beyond words.*

Looking at her friend, she watches the candlelight shift in his deep eyes and bathe his aging face with amber light. Like a spirit, the light moves over the table and the plates before them.

"I had hoped . . ." Torrez speaks, finally, "I had hoped that you might take this bread down to the village children." He looks at her as if he were measuring her.

She surveys the bounty on the table and looks back at him again. "Yes," she says. "I will. Yes."

The archbishop had understood her when she had not understood herself, in that time of confusion and loss—those days when she woke up shaking; those nights when she sat up, sleepless, wrapped in the sheets. Giving the bread to the children—this was her first contact with the villagers, the beginning of her long, deep relationship with these people she had grown to love.

"I spoke with Don Carlos at the Human Genome Center," he had said with a knowing look of concern. "You can't keep yourself locked up in here forever." He paused, as if turning a stratagem in his mind. "If you're no longer happy there, I know a small base-community hospital that could use some help. Perhaps there's something there for you, my child, at the administrative end, of course, only until you get back on your feet."

Better to concentrate on somebody else's pain.
She had accepted, at first working long hours in her
office, but always taking time to visit the children,
making her rounds, lingering, her feet dangling off
the side of their beds, reading them stories. She'd
studied the children's faces, watched them wince as
their storybook heroes muddled through perils and
laugh as their heroes soared on to glorious heights.
The older ones, alert and entranced, listened raptly
while the little ones, after only a short while, crossed
their sleepy eyes and nodded helplessly away as if
slipping under a narcotic spell.

"Carla! . . . *Mammacita!* . . . Carla!" She had found
favor in their eyes. And to her, the children were
tender, strong, bright as a thousand strands in a new
weaving—one she wrapped herself in now—now,
when she felt most alone. Here, in Pachuca, in this
tiny base community of working poor, she beheld a
forgotten dream. These were not her children, and yet
they were. They had something in common, Carla
and these little ones. They needed each other
desperately. And she soon discovered that she needed
them far more than they could ever need her. This
gradual realization was at the heart of her decision to
devote her life to this place. She had at last found a
path with heart. It was a realization born of her
gratitude to God. By His grace, she had found her
place. *Lord, I have nothing left to ask for. I pray only
my love to You, that I may be made an instrument of
Your will.*

Her first words to Torrez months later were
halting. She spoke to the archbishop about staying

in the community. *I think . . . I feel . . . maybe I'm supposed to be here . . . ?* The warm smile on his face signaled that, once again, the old man understood.

Carla wasn't going to make the same mistake her mother had made with her stepfather. No marriages of convenience. No desperate entanglements with other, lesser men. This ministry, instead, would be her life. Here, she knew she had found her center. There were no boundaries to protect her, no vain glory to compete for. Often now, when she prayed, she felt an odd buoyancy—a lightness and union with God she'd not known before. In losing all, she had, to her astonishment, been found.

▼

"We need you there, in Rome; we need you on the *inside*," Torrez' voice was tense. He quieted himself as Margaret, his matronly assistant, placed two steaming cups of coffee before them, then left the room. The woman quietly closed his office door behind her.

"Look, we don't have much time. We need you in Rome . . . now. We need someone, someone we can trust, on the inside, someone to keep an eye on things, to keep us informed."

Carla interrupted, "It's not why—"

The archbishop raised his hand. "I know. I was there."

"I did not turn my back on my career to—" she stuttered and her voice broke. Wearily, she continued, "*This* is why I joined these people. You know I have no ambition." Her eyes brimmed with tears. "And I resent you using our *friendship,* putting me in this position, for all your maneuvering you're . . . you're *forcing* me against my will, Alejandro."

She paused then went on plaintively, "I can't believe you're doing this! Can't you see what you're doing? Is all this political intrigue so impor—"

"I and a great many others *believe* in these communities." He stepped around from behind his desk. "But it's bigger than that. Our beliefs are vain unless we act on them. The Church has grown vast; unfortunately, where the fortune is great, so is the potential for corruption."

Carla looked away.

"This is not just threatening the dignity of the Church—"

"Money!" She turned, nearly spitting the word. "That's what this is all about. Just another vulgar attempt to redistribute the wealth. Where's your sense of history, Alejandro? You sound like some Marxist revolutionary. Maybe nobody's told you, but Marxism went out with the dinosaurs."

"It's more than wealth distribution. We're not materialists, and you of all people should know that."

"*Regnare Christum volumus!*" Carla said only half mockingly, taking a sip of her coffee.

The archbishop pulled away from his bookcase and nodded. "Exactly right! We want Christ to reign! Here! Now! The kingdom is upon us, Carla. You've seen it with your own eyes." The old man's expression seemed electrified. He drew in a deep breath and folded his hands into the cuffs of his sleeves. "Believe me, I do not ask this of you lightly. I call on your faith, as if you were my own daughter; please trust me in this."

He stepped toward her. "There are very important reasons for you to go. This is not about politics or economics or ambition or anything secular for that matter. This is a spiritual matter. *Spiritual.*" He pronounced the word slowly, extending his hands. "Important spiritual changes are taking place. We live in extraordinary times. I believe this pope may be the last; this ancient organization, promised to endure against the very gates of hell . . . Go for us, my daughter. Go for us." He took her hand.

Carla looked at him. It seemed a long time before she could press his hands, dry and fragile as November leaves.

Carla shut the door of Torrez' office and walked down the hospital's wide central corridor toward ultrasound therapy. *Our beliefs are vain . . . unless they are backed by our actions. Someone . . . on the inside,* Torrez' words grated on her. *What have I become . . . a spy?* She felt a darkening cloud enfold her, *Lord, help me to see.* Looking up, she at once recognized the skinny form, the familiar crumpled blue flannel pajamas approaching her.

"Hey . . . Carla . . . what's going on?" asked a raspy voice. Before her stood a child barely more than three feet high. Eddie was suffering from renal failure. Though he was twelve, his mind and body had been arrested in development, leaving him at this point six years behind where he would have been if not for his illness.

Carla smiled as she looked down at the sad dark eyes flashing up at her from the tiny fuzzy-headed fellow who had struck her as a precocious hatchling from her very first day on the job. His black hair stood straight up on end at the top of his head. There was no mistake about it, Eddie looked like a baby bird. "You mean you don't know?" she asked, ruffling his downy hair.

"Well . . . I heard," Eddie said, sliding both hands under the elastic waistband of his pajamas before he began shifting his weight on his small bare feet. "I don't want you to go," he said, his eyes welling up with tears. He turned away and wiped them with his sleeve.

Her chest tightened. "I'll miss you too, Eddie." She bent down, lifted his nearly weightless body onto her hip and gave him a hug. She pressed her face into his fleshy cheek. For a moment her own eyes blurred. She drew in a deep breath and smelled the familiar, sweet, fresh-scrubbed aroma of this child she had grown to love as her own. "Hey," she cleared her throat, "aren't you supposed to be in therapy?"

"Yeah," he admitted reluctantly, without loosening his embrace.

"Well, come on then. Let's get a move on."

Two doors labeled "Ultrasound Therapy" swept open as Carla and Eddie passed the infrared sensor. Inside, the room was austere. A small, elevated hospital bed sat against the far wall. Four nurses trained in clinical ultrasonics stood smiling by the bedside.

"*Señor Eduardo!*" the heavy-set redhead spoke for all, "*Como está?*"

"Hey . . . I'm okay," Eddie slid down Carla's side. He padded to the bedside and crawled onto the bed. Instantly, eight hands ruffled his hair, pinched his cheeks, tickled his puppy-belly.

Carla smiled, watching him giggle and squirm.

Just then, Dr. Bukovsky stepped into the room and rolled a holographic recorder into place at the foot of the bed. "You might want to stay and see this," he said, speaking aside to Carla.

The machine seemed an older model. A prototype, Carla figured. It stood three feet off the floor, like a redwood doughnut balanced on four silvery legs of chromium tube steel. Bukovsky fidgeted with some switches before a multiplexed image of various colors and cross hairs shot into the air from the center of the ring.

"My colleagues at the Texas Institute for Human Studies at Austin are very interested in this case."

Carla looked down at Eddie. His eyes widened at the sudden appearance of his own hologram while the nurses helped him out of his pajamas.

The doctor signaled for her to step over to the foot of the bed. From there she watched Eddie's image transformed to a three-dimensional display of throbbing colored light. The boy's body became a misty haze of flickering bluish white, streaked from within by what appeared to be a bile-green skeleton. The putrid skeletal glow pulsed at his center.

Eddie tugged on the nurse's robe. "Hey . . . That's my spirit isn't it?" he whispered.

She turned to Carla for help.

"I don't think you can see a spirit, do you?" Carla asked, stepping from behind the image.

The expression on his face said he wasn't quite certain. He turned back to face his own hologram. Carla smiled and stepped back out of the way.

The nurses drew in close and rubbed together vigorously what appeared to be defibrillator paddles. "They're priming," the doctor explained, repeating his words in Russian for the benefit of the recording being made. The nurse standing at Eddie's head placed one paddle over each of his clavicles at a distance of about three inches. The two women at his sides interlaced theirs, in a line parallel with his spine, to a spot just above his pubic area. The doctor translated into Russian quietly the action that followed. "The clicking sound you're hearing now is actually a series of ultra-high-frequency sonic pulses. . . ."

Like a Geiger counter in a uranium field, the clicks began to come more rapidly now, until they seemed to blend together in a fuzz of white noise. Bukovsky continued in his native tongue: "The delivered pulse is actually a full spectrum—"

The hologram's imagery shifted noticeably. The child's form began to pulse in a rapid, periodic rhythm.

"Results in past cases we've observed have been quite profound," Bukovsky continued. As he spoke the child's hologram slowly changed color, at first emanating a brilliant white pin-prick of light at each paddle point. Gradually, the six light points reached like long probing fingers deep into Eddie's spectral form, eventually reaching his center, transforming the sickly green vapor at the center of his form into a faint, flickering cobalt blue glow.

Forty-five minutes later, Eddie was fast asleep. Carla picked him up and cradled him in her arms. She nodded to the nurses and smiled, then carried him out of the room.

Eddie's room was crowded with drawings and banners from all the birthdays and holidays he had spent in the hospital. Everybody loved him, even the other children. Eddie had a disarming way of foraging in everybody's business that was always lovable, always welcome. Now, Carla looked down at the little boy sound asleep before her and covered him with his favorite Superman blanket. *Eddie could melt the stars,* she thought, sitting on the side of his bed to stroke his hair. He stirred briefly and sleepily opened his eyes.

"Carla, what's it like to die?" he asked matter of factly, keeping his hands underneath the covers.

She raised her head, looking up at the starlight shining in through his window, and struggled to find the words, "Well, Eddie . . . at first it might be a little hard to breathe. But you try to relax . . . and it feels like you're going away. And then . . . you . . . you just sort of keep going. Out and out and out and farther and farther away . . . until . . . until God meets you and keeps you with Him." She paused for a moment to swallow. "You don't have to be afraid." She held her head completely still for fear of spilling the tears that had suddenly filled her eyes. After a few moments of silence, she glanced down and wiped her cheeks. Eddie had again fallen asleep.

Carla turned out the light and paused. Soon she would be seeing the lights of Vatican City. "Don't be afraid," she whispered.

Chapter

3

Montreal, Quebec
October 5, 2065

"Take some time," Henri said, his voice fatigued and scratchy. "Do you some good. Get out, get some fresh air. There's nothing more you can do until tomorrow anyway. Believe me, Lane's not going anywhere. Besides, I'd like you to talk to her." Henri stepped slowly behind his desk. "Kids," he shook his head. "Where'd she say she'd meet you?"

"Where else?" Sandy smirked, working the tension out of her neck and shoulders as if she were struggling with a Gordian knot. Finally, she stopped, lost in the recollection of Masako's words: *You've got to see this, Sandy. The animals are going crazy around here.*

"Please. Talk to her."

"I'm sorry, Henri." Sandy shook off her daze. "It's just hard to focus, you know. I mean, we're on the phone, she's going on and on about this new zoological director of hers, animal behaviorists in from Boston, forecasts of imminent seismological events, and all I can think of is—"

Henri peered over the top of his glasses. "Earthquakes?"

Sandy rolled her eyes.

"That child." A moment passed. Henri cleared his throat and shuffled disenchantedly through some papers on his desk. "Listen, before you go; who's this—" he held up a pink message slip and stepped toward the door, "Carla—" he looked down to find the surname through his bifocals, "MacGregor?"

"Oh, yeah." Sandy followed him into the hall. "I've spoken to her. Vatican's Consultant for Scientific Affairs. Nice lady."

"A fanatic?"

"No-no-no. Solid." Sandy chuckled. "I remember she emphasized the word *consultant* in her title. Modest . . . actually humble. Refreshing really. Very strong science background, a Ph.D., Harvey Mudd, I think, that's why the Vatican tapped her. Been following our work—clinical applications—from the beginning." Sandy waited for the elevator doors to open, then stepped in after Henri.

"Body shop," Henri announced as the doors closed.

"You know how it is," Sandy continued, "the usual dealings with Rome. Keep them apprised, that's all."

"That's a relief." Henri stepped out into the lab and raised his voice over the clamor. "We don't need more fanatics."

Sandy smiled. "No, Henri, Carla MacGregor's no fanatic." She followed Henri to the glass amnion at the back of the room. "Late tomorrow . . . we know," she said, adjusting the bandage above her ear. Wincing, she looked around at the bizarre jungle of machinery in the prosthetics laboratory: coiled accordion hoses and glass tubing and cables and wires and blinking lights. The body shop resembled the entrails of a great mechanical beast. An unctuous scent—benzene and polyethylene glycol—belched into the air on sporadic bursts of steam.

"Lord, help me," Henri murmured under the crackling noise, his gaze fixed on the glass bubble, twelve feet in diameter, suspended between two shiny steel rings high in the center of the jam-packed room. Inside the zero-gravity bubble, a swirl of chemicals clouded the epibolic body work being done by three slender robotic arms. The computer-controlled arms balanced three dog's-head-shaped nozzles that exuded microfilaments like spiders spinning webs. Once irradiated, the microscopic threads combined with the chemical matrix in the bubble to perfectly replicate the form and function of living cells.

What have I done? Henri thought, recoiling at a sudden discharge of electricity inside the bubble.

"Van de Graff effects," Sandy shook her head at the erratic flurry of electrical activity. Hair-thin tendrils of lightning crawled over the inner surface of the bubble like the fine blue wisps of an electric dandelion.

Henri stepped over a thick conduit of cables, removed his glasses, buffed the lenses on his lab coat, and peered up into the opalescent globe. Barely discernible at the center of the bubble, Lane's new nervous system hung vertically suspended like a man-sized tadpole in the smoky, zero-gravity atmosphere. Brain, spinal nerves, autonomic nerves, optic nerves, eyes fully formed, the entire neural network complete. As the swirling matrix cleared in pockets, Henri could make out what would ultimately be Lane's new body shape. There in the mist, the tangled brachial structure of the world's first synthetic human being was taking form, one cell layer at a time. Arms outstretched, legs asprawl, the macabre, branching anatomy took the form of an inverted five point star. *I am become Man.*

"You know, I was wondering," Sandy's words drew Henri out of his contemplative moment, "what do you think the odds are that Lane is somehow still conscious?"

Henri turned away from the amnion and peering over the top of his glasses fixed his gaze on Sandy. "I don't follow."

"I mean, during the mapping process, we don't really know what takes place. What if Lane's consciousness is suspended within the computer? His thoughts, feelings, everything that makes him unique, a thinking creature—somehow frozen at the point of transfer like a freeze-frame photograph."

"We built a computer *map* of his mind, not a Jericho head. It's a schematic, not a spirit trap." Henri turned and glanced at the large digital clock on the wall, then at the holographic bio-map display that mirrored the globe at the far end of the room.

"Ossification should begin any time now." He shook his head and stepped away from the glass. "Organic soup!"

"Who's to say? Maybe Lane was right. Maybe this *is* how the Creation—" Sandy caught herself; Henri moved toward the door. "I mean, any energy moving through a system acts to organize that system—"

"Some organization."

Sandy followed him through the door and down the hall, "Alpha . . . and now Omega," she muttered, playfully.

"Be careful," Henri said quietly.

"No disrespect intended," Sandy apologized.

Henri bowed his head almost imperceptibly and then checked his watch. "I've got to make some calls. Two days and I haven't even talked to my daughter yet."

"Some father."

"I make no pretenses on that score." Henri sighed. Wearily, he raised his hand to the scanner; his office door hissed open. "She knows me."

▼

Masako Nakasone, Henri's daughter, stopped at the railing and gazed into the darkened cave, her thoughts on the sound of fatigue in her father's voice. She sensed his strain, anxiety.

Off to one side, a small brass sign, pressed into the ground and nearly hidden by the trees, caught her eye—black letters embossed on dull yellow metal: *Panthera (felis pardus)*.

She sidled tentatively along the railing and surveyed the empty lair of a black panther—a sheer rocky bluff towering over the swirling white water of a man-made stream. Again, something pulled her gaze to the cave. Somehow, the shadows shifted and changed. For a moment, everything around her seemed luminous, even the silence. On the trees, the leaves rustled and whispered. She shuddered, as if the shadows themselves were speaking to her. She thought she recognized the voice. . . .

A sharp, phantom pain lacerated her neck. Masako gasped. The fleeting diaphanous image of a decapitated body, bloodied—vivisected—formed a grim augury in her mind. . . .

"What is it, Masako?" Sandy asked, "You are *pale.*" The odd look of concern on Sandy's face mirrored her own; Sandy pushed Masako's hair away from her face and gazed into her dark, hooded eyes.

"I'm okay," Masako quickly averted her glance, trying unsuccessfully to hide the inchoate terror she felt welling up within her. She stepped away from the railing and slowly turned her back on the panther's pit. "I'm okay."

Sandy sensed Masako's change of mood, as if her quiet, contemplative state of mind had become suddenly adumbrated by something threatening, sinister. "What—?"

"I said," Masako interrupted gently, her hand raised in an admonitory gesture, "I'm okay." She pulled away and started down the wide cobblestone path. She'd walked some distance before she finally spoke, her voice dispirited. "I'm really worried about my father."

"What do you mean?" Sandy slid her hands into her pockets and lowered her eyes to the ground.

Masako looked at her thoughtfully. "This insane opposition to his work. The lunatics. The media. And now Lane's been hurt! There's something ominous, something oppressive about all this. I can feel it. Even the animals can feel it!"

"Your father is a pioneer. Pioneers take flak," Sandy answered flatly.

Masako walked a bit farther, lost in her thoughts, disconsolate.

Sandy came abreast of her, gazed into her eyes, and taking her hand from her pocket, lightly touched her cheek. A maternal tone edged her voice. "Masako?"

Despite her lachrymose mood, a faltering smile came to the younger woman's lips. For the first time she saw Sandy as the simulacrum of her mother in *her* youth. "I don't know. It's my craft, Sandy," she explained, her voice soft, almost apologetic. "It's like I feel everybody else's pain . . . Literally, I *feel* it. I was thinking about Lane, about my dad, I saw the blood and . . . It's wearing me down. I'm so tired." Her words ran together, taking on the desperate cadence of a confessional flood. "I can't study. I rarely sleep anymore. I haven't touched my doctoral thesis in weeks. I feel something . . . *something*—almost like a storm approaching. Dreams. Visions. The animals. I *hate* this! It's a curse!"

"Perhaps you need to take some time off," Sandy stepped out in front of her and gently grasped her shoulders. "A sabbatical."

"My father would object," she said with a sigh.

"I'll talk to him." A gentle smile crossed Sandy's face as she dropped her arms to her side. "He'll understand."

Masako shook her head. "You know him, Sandy. He's *Nihonjin.* You know, born Japanese means more than born in Japan. He'll say there'll be plenty of time for sabbaticals *after* my dissertation has been—"

A shrill siren instantly stifled their conversation, rising and falling in undulant waves, blaring into the air from bright yellow trumpets suddenly apparent in clusters of three in the trees and atop the light posts.

Sandy grabbed Masako by the elbow and jerked her out of the roadway as two red and white jeeps retraced the path back toward the panther's lair, their flashing lights and ululating sirens growing brighter and louder as they approached and then fading gradually beneath the din of the warbling alarm as they disappeared behind a dense stand of trees.

A team of zoo employees scrambled past at a near sprint in their wake. "What is it?" Sandy called out, prompted by chatter that someone had just been mauled by a cat.

"Folks, just stay back," the last man called over his shoulder as he ran by.

Masako looked through the van's windshield toward the LMC Research Park, her gaze following dead leaves blowing across the neatly landscaped grounds surrounding the entrance. She watched the scraps of color rise into the air, like sparks from a bonfire, before they collected at the feet of a boisterous crowd gathered at the gate. Their muffled protests rose and then faded as the van passed by.

"Fanatics," Masako muttered, watching the mob recede into the distance through the side view mirror. "Where do these people come from?"

The van's engine sounded a muffled purr as it slowed into the heart of Montreal, past a handful of ancient cathedrals that stood out like precious gems against the backdrop of this modern city of tall steel and glass. A wondrous play of light and shadow moved against the white polished stone surfaces—curved, linear, austere. A strange geometry of modern and gothic motifs combined in a dizzying display of architectural éclat. High in the city's vast open spaces where there was no stone, luminous tinted glass surfaces reflected the feathered edges of clouds set ablaze by the sunset. From remaining ancient buildings, the implacable chiseled faces of seraphim and gargoyles gazed over the city below, where the rush hour crowds made a slow-moving mosaic on the gold, silver, blue, and green glass canyon walls that lined the wide boulevards. Lush green parks, surrounded by the colorful, connected city homes of the affluent, carved out what little neighborhood space was available along the St. Lawrence.

The van slowed and pulled into the pot-handle drive of Dr. Nakasone's spacious town home. "Want me to come in?" Sandy asked, as Masako hopped out.

"No, thanks anyway. I'll be all right." Masako closed the door and walked around to Sandy's side of the van. "Thanks, Sandy," she gave her a pat on the arm and then turned toward the house.

Sandy leaned out through the window. "Talk to your dad."

Masako waved and then disappeared into the house.

Masako tossed the magazine on the coffee table, leaned back, and closed her eyes, only barely aware of the holovision broadcast of the eight o'clock news. "We've had a couple of attempted break-ins." The guard's voice was strained as he attempted to cover the camera's lens with his free hand. "That's all I can say."

She sat up, reached for the control wand, and turned up the volume. She peered at the jiggling hologram obviously being broadcast live. "What?" she mumbled.

A sudden trill tone interrupted the broadcast. At once, Henri's image flashed onto the screen. Hair blowzy, eyes puffy, Masako's father gave the appearance of one who'd been awake for several days.

Masako hit the COM panel. "Daddy, I've been worried."

"I'll be home in about an hour," Henri said, his voice flat with fatigue. "We'll talk then."

▼

The evening seemed to darken the ugly mob surrounding Henri's van. He leaned forward and flipped on the auto-driver, tensing his jaw and sinking back in his seat as the crowd slowly parted, their voices raised in an obstreperous, malevolent chant.

Henri jerked around at the sound of something smashing against the van's side panel, his veins filled with an unwelcome rush of heat and anxiety. He craned his neck, looking over his shoulder through the passenger side window. He watched with growing impatience the holographic television crews scramble to get their lights and cameras into position. "Most unpleasant," he muttered, recognizing the international news logo on the caps and jackets of the crew.

The van inched forward, hesitated, then jerked to a stop. The crowd grew more boisterous. It seemed to swallow the van. The chanting intensified. Henri gripped the armrests to catch his balance. The van bounced on its shocks, rocking wildly back and forth. He felt hot and tired and anxious. Again, the van lurched forward. Henri wiped the sweat from his face as the last wave of protestors reluctantly gave ground, their faces demonic, dark shadows at the hollows of their eyes and cheekbones, their features distorted by amber candlelight as they marched and chanted, "Satan! Satan! Satan!"

The van finally wrested free from the mob, peeling out of the LMC entrance and accelerating onto the throughway with wheels screeching; Henri was shoved back against his seat. At speed, he reached for the control console, hit a switch, and let the forward windows down a crack. The van filled with the fresh loamy scent of chill night air. Henri drew in a deep breath; the nutty aroma of burning leaves from some distant autumnal fire soothed him.

Who were these people? he wondered. His mind flashed to the mob as the van's headlamps illuminated the lonely stretch of highway with sweeping cones of yellow light. The trees loomed like shadowy giants along the winding road. *More misguided believers.* Henri answered himself. And what did *he* believe in?

He thought of Lane's beaten and bloodied face. *So . . . mortal.* Henri slowed the van. In an instant the awe, the respect he had felt for Lane's towering intellect evaporated, replaced by a compassion he had previously felt only for his own family, for his wife and his daughter.

And what now? "If" we succeed, we will have done it all. What is left to do? For a long time it seemed, Henri was still, drawn into himself. *Misguided believers.*

It wasn't until the van pulled into his driveway and had come to a complete stop that his thoughts turned to his own misguided daughter. He pictured a teen-age Masako reading excitedly from her borrowed tarot cards.

How many arguments had they suffered through since those days on account of her so-called "mystical" beliefs? It had become quite a sore spot with Henri. At first he was simply annoyed. But now, he was worried, guilty. Had he been a better father, spent more time at home, he might have been better able to help her set limits and avoid such vain and dangerous pastimes. Lately, their arguments had ended in tears. She claimed her father just didn't understand, claimed she was just more "spiritual" than he was.

"Spiritual." Lord, she's twenty-five years old. Is it now too late? Am I a fool to trouble myself now with trying to change a behavior that I've already tolerated for far too long? Forgive me, Lord. What I should have detested in strength, I dealt with in weakness; fearing confrontation, mine was the coward's path masquerading as benign resignation. How much damage have I done? Enough weakness, Henri'san. Enough! Time for tougher love. Lord, be my guide.

Tough love. Spiritual. As far as Henri was concerned, *spiritual* meant only one thing—faithful service to humanity informed by an unfettered worship of the Lord. For Henri, selfless service was the essence behind the revelation of God on earth, the whole purpose behind the Word made flesh, the Creator Himself entering His creation so that His fallen creatures might be redeemed.

Redemption. It frightened Henri the way his daughter continually criticized his faith in a personal God. "Too pedestrian," she had said, "too naive." But what did that say about her beliefs? If she had studied the Word with the same enthusiasm she mustered to pore over her mystical manuals, she might find herself part of a real miracle. But it was hard to talk to one so "sophisticated." A troubled, struggling postgraduate student at odds with her eminently erudite father over his "pedestrian" beliefs.

Ha! Others may fear what they have done; I fear what I have failed to do. But no more. No more. His daughter had seemed to hunger after the mysterious. There was an immature, magical aspect to her personality that Henri hoped and prayed she would soon outgrow. He wondered how patient he could continue to be, having to endure her strange ways, her continual assaults stemming from this overdeveloped interest in occult nonsense—tarot cards, psychic readings.

"Wands," she had once begun, attempting to explain the card that she had placed across the King of Pentacles, the card that she had claimed stood for her father. Henri couldn't remember which wand, only his daughter's youthful voice as she had read from her dogeared paperback copy of *The Tarot Interpreted.* "The pain of Alexander, who, in surveying his worldly dominion, becomes mortified when he realizes he has nothing left to conquer."

"Be careful, Masako," he had replied, somewhat forcefully. "Be careful of what you hold close to your heart. There's more to the world than even *you* know. You want mystery, magic? Try meditating on the image of Him who created all that is from nothing. Hold His image in your mind's eye, not these wands and pentacles. They are evil. Search your heart, Masako, lest you become what you worship."

Henri drew in a heavy sigh at the recollection of his own advice. Exhausted, he stepped out of the van and headed into the house.

Chapter

4

"He's 'locking in.' He's like a fetus now. He'll be squirming for quite a while yet," Sandy said flatly, her gaze fixed on the flickering spherical amnion below.

Lane's new anatomy, now fully formed, was submerged and unconscious in the milky serum, strung like an inverted marionette on invisible wire supports. A barrage of ruby laser sensors illuminated his flesh like so many pins in a voodoo doll. The amnion reddened like a fiery autumn sunset, blushing orange and peach by turns, marbleized by flowering swirls of ashen smoke.

Sandy stepped away from the glass bulkhead and returned to her work station, her eyes trained on the triptych computer screens in front of her. Data from Lane's heart and metabolism scrolled across the side screens in an endless stream of jagged lines while a three-dimensional image of his brain pulsed in midair at the front of the center screen, a luminous explosion of primary colors. Except for the rattle of a high-speed printer in the far corner, Surg Op Control was quiet, well insulated from the belching hiss and spray of the labyrinthine mechanical womb on the other side of the glass.

"What time does Dr. Nakasone get in?" Azeem asked, his long hair hanging down around his shoulders as he scribbled something into his log.

"Any—"

The doors hissed open, cutting Sandy's words short. A machine-like industrial clamor sounding in three-four time preceded Henri into the room. Sandy looked up, peering over the top of her glasses. "*O tosan!* Your baby's kicking!"

"*Our* baby's kicking, *O kasan,*" Henri said with a smile, dropping his leather bag down on the vacant counter.

"*O hyio gozai imasu, Azeem'san.*" Henri nodded smartly, delivering his usual morning salutation in Japanese. He stepped behind Sandy to get a look over her shoulder at the computer screen. "I see. Very good. Very, very good." He tilted his head back a little and squinted through his bifocals. "Hmm . . . How's *your* head?" he asked, his voice soft and empathetic as he gently probed her bandage, feeling underneath her jaw and along her neck with the fingertips of both hands.

"It's just a bump, Henri! Lighten up!" Sandy pulled away with a bemused chuckle and shook her head.

Henri straightened up, a concerned paternal frown now evident on his face. "One of us must worry about you. Are you taking anything for that?"

"Pain block. I appreciate your concern, Henri. But really, I'm okay."

Henri paused a long moment and stared at Sandy's bandage. "I see." Abruptly, then, he grabbed a chair, sat down, and after a moment of adjusting his seat height, focused his attention on the center screen, switching scales and resolution on the computer like a child flipping through holovision channels.

"What do you think?" Sandy asked, watching the familiar cerebral form change from a panoply of vivid reds and blues and greens to a shapeless twinkling constellation of lights, like a bare tree strung with Christmas bulbs. Henri rotated the image, slowed the computer scan, and followed the magnified electrical impulses along the chains of nerve cells with his finger.

"Neurotransmitters appear to be functioning," he said, and then switched his attention to the smaller screen, "Neurosteroid level is optimal." After a moment of silent study he turned away from the screen, "Looks like he's ready for a little . . . stimulation."

Sandy smiled. "I'd say so." She watched the muscles in Henri's jaw tighten and relax in spasms as he turned back and scanned the screen—a feeling of excitement seemed to build within her. She clenched her own jaw.

"Azeem," Henri said, "let's go ahead and set the pulse code."

"Set and ready," Azeem replied.

"Ah, so desu ka," Henri nodded appreciatively, "I see," he turned to Sandy. "Your team—"

Sandy craned her neck and looked down into the lab. She seemed to be counting. Henri followed her gaze and saw for himself a congregation of men and women in green scrubs, white lab coats—the entire surgical staff standing ready at the base of the bubble.

"Excellent." Henri stood up, reached for the gooseneck microphone at the wall and flipped a switch. His voice, although amplified, sounded muffled through the glass barrier. "Please, everyone . . . your attention please."

All eyes lifted toward the control booth, to Dr. Henri Nakasone's blocky figure standing at the glass in mint green scrubs, unfastened sterile cap that hung down around his neck like an aviator's helmet. Henri gave a slight bow, then lifted his voice like an ancient Japanese warlord calling his shogunate to arms. "We have come a long, long way together." He cleared his throat. "Let's keep sharp. Together! Remember, we are . . . *family!"* he paused a moment and met each team member's gaze in turn. "We will begin the birthing pulse on my mark. We reach threshold in—" he turned to Sandy.

She leaned forward and checked the monitor. "Forty-six minutes."

Henri turned back toward the glass and repeated for the benefit of the team, "Forty-six minutes. Threshold. When it is time, get him out and get him out fast." He let the words hang in the air a moment before continuing. "We are dealing with deep subconscious. Brain waves indicate he is comatose, but, I remind you all, this is new territory. We cannot be sure what Dr. Balcourt is going through mentally, if anything." Again, he paused. "That so, I want to keep him completely under until we get him out of the amnion and off life support."

"Okay," Henri said with his lips. With his heart, he had already begun to pray, *I have formed with my hands what I did not understand, things too wonderful for me, which I did not know.* Directing a backward glance toward Sandy, he spoke over the open microphone. For a moment his voice cracked. "On my mark . . ." he raised his hand momentarily and then dropped it abruptly, "we begin!"

Sandy spoke into her star-set mike, made a few adjustments to the instruments in front of her, and then looked down into the body shop. A gauzy, reddish-gold *quattrocento* halo appeared in the fluid around Lane's head, emanating from the laser sensors lining the platinum band that crowned his hairless skull. The amnion began to strobe from within, hair-thin tendrils of lightning crawled like spiders over the inner surface of the globe.

Azeem's voice broke the silence. "Laser's set," he called out. "Pulse wave . . . normal."

Henri stepped away from the glass and looked over Sandy's shoulder. "How's the signature compare?"

Sandy compared the patterns of the pre-op brain scans with the new scans from the amnion. "Perfect symmetry," she answered, biting her still swollen bottom lip. She kept her eyes focused on the screen. "He's there . . . somewhere."

Henri returned to his seat and sat down. He was still, his back erect, hands cupped on his knees. His eyes focused on the monitors that displayed the electrical excitation level of Lane's brain. Minutes passed as the relentless jagged patterns scrolled across the screen. Watching, Henri still felt fatigued. He leaned back in his chair and took another look at the luminescent amnion below him. The globe had been rotated. Lane's body was now clearly evident, upright in the position of Da Vinci's *Vitruvian Man,* his head crooked to one side, chin on his chest, arms and legs extended at his side, somnambulistic. Abruptly, Henri saw not the amnion, but himself, long before—a time of peace, a sheltered place.

He is three years old, intently rocking back and forth on that great, beige futon in the living room, listening to the milk slosh mysteriously within his stomach. He is comfortable here, keenly aware of the sweet-scented furniture polish on the surface of the dark lacquered table at his feet. The reflected flames from the fireplace play on the slippery surface of the tabletop. An ancient kiln-fired clay mosaic ashtray, always clean and unused, sits at the center of the table. A silver and ebony bas-relief of Christ on the Cross hangs on the wall over the couch end. Henri spends hours admiring the tragic little man nailed to the cross. There, rendered in silver, he sees the solemn destiny of man. The relief's only blemish is a coarse break gouged from the center of the dark wood, evidence of Henri's earliest explorations. In an instant, he'd managed to push a sharpened pencil through the brittle ebony upright, losing his pencil lead in the process and earning a paddling on his padded end besides. He had been relieved to find the silver face still intact.

The child treasures his solitude, hoping it will not be invaded by the big voices of adults.

"Don't talk to me," he'd lisp in his native Japanese. "I'm the Stranger."

The "Stranger" was somehow his way of seeing himself. His mother, confused and flushed, her voice a little too bright, had asked him repeatedly what exactly he meant by saying that he was the Stranger.

The child didn't mind talking to his mother so much. She hadn't bothered him the way other adults did. But he couldn't answer her question. All he knew was that he liked the way his favorite hologram Westerns portrayed that one mysterious character who later would become a metaphor for his adult life . . . that was the Stranger. The guy walks up to the bar—he's new in town, a man of few words. The bartender says, "What'll you have, Stranger?"

"Whiskey," he says . . . and that's all he says.

Little Henri liked the space the townspeople gave the Stranger. The distance. Nobody ever crowded the Stranger. That's what he was after.

"Impossible!" Sandy muttered for the second time. Her voice was bright, nervous. "Henri! Are you looking at this? Don't you think something's just a little funny here?"

Henri snapped into focus. "What?"

"Just dawned on me. The symmetry . . . it's absolutely . . . perfect! No noise; no data clutter! It's . . . It's *immaculate!* Absolutely flawless! Look at this."

Henri rolled his seat over to Azeem's console. "Trouble?" he asked, checking the screens.

Azeem shook his head solemnly.

Henri looked across the room and read the worried expression on Sandy's face. He turned his gaze back to Azeem. "You're *sure* we're not just watching a duplicate data stream?"

Henri's voice was tense. His eyes now on the identical data streams at the center of the screens, one marked pre-op the other post-op, one indistinguishable from the other. "You're *positive* this is coming from *him* and not from our own computer?"

Azeem made a quick check, his hands a blur on the keyboard. "Dr. Nakasone, sir, of that I am positive."

Azeem looked at Sandy; her face was pale. "It's . . ." he began, then turned his attention back to Henri, "it's impossible to overlay a loop track with this data, I set this up to feed from two separate sources—parallel systems, sir. There's no possibility of contamination. I assure you, sir, this is *definitely* not a loop."

"Threshold," Henri said *sotto voce*. A shiver raised the hair on his back and arms. He moved nimbly to the glass bulkhead, grabbed the mike and flipped the switch. He spoke hurriedly, his voice sharp, demanding. "Attention! We have an early threshold response. Get him out of there! Do it now!"

Three men in scrubs rushed to the amnion, a blur of green obscured Henri's view as the technologists moved their hands over an illuminated panel of instruments. At once, the steel support rings began to rumble, rotating to a position perpendicular to the ground while the sanguinous amniotic fluid drained out of the bubble through a broad lucite pipe in the floor. The top of the amnion opened up like a giant glass eyelid as the sphere locked itself into a recess within the base and telescoped down to bedside height. There was a frenzy of activity as the lights inside the globe went dark. Lane's head jerked spastically just beneath the surface of the fluid like a bobbing apple.

"Sandy, come," Henri said, walking briskly toward the door.

Sandy followed Henri into the elevator.

Henri continued, "I want you to start a peripheral IV. Keep him comatose."

Sandy nodded. They stepped out of the elevator just as the surgical techs lowered Lane's drenched, flaccid body to the gurney, his mouth gulping air like a fish out of water. Lane's expression was walleyed, stunned.

"Get him suctioned!" Sandy barked, approaching the gurney as one of the techs slapped a set of adhesive electrodes to Lane's chest. "Hook up!" she said, ripping a sterile IV rig from its plastic wrap and then nimbly threading the catheter into a vein on Lane's hand.

A nurse leaned over and clipped a set of leads to the electrode patches on his chest and flipped the switch on the cardiac monitor. At once, the familiar *blipblip . . . blipblip . . . blipblip* of Lane's heart broke the silence.

Rolling him over onto his side, the nurse fed a floppy rubber tube into his nostril. A loud, gurgling sound rose into the air as a thick stream of pinkish serum emptied into the suction canister.

"He's clear, he's clear," Sandy said as the canister began sucking air, watching as Lane gasped and vomited serum onto the floor.

Henri stood back out of the way, waiting while Sandy quickly hung a bag of Pavulon. Slowly the fluid dripped into Lane's bloodstream.

"We'll have him under in a moment," she said, stepping to the opposite side of the gurney, her eyes darting from Henri to the IV to the monitor at Lane's head.

Henri sat down and rolled his chair to the head of the gurney. He ripped open a sealed plastic bag and, with a chrome instrument, deftly guided the clear plastic ET tube deep into Lane's throat. Sandy leaned over, taped the tube to Lane's face and then connected it to the ventilator. At once the room was filled with a rhythmic sound as the ventilator's cylindrical bellows pushed a measured volume of air into Lane's lungs.

Henri stood up as the coma-inducing medication slowly dripped into Lane's bloodstream. He could hear his own heartbeat quicken, a counterpoint to Lane's cardiac monitor and the slow-going drone of the ventilator.

"We're losing him!" Sandy screamed at the sudden high-pitched alarm that replaced Lane's pulsing heartbeat.

Henri's eyes immediately went to the cardiac monitor. The familiar scrolling pattern was gone, replaced instead with a flat line.

"Paddles!" Henri stepped forward and held out his hands for the defibrillator.

Sandy disconnected the ventilator, reached under the gurney for an ambubag and connected it to his ET tube.

"Hang on, Lane!" she said, rhythmically working the ambubag by hand, filling his lungs with air.

Henri gripped the cardiac paddles and twisted them into the conductive jelly on Lane's bare chest. He moistened his lips and looked up at the waiting team. "Clear!" his voice was tight. *Lord, I lay my hand upon my mouth.*

Sandy stepped back, a thin stream of sweat rolled down her back as Henri repeated the process, delivering a series of stronger and stronger electrical jolts to start Lane's heart pumping again. Lane's body arched in one violent convulsion after another. The muscles and veins in his face and neck bulged as his head slammed back hard against the table. Henri wiped the sweat off his brow with his sleeve and rubbed the paddles together before twisting them onto Lane's chest for the third time.

"Clear!" He ordered, his tone desperate. Again, Lane's back arched, the webbed cloth restraints dug deep into his flesh, his head thrown back like a man falling to earth through tremendous G-forces.

▼

Blinding white light shone into Lane's right eye, then his left, dazzling, painful light that rendered Henri Nakasone a shadowy chiaroscuro before him. Lane tried to speak to his old friend, but he could not. So he listened, his vision darkening again as the sound of his own name echoed in his mind. Lane! . . . Lane! . . . Lane!"

What came next pierced him, penetrating deep into the marrow of his bones—a rapid, periodic buzzing, coming at regular intervals, sounding near, as if it emanated from inside his own head, then far removed, alternating like the whirling buzz of an ancient helicopter. The noise grew louder and louder, its intervals growing closer and closer together, until what had become a great din abruptly vanished into silence. . . .

Lane felt dizzy, mildly nauseated, his head faintly abuzz. He opened his eyes, blinking to clear his blurry vision. The night air was crystalline, surreal, shattered intermittently by sudden flashes of light and the rumbling of thunder in the distance. He looked down at his feet. I must be dreaming, *he thought, marveling at how his bare toes dimpled the russet dust. His eyes followed the bony arch and curve of his skin above his ankle, up the lean form of his leg to his thigh, slightly thick, muscled, and above . . .*

A slow smile came to his lips—discovering, exploring—he slid his hands up his rippled abdomen to his chest, his neck, his face. There seemed to be eyes in his fingertips, lips too.

Feel! He clenched his fists and tugged at his hair, an open smile now on his face as he looked out over what seemed a great, parched desert extending as far as he could see in every direction.

The ground was barren, cracked like drying mud, and covered with powdered sand as fine as talc. He dropped his hands to his side and stared off into the distance along the stark, straight line of the horizon. Feeling boundless, the center of his consciousness seemed to move with the focus of his attention. At once, he was everywhere . . . ubiquitous.

Slowly, he raised his eyes to the pulsing sky and watched the lightning illuminate the gathering clouds. Great billowing cumulus shadows, slow, roiling, coming alive and dying like a firefly's tail, blinking like molten gold beneath the dross. Partially obscured behind the clouds, three moons showed shimmering feathered slices. As he beheld the chalky planets, Lane felt himself rise into the clouds like a great winged bird. From an eagle's vantage, now, above the blinking mist, he felt himself expand, stretching his arms out wide as if to measure the breadth of the three silvery orbs—one above, two below.

A buoyant pride swelled in him, he rose even higher. I am. I am . . . and all that I see is mine! For a moment, he hovered there, lucid, ecstatic. The instant he turned his eyes back to the desert floor, he was earthbound.

Off in the distance, sudden streaks of lightning split the sky. Like fabric, the darkness *seemed to tear. He looked down at his own form, observing how the bizarre play of light put a crisp edge on the outline of his body. Studying his nakedness, he marveled. Under the moonlight he seemed more three-dimensional than before, separate from the stark, cracked earth upon which he stood, yet somehow more connected to the space that contained him and all that he surveyed.*

Odd, Lane thought, the light differentiates . . . but there's no illumination. *He quieted his mind and for a long time watched the slow-motion storm of clouds, beginning to understand that he had indeed entered a strange land. He understood that he was dreaming, that he could not wake up. He had become a lucid prisoner, locked within the landscape of his own unconscious mind. Alone. Here, where there were no voices to comfort him, no winds to soothe him, he felt released and contained at the same time.*

Finally he spoke. "I am! I am! . . . I am the center of all that is, the one true worth, and all that is is mine! Mine. Mine. Mine. . . ." *There was an echo and simultaneous flash, consuming him in a thundering apotheosis of fission unchained. Then, a deathly absence of color, of light, of form—a darkness so intense he could not breathe.*

▼

Sandy checked the digital clock over Lane's bed: 18:15:37. On her clipboard she marked the elapsed time since his removal from the amnion. Her gaze went to the brain-wave monitors. Sudden spikes appeared and then disappeared in the otherwise rhythmic patterns. *Must be having one nasty dream,* she thought.

She turned to the duty nurse standing at her side, tapping the monitor with her pencil. "Look at this output."

"Something's wrong?" the nurse asked, checking the two leads connected to the platinum band that encircled the circumference of his bald head.

Sandy leaned against the mattress and looked down at Lane, motionless on the bed. "Everything's wrong," she said, her voice heavy. "I just don't understand this scan."

The recovery room door swept open. Henri nodded, looking up at the clock. "How are his stats?" He took the clipboard from Sandy's hands.

"No change," she said, nodding toward the bed. "He's still comatose."

Henri stopped abruptly at the bedside and rubbed the bridge of his nose above his spectacles, "He should be alert."

"You don't look so hot." Sandy said.

Henri looked up from the clipboard. "Migraine."

Sandy shook her head. "Maybe you should—"

"Aaaahhhhhhhhhmmmm!" Lane moaned through his ET tube, writhing as if he had sustained a tremendous electric shock, his head whipping violently from side to side, his eyes rolled back into his skull. A sudden medley of high-pitched alarms filled the room.

Henri jerked around, dropped the clipboard, and grabbed Lane's head, holding it still against the pillow while Sandy stretched the restraints across his chest.

"Maybe this is it," Sandy said. She reached up over Lane's head, switched off the alarm on the cardiac monitor, then checked the connection to the ventilator. She switched off that alarm as well. Lane's screaming trailed off into a series of garbled choking sounds as he twitched and jerked like a fish on a hook back into what appeared to be a disturbed sleep.

"I'm afraid he's going to rip this thing out and do some real damage." Henri's voice was muted. He reached his fingers into Lane's mouth and tugged gently on the ET tube. "He's reached the dream state. Why isn't he coming out of it?" Henri wiped his fingers on the bedsheet, then gently lifted Lane's eyelids, shining his penlight into each pupil. "I don't understand."

Sandy disconnected the tube and shook out the condensation. The tube made a faint whistling sound as she swung it toward the floor. She snapped the tube back in place, then picked up the clipboard off the floor. "Maybe he's not locking in," she said, brushing her hair from her eyes with the back of her wrist. "Maybe he's gone."

"Locking in?" the nurse asked, her hands still trembling.

"Dr. Balcourt anticipated a lock-in—a violent surge in sensory input to the conscious synthetic brain," Henri explained, returning his penlight to his pocket.

Sandy adjusted the controls on the EEG. "I wonder if the hyperstimulation from the mapping and disengagement process was too much?"

"Sounds like he's in pain," the nurse said.

"No way of knowing . . ." Henri's voice trailed off. After a short pause he began again. He turned to Sandy. "They were *his* plans, *his* designs. I followed them exactly . . . exactly."

"This *is* the first attempt, Henri," Sandy responded.

"That's what bothers me the most—not knowing what to expect. If he could have just had a little more time to complete his notes . . ." Henri looked down at Lane.

Sandy nodded her head in agreement, her eyes drawn to the sound of a telephone ringing. She kept silent as the nurse left the room to answer the call. "You remember what Lane said, early on, when we first started talking about the transfer?" She waited for his nod, "Didn't he say that the convergence of stimuli on the new brain might be overwhelming, that it might cause . . . What were his words? A brutal kind of firestorm within the brain? What's that sound like to you?"

Henri looked confused.

"Firestorm, brutal firestorm—he used those words." Sandy's voice was insistent.

"An epileptic episode?" Henri's brows furrowed. "Is that what you're getting at?"

Sandy stepped out from behind the bed. "Grand mal." She stuffed her hands in her pockets.

"So?"

"So why don't we treat it the way they used to treat seizures?"

"Shock." Henri's voice was flat. It was less a question and more a statement of disbelief.

"Why not?"

Henri thought about it for a moment. "I'm trying to save him, not torture him."

"I don't know." She paused a moment before continuing. "Check his brain scans, Henri. What are we going to do? Where do we draw the line? Great! We built the world's first immortal vegetable. Look at him. There he is, completely cataleptic—maybe for eternity thanks to modern technology. Unable to move, unable to eat, unable to breathe on his own, locked in who knows what kind of semi- or unconscious mental state . . . Henri, that's what *I* call torture."

Henri motioned back toward the observation room. He waited for the doors to slide open and then followed Sandy inside. "One week," he said, his voice unusually tight as the doors swept shut at his back. "One week. We'll either bring him around or—"

Sandy crossed her arms. "Or what?"

"I don't know."

PART TWO

Chapter

5

Henri got up from his chair in the darkened recovery room and stepped over to the glass wall. He flipped a switch and waited in silent prayer as the electric shades slowly twisted open, his eyes lifting toward the starry, predawn sky.

Lord, take me into your arms. Deliver me from this servile fear. I am so . . . so lost in darkness and confusion, how dare I step farther without Your grace and guidance? After a long, quiet moment, Henri turned toward his unconscious friend. The silence seemed to beg. Again his eyes went to the starry sky.

"What do you want me to do?" he asked, his voice weary, cracking from the strain of the last week—day after day, hour after relentless hour, speaking to a man trapped within the prison of his own mind. Henri's voice was ragged now, strained from constant talk, trying to trigger *something* in Lane's mind that might bring him out of his coma. He turned his gaze back to Lane, motionless in the bed. A faint greenish glow from the monitors kept Lane hidden in shadows. "What do you want from me?" Henri's voice broke. He cleared his throat quietly and returned his gaze to the window. "What more can I do?" Lifting his eyes skyward, his tone became quietly ironic. "What?"

He let his gaze drop to the sprawling, dew silvery lawn. The starlit scene seemed cold, dreary. Henri felt something like the approach of winter in his bones. He felt it combine with the stress of the past seven days like a malevolent weight bearing down on his shoulders. He felt old and tired and spent. For a long time he stood there at the window, silent, looking out into the early morning darkness. Finally he let out a deep sigh, stepped back to the bedside, and began again, "Lane, can you hear me?"

Silence.

"Lane? Something—you've got to give me something!"

Silence.

Henri sat down on the side of the bed and took Lane's hand. It was flaccid, unresponsive, still; Henri gave him a firm squeeze. "Lane, reach out, talk to me. Talk to me! I've tried everything I can think of. I've pored over your notes. This—this should not be happening."

Silence.

Henri dropped Lane's hand gently and slid his glasses down a bit. He closed his eyes and pinched the bridge of his nose. The heartbeat in his fingertips echoed the sharp, throbbing pain he felt just behind his eyes. For some moments he allowed himself to float, drift, past the lab, past Lane. *Let it go . . . let it go.* Over the years those words had become cathartic.

Henri's grandfather is wearing his traditional gray, broad-sleeved yokata. *He clasps his hands in front of him and smiles. Thin gray hair, dark, wide-set eyes completely hooded by his tawny, wrinkled hide. A fresh smell of soap and orange blossoms rises from his skin. He wears open sandals over his fluorescent white* tabi.

A devout Christian, he had told the boy of his ancestor's custom for the coconut-shaped Buddhist talisman; the Daruma—the Bodhiddharma—*a round, ball-like doll with a painted face. The doll was long ago believed to be graced with the power to grant wishes. The* Daruma's *eyes are white, blind. "They believed you paint one eye black when you make your wish, the other when your wish comes true," the old man had said, smiling at the ancient superstitions.*

Henri's grandfather had lived an exemplary Christian life, having worked with humility and a holy fervor most of his adult years to acquire the virtues the Savior had set forth as the end of our care and labor. Henri loved the old man, his quiet wisdom, his gentle heart, his patience, his meekness, his tenderness and his understanding. The old man had embraced Christianity as the one true faith as had his father before him and his father's father before that. For the Nakasone family, Buddhist artifacts like the Daruma *were*

*honored for their place in the Eastern culture and
not as religious icons.*

*"I have a very big wish, Grandfather," the
child says energetically, bringing a painted,
homemade kite from behind his back in a quick
but clumsy attempt at prestidigitation. The image
of a one-eyed Daruma is painted in black and red
and yellow and white on the face of the kite.
"Come! See!" The boy leaps forward, running for
a grassy hillock nearby.*

*The old man is slow to follow. Young Henri
turns and for a brief moment he watches the old
man climb the lush green knoll, the wind tossing
his hair and robe as it ruffles and bends the long,
slender-necked grasses. The sky is a deep blue
scattered with puffs of smoky clouds. The air is
sweet, fragrant with the drift of meadowland and
white spring flowers on the breeze. Before the old
man reaches the top, the boy launches his kite and
watches as it stitches its way high into the air.*

*"See," the child thrusts out an open handful
of small stones and pebbles. "I will grant my own
wish. I will mark the other eye with one of these
stones, then . . . it will be so!"*

*They look up. There is the gentle stitching of
the circular kite against the sky; the knotted
fustian tail, serpentine in the breeze; the graceful
bow and play of the twine; the parabolic trajectory
of the stones as the child hurls them with all his
might against that furtive blinking face, only to
watch as they plummet to the ground, one after
the other. All in vain. The day is too good for*

Daruma *kites, and it soars far above him, out of reach.*

The old man watches everything—the boy exhausting his hoard of pebbles, then frantically hunting for more in the tall grass, his body barely a head and shoulders higher than the tallest blades. Finally, the twine snaps against a strong gust and the kite tumbles away like a leaf on the breeze. The child runs into the old man's arms, his face shining wet.

The old man lets him cry. "Let it go," the old man says. His voice rings warm and reassuring. Soon the tears turn to whimpers. The old man lifts the child away from his chest, looks deep into his watery eyes, and dries his face with his thumbs. "Some things are not ours to decide, little one. Such is the mystery of our Lord's will. Amen—so be it."

Henri looked down at his watch: 4:27 A.M. *Still a few hours left.*

"Lane, listen. Listen carefully. How many years have we worked on this? *Remember! Think!* Think of all you've been through. You've done it, Lane. *You've done it!* Now just . . . wake! . . . up! Wake up!"

Silence.

Henri let a few moments pass before he began again, "I can't help you if you don't reach." He stood, took the damp cloth from the bedside and dabbed at Lane's brow, his voice continuing, exhausted. "I . . . I don't know how."

Henri dried his eyes on his sleeve. "Tell me how to help you. Lane! We only have a few more hours. You know I can't let you linger like this. I *won't* leave you like this . . . not like this." He dropped the cloth on the bedside tray, drew a pen from his breast pocket and wrote slowly across Lane's chart, "No heroic resus."

For a long time Henri stood there, staring at the chart. *No Hero . . . No Hero . . . No Hero.*

"This," he finally said, "is all I can do." He let the chart down quietly, his gaze moving over the man in the shadows. "Reality, Lane. Fifteen years. Drop the mask, you used to say." There was a long pause before he continued. "Ura . . . I—" he choked on his words, ura. Face was so important. He paused and then began again, his voice slow and deliberate, the words difficult. "I . . . envied . . . you. I envied your paralysis—" A spontaneous chuckle cut his words short, his eyes filled. "Hai. Fifteen years, I became your arms, your legs. You . . . you were my mind. My higher mind, my higher self. I watched you, unable to move, your genius, the energy you felt for life—boundless." Henri thought about it, drew in a deep breath and spoke with a sudden thrill, "It was . . . infectious!"

He wiped the corners of his eyes twice and stepped back to the window. For a long moment he kept still, watching the mist rise from the reflector pool, crooked, swirling, like an inverted rainfall. "I needed that from you. I needed your energy. I became . . . addicted to it." He let his head fall back and looked up at the stars through watery eyes. "We were made for each other, you and I, Lane'san. You, unable to feel your body; I, unable to feel my life. My life . . . what *is* my life? Who knows the answer to that question, old friend? The nail that sticks out is hammered down! *Watashi wa Lucien Machine*

Corporation no Nakasone desu." Henri pulled away from the window and looked back at the bed. "I am Lucien Machine Corporation's Dr. Nakasone. *That* is *honne,* the unspoken truth. We are what we do."

Henri looked over at the darkened bed, a dim greenish glow fluoresced the gentle white linen folds. He felt a strange twinge of envy again. *When I do this, which one of us dies?* Slowly, reluctantly, he removed the accordion respiratory hose from Lane's ET tube then switched off the ventilator. Henri's awareness of the darkness and shadows crossing the room heightened as the drone of the bellows abruptly stopped. There seemed a conspicuous absence of light.

Using an empty syringe, he deflated the balloon cuff that had kept the ET tube lodged in Lane's trachea and, with both hands, slowly pulled the curved tube clear from Lane's mouth. Lane gagged, coughed, and then began to breathe on his own. Henri reached up and switched off the bank of monitors. He didn't hear the door, only Sandy's quiet, plaintive voice as she entered the room.

"Henri, you've been at it long enough."

"I just disconnected him," Henri answered, quickly collecting himself. His head held slightly back, he seemed self-conscious, afraid he might spill his own tears.

Sandy stepped quietly to Henri's side. "We really came close."

"Hai," Henri's reply came out like a scratchy whisper. He reached for his penlight. "He's in there, Sandy," he said, clearing his throat, gently prying open Lane's eyelids, alternating the light between

Lane's eyes. "I know he's in there. I just don't know how to reach him."

"You've done everything you could. We all have. You said it yourself, Henri, we can't stand by and let him linger in this vegetative state forever."

Henri returned his penlight to his pocket and motioned toward the observation room door. "And it would be forever," she continued, following him into the small glassed-in room.

"He has refused to die. How can we do less?

A brilliant burst of morning sunlight came from the window in the recovery room. Sandy squinted and shook her head, recoiling from the sudden glare, "You left the shades open! No light before coffee, you know that." She stepped out the door and stopped cold. *"Henri!"* her voice was suddenly bright.

Henri looked out through the glass partition and then leaped out of his chair, his eyes wide as he entered the room. Lane stood naked at the center of the glass wall, his slender body a dark silhouette against the rose-colored dawn. He turned. Slowly, he raised his arms to Henri. The platinum band encircling his hairless skull glinted in the morning light. A full third of the wire leads dangled loose and disconnected over his shoulder.

Henri buckled as an unexpected wave of heat surged through him. He tried to say something but his voice caught, his breathing suddenly reduced to a confused stutter. Slowly, he approached his friend, his throat tightening with each step. The last few steps closed quickly. He locked his jaw and embraced

Lane, fighting and failing with everything he had to hold back his tears, his heart overflowing with wonder and gratitude.

Lane's arms gathered him in. Henri felt elevated and dwarfed at the same time. For a long silent moment neither of them moved. Henri clutched him, tightly this time, before he finally pulled away and gazed into Lane's eyes. Henri wept. Lane's eyes, too, were wet. His expression was radiant, blissful, benign. Henri held his gaze and nodded before he ducked under Lane's shoulder, gesturing to Sandy for help. Gently, they helped Lane back to his bed. The tears all three spilled as they crossed the room spoke the only words necessary.

Lane struggled to keep his eyes open as his friends tucked him into bed. He strained to focus on the two blurry figures standing before him. Then he realized that he was actually touching flesh.

Hands! he thought, amazed. He squeezed Henri's hand. Sandy quickly reached for Lane's other hand. He squeezed hers, a slight smile creasing the corners of his mouth. He felt the linen sheet against his skin, his back pressed into the mattress, his hands clutching Henri on one side and Sandy on the other.

The sense of Sandy's touch crept through him. He closed his eyes and savored the barrage of physical sensations, then drew in a deep lingering breath. The air tasted like heavenly flowers, like spring, like summer, like no air he had ever known before. He smiled faintly, and even as he drifted back toward sleep, he smiled.

Chapter

6

Vatican City
October 13, 2065

Carla lolled cross-legged on her bed, poring over the now-dated news headlines. "THE LAME WALK! THE BLIND SEE! THE MEDICAL MIRACLE OF NEURAL SYNTHESIS!"

She felt morbid, nervous, despite the delicate drift of the Brandenberg concerto rising like a lullaby from her stereo against the wall. *Alonealonealone.* Drawing in a deep breath, she let her head fall back and closed her eyes. Tonight, like every other night, she was alone, immured in her room like some half-demented solipsist, her nose buried in a stack of medical reports and scientific journals six inches thick, assiduously trying to cull meaning from a collection of texts chockful of long forgotten terms-of-art, mathematical formulae and abstruse scientific jargon that read like so much intellectual legerdemain.

Impulsively, she rolled her head back and forth along her shoulders. *Relax,* she told herself, wincing at the gristly crack of bone and cartilage in her neck and back. Looking up, a minuscule flash of blue light on her bedside COM panel caught her eye: a telephone call. She lifted the control wand off her lap, silenced the stereo, leaned across the bed, and slapped the COM with her free hand.

"Dr. Henri Nakasone calling from Montreal," said the cool computer voice at the other end.

Carla sat quickly at the edge of her bed, modestly tugging the bottom of her t-shirt over her underpants. She cleared her throat and removed her reading glasses. "Yes, Dr. Nakasone, thanks for getting back to me." She nodded, listening intently to the haggard voice at the other end. "Yes, I understand. I understand." She waited for him to finish. "Doctor, I called to follow up on an earlier conversation I had with Dr. Sandy Benson. Just a few questions, really. If you don't mind."

"Not at all," Henri's voice cracked, again betraying his fatigue. "Shall we go to image?"

"Uh—one second," she said. Carla quickly foraged through her papers before slipping into a pair of washed-out jeans. She snapped her pants at the waist, leaned over, and touched the visual panel. Henri's hologram appeared in the empty space between her bed and her desk. He wore wrinkled green hospital scrubs.

"You'll have to forgive my attire," she said, slightly winded, "I was catching up on some reading. Your work, mostly."

"I'm sure that can get to be very tiresome." He smiled wearily. "Take it from me, it's much better to do the work than it is to read about it."

"I can only imagine," she said, then, feeling a little doltish at the awkward silence that followed, she continued. "Dr. Benson and I had discussed—when was it? All the way back in Stockholm, I think—your plans for . . . well, for moving into medical therapeutics. From what little I've read, your work seems to be moving forward—now, correct me if I'm wrong here—maybe even a bit faster than you had initially thought?"

"Yes, that is certainly true."

"Ah!" His answer pleased her. She went on. "Are we close to seeing any therapeutic applications outside the orthopedic and vision areas?"

"Soon." Henri sounded relieved. "We'll be doing some organ implants very soon. Kidneys—"

Carla interrupted: "You did say kidneys?"

"Yes—" Henri was caught off guard by the alacrity of her response. "That will be our focus, therapeutic replacements, organs mostly."

"You say therapeutic—I assume you mean new drug therapy."

"Well, perhaps therapeutic is a misnomer. With neural synthesis, we're not really concerned with remedial treatments. No. We're surgeons, medical engineers. We'd rather replace a diseased organ entirely . . . use an engineered organoid and do it all in one surgery. Get in and get out—straightforward. That way we avoid the medical risks inherent with the 'multiples' required of more conventional therapies."

"Multiples? I'm afraid I don't follow."

"Very sorry—I'm referring to multiple surgeries. If we approached patient care as traditional medical therapists, concerned ourselves with rehabilitating diseased systems instead of engineering totally new ones, we'd have to make multiple surgical intrusions. Each time you go under the knife, that's a risk. I think you can see, that's just not an optimal approach. The way we look at it, why make numerous intrusions just so you can tweak what will most likely be—in the end—an unstable composite anyway: this part biological, that part synthetic. *Synthetic . . ."* Henri mused out loud. "That's not really a very good word is it? I should think we need to come up with a better term," he muttered.

Carla cleared her throat. "I ask, Doctor, because . . . well, it's just that I have a . . . a very . . . *special* friend back at the children's hospital in Pachuca. A little boy. He's suffering from renal failure."

"I see," Henri turned away for a moment and answered someone's question off-camera with a brusque nod, *"Hai!* Very sorry. Problems," he shook his head, his face pensive. "Okay, where were we? Ah, yes—why don't you have your friend's case history sent to me? We'll have a look at it."

Carla broke into a wide smile. "You're serious." A feeling of relief washed over her.

"Of course."

"Right away, then! I'll have it sent to you right away. If there's something there, something you can do—"

"Send them along. I or Dr. Benson will get back to you with our findings. We'll talk about it then."

"Thank you so much, Dr. Nakasone. You don't realize how much this means to me." Carla beamed, her voice tense, excited.

"We'll do what we can. Was there anything else?" Henri asked, his attention again drawn off-camera.

"No, that was it, Doctor. I'm trying to get this report filed. Just interested in how far you'd come, your plans—"

"Very well, if there's anything else, feel free to call," Henri replied, his hand raised in polite farewell as his hologram vanished.

Carla tapped the COM, stood up, and began to pace. She spoke to the monitor. "Get me Archbishop Alejandro Torrez in Pachuca."

▼

Archbishop Torrez took the call at his desk. "Carla, you must have read my mind, child. I was just about to give you a call." He smiled warmly as Carla's hologram materialized at the side of his desk.

"Alejandro, I've got some *very* good news," she said, aware her words were coming out in a rush.

"Maybe you should hear *my* news first."

Something in his tone made her go still. She was in no mood for his political wrangling. "What is it, Alejandro?"

"I'm afraid it's Eddie. He's—he's worse, Carla."

"Oh, Alejandro—"

"He's been taken into the critical care unit."

She kept silent, suddenly lost in a kind of darkness, struggling to keep her composure.

"I thought you'd want to know," Torrez said.

"I wish I'd never come here—" the words sounded distant, flat, weak to her.

"Carla—"

"The timing, Alejandro," her voice cracked, "the timing's unbelievable!" Again, for a long time she kept silent, "I called," she finally continued, her desperation fulminating in tears, "to tell you that Dr. Nakasone asked me to have Eddie's records forwarded to him in Montreal. I thought Eddie might . . ." Her face was wet, gleaming. "I'm coming back. I'll talk to Cardinal Verrechio right away. I need to be there."

The connection broke. For a long time, it seemed, she just sat there. And then she was peeling off her clothes, she was standing in the shower, crying, as the jets of water stung her cheek. Eddie's face. It seemed to hang before her. The pope's face, her audience with the enfeebled Holy Father. Eddie's face. She needed to be there, with him. She wanted to clutch his tiny hand in hers. She wanted to kiss him and make him better. Then, the ultrasound, his pathetic little hologram turning before her. Carla put her hands to her face and tried to wipe away the negative image. *Touch him! I'll touch him!* she concentrated until her head pounded. *Lord, I love this child. If it is Your will, please, God, spare him to me.*

▼

Cardinal Verrechio stood as Carla entered his office. The walls were covered with leather-bound books, and the room smelled of pipe tobacco, sweet and pungent at the same time. A rustic globe that normally concealed a crystal cognac decanter and glasses sat open at the side of his wine-dark mahogany desk. An empty snifter rested on top of the black kidskin folio at center. Carla nearly tripped over a Persian carpet where the corner had lifted from the floor.

"I'm sorry. I've got to have that tacked down," Verrechio said, extending his hand.

She kissed his cheeks in stiff European fashion and then followed his gesture to one of two wing-back leather chairs. "Thank you, Excellency, for seeing me on such short notice," she said, as Verrechio took the other chair.

He smiled. "Nonsense." The cardinal reached for the twisted briar pipe and gold lighter that rested on a small table at his side. "Now," he spoke with patient forbearance as he ignited the laser match and drew on his pipe, "what is it that is so urgent?" He returned the lighter to the table before giving Carla his full attention.

"I've a friend, a little boy . . . I just got word . . . he's very ill," she explained, barely able to control her own gnawing feeling of bereavement.

"I see. One of your children from the hospital?" he waited for her to nod affirmation, "I'm sorry to hear that."

"I must return to Pachuca."

The cardinal exhaled a billowing cloud of smoke over both their heads. "Of course. How long would you be gone?"

"That's the thing. I don't think I'll be coming back," she said without lifting her eyes from her hands.

Verrechio cleared his throat. "Have you thought this through, Carla?"

"I'm confused, I'll say that much," she looked up and reluctantly surveyed the room. "I just think I belong with my own people. It's where my heart is." She felt something corrosive well up inside her, like guilt.

"I see." He withdrew the pipe from his mouth and placed it gently on the table. The cardinal paused a moment before continuing with equanimity. "I can understand the strength of the feelings that must tug at your heart. Has the archbishop counseled you in this?"

"I haven't told him yet. Only that I'm coming back. Now. I'm sure he just assumes that it's a temporary visit." Her eyes reddened and blurred.

"He'll be disappointed."

Carla nodded.

"Well, I'm sure you understand what difficulties your decision would mean for us. You know our contract carries certain responsibilities. The primary of which *is* your presence here in Rome. At least until you complete your report." He looked away for a moment. "I wish you'd reconsider. We've all lost loved ones. It's hard. I do know. But please consider our situation here. We can barely keep abreast of the news coming out of Montreal as it is. We need your help, Carla. Your work is excellent. We do so much appreciate your service—"

"I seem to be of very little service here," she interrupted, dropping her gaze once again to her folded hands.

Verrechio uncrossed his legs and leaned forward in his chair, his elbows resting on the armrests. "If I'm intruding, please—stop me. My role with you here, Carla, is strictly to act as your . . . *liaison* with this lumbering old organization. I have no authority other than that which you allow me."

Carla stirred uncomfortably in her seat. *This is getting nowhere.* She sighed and looked out the window.

▼

Hours after his meeting with Carla, the cardinal's telephone sounded a trill tone, disturbing him from his work. He tapped the COM absently and continued poring over the spread sheets laid out on his desk before him. "Yes, what is it?"

"Dr. Sandy Benson calling from LMC in Montreal," the computer announced.

"Put her through," Verrechio said, touching the switch that controlled the door locks to his office.

Sandy's hologram materialized in front of the open cognac globe as the mahogany doors silently swung shut and locked with a muffled concatenation of clicks. "We've done it, Massimo." She smiled. "We've done it. I can't believe it. Death's door and back!"

Verrechio leaned back in his chair and rested a slippered foot on the side of an open desk drawer. "He's conscious?"

"Conscious." Sandy beamed.

Verrechio kept silent.

"By the way," Sandy surveyed the dimly lit room, "What's keeping you at the office? You're working late tonight, aren't you?"

"I had to get through this infernal paperwork. Part of this whole reorganization fiasco. We're trying to liquidate our assets and redistribute the treasury. Everybody's got a hand in it. This Liberation thing's a mess, I'm telling you!"

"How's that going to affect *our* arrangement?" Sandy asked.

"LMC is a blue-chip security. Blue chips are considered liquid. Won't affect it at all. But I do think the LMC holdings will remain with us . . . that is . . . in Rome." The cardinal smiled.

"Good." Sandy seemed pleased. "Good. That's one less thing to worry about."

Verrechio reached up and stroked his collar. "So . . . he's alive; he's conscious."

"Oh, he's conscious all right. We were speaking with him just a few hours ago. He's up, walking around. He's . . . ," she laughed, "he's something else, Massimo. You've got to see this to believe it."

Verrechio nodded his head almost imperceptibly. "Maybe it's not too late, after all," he said to himself, looking off to the side.

"What's that?"

The cardinal leaned forward in his chair. "What about his chances from here on out?"

"We have no idea. I mean—none. Nobody does. Fact is, we're all trying to assimilate the shock, trying to get over how the transfer has gone this far without any glitches. I guess it pays when you're on the side of the angels."

The cardinal pushed back his chair and stood up. "Interesting, Sandy. That depends on which angels you've sided with. I think we may have to reconsider our options. The Liberation *is* contingent on this Holy Father being the last."

"Cardinal! You're a devil," Sandy interjected.

Verrechio continued, somewhat less than enthusiastic with Sandy's appellation. "What can we do to make sure the Holy Father will be next in line?"

"Say the word."

Verrechio reached for his pipe and lighter. "I can hear the Liberationists howling already."

A look of bemusement appeared on Sandy's face. "I don't see what their gripe could be. I thought you said they agreed to maintain and support the papacy for as long as this pope lives."

Verrechio ignited the laser match and took several nursing draws on his pipe before exhaling a billowing cloud of smoke over his own head. "Easy concessions to make with the Holy Father on his deathbed."

He stepped around to the front of his desk and leaned back on the edge of the desktop, studying Sandy's smiling face in silence before speaking. "Strange . . . ways . . . indeed." He took another long draw on his pipe, his eyes on the handpainted medieval map of the world off-kilter on his opened globe. "What does this involve?" he asked, finally, refusing to face Sandy directly.

"We're dealing with a five-step procedure," Sandy began.

"Please," Verrechio said expectantly, turning away from the globe. "I'm listening." He removed his pipe and with his free hand carefully plucked a morsel of tobacco from his moistened lips.

"First, we gain surgical access to the brain," Sandy explained. "This is accomplished with the laser microsaber. We need the precision offered us by the laser's robotic controller." Sandy waited for Verrechio to acknowledge that he was following along. "Next comes the actual capture. This step takes us close to twelve hours."

Verrechio lifted his eyebrows and nodded.

Sandy paused for a moment, then continued. "During the capture phase, we use the laser to excite the brain one cellular level at a time. Ultimately, the tissue is destroyed. However, if we're successful, the bioelectric signature will be captured and held within the computer for future integration into a schematic map of his mind."

"The tissue's destroyed." Verrechio furrowed his brows. "I thought you were using drugs to excite the brain."

"Too shallow. We only used drugs to *emulate* capture. We can't get the map without the microsaber. No map, no synthesis."

Verrechio shrugged. "I get the image of you peeling the brain like an onion."

"Now you sound like Henri." She smiled, nodding. "Not a bad way to look at it. Anyway, after the capture comes the body synthesis. That takes several days. Only the vivification process remains after that. We need to give the system a pretty good jolt to get it functioning. Hopefully, the shock won't disturb the higher brain functions. I mean, we're not interested in saving a residual aspect of our patient's personality; we're trying to save the patient . . . intact."

Verrechio leaned farther back on the desktop, one foot now dangling off the floor. "Best to be careful not to peel the onion too far," he said, a smile disappearing as he took another draw on his pipe.

Carla leaned back and closed her eyes. She felt the buoyancy of the solid rubber tires through the structural steel struts underneath her seat. An erratic *clickcrunch!* of metal, like a fatigued shock absorber, punctuated the rattle and shake of the lumbering aircraft as it rolled down the runway at speed. *Just a few hours. Hold on, little one, hold on.* Carla felt a dull pressure on her chest as the air shuttle lurched upward and then suddenly lifted off the ground, pushing her back and down into her seat, the entire plane vibrating for a brief moment as the wheels retracted and disappeared into the underbelly of the aircraft. The drone of the in-flight computer, a mindless vocalization of emergency landing procedures, faded beneath the roar of the jet engines.

Everything around her seemed to combine in a mellifluous swirl of rushing air, a blurry, white-noise backdrop to the plaintive voice in her own head.

What am I doing? she wondered, *What?* She lingered for a long while in a gauzy, cataleptic realm, not much more than a brainless, breathing organism occupying vacant space. Numb. Insensate. Self-absorbed. A sudden rattle from the serving tray rolling up beside her jolted her awake and into focus.

"Excuse me." The young steward smiled, juggling a tray in each hand. "Will you be having a snack?"

Carla adjusted herself in her seat and nodded. She pushed her glasses back on her nose and made an effort to survey the hors d'oeuvres tray placed before her. A collection of hard and soft cheeses—wedges individually wrapped in silver and gold foil—a plum-purple cluster of Concord grapes dew-moistened from the refrigerator, a crescent of honeydew melon topped by a sprig of peppermint, and a plump, red strawberry completed the complement of garden color neatly arranged on the rectangular white china plate. Off to the side, a small osier basket held dinner rolls—light and dark—and three sesame covered bread sticks on a bed of lilac tissue. A miniature twist-top bottle of mineral water—*Deutschewasser: aufgasse*—crowned the setting next to a glistening water goblet that seemed to cry out to her for its fill, a thin lemon slice its only garnish. She reached for the bottle and opened it with a quick twist, pouring its sparkling contents full into the glass. She dropped the lemon slice into the water, lifted the glass to her lips, and lingered on the clean citrus aroma, tinted with ice, before she took a sip; the cool ambrosial liquid spilled quickly down her throat. She swallowed. Drawing in a chill breath, she closed her eyes, her mind replaying her visit to Rome.

A cardinal . . . Carla studies the old man as they walk. Even in street clothes he would seem a prince, a prelate.

She follows the old cardinal as he shuffles up the papal stairway, the gentle sanding of their shoe soles against the stairs echoing through the richly ornamented Clementine hall. She looks up from the sun-washed gray marble floor, her eyes drawn to the magnificent painted ceilings. The midday sun illuminates the ancient lunette frescoes, bleaching the milky flesh tones of the cherubim, while highlighting the perfectly formed human figures draped and veiled in flowing robes and mantles and tissues of powder blue, apricot and saffron, amethyst and crimson. She notices the arched windows. Their gauzy white draperies hang open, the length of the floor-to-ceiling smoked glass, and seem out of place in comparison to the heavy, gilded opulence of the surrounding architecture. The modern light fixtures, collected in triplets every ten paces or so, join with the draperies in a refusal to blend in.

Carla feels her heart sink. She feels like a child who has eaten a rich dessert to the point of surfeit. The children. She looks up at the panoply of plump-bottomed cherubim. Winged . . . perfect. She sighs quietly as the haunting image of her own imperfect children at the hospital now come to her mind. Real children . . . children you can love. By comparison, these paintings seem cold and unreal. She glances over at the old cardinal and notices

something unreal about his expression, too.
Pampered . . . wealthy. *She thinks of the weathered,
brown faces of the poor people she left behind at the
base community. She smiles to herself when she
thinks of the old man in the sombrero. She recalls
watching him in conversation, his gestures genuine
and sharp. She can, for a moment, see the salt-white
flash of his smile, and, thinking of it, she smiles
herself.*

The old cardinal, watching Carla, nods at the
painting. "It is beautiful, isn't it?"

"Oh, yes," she hurriedly agrees. "Beautiful."

*As the two approach the papal chambers, Carla
switches her attention from thoughts of home to the
approaching meeting—her first official audience with
the Holy Father. The sight of the Swiss guards—two
translucent cylindrical sentries who stand like Roman
columns at the entry to the anteroom leading to the
papal suite—grips Carla with anxiety. Their
microcircuit innards can be clearly seen through the
sparkling outer surface of their lucite skins, like the
guts of a fine Swiss watch, except for the three-foot
square scarlet field at their centers, embossed by a
single white Swiss cross. She touches her moist palms
to her dress as the two robotic sentries scan her
identification badge with a luminous cannonade of
ruby-red laser light.*

An electronic female voice speaks; its tone calls
to Carla's mind a state of sedation. "Thank you . . .
The Holy Father . . . will see you now."

*They pass the guards and walk through the
papal salon without a word. The room is furnished
in an eclectic mix of old and new, mostly giving the
impression of an ancient Parisian stateroom. A
group of cardinals gathered around the window
ledge is engaged in a hushed debate. They seem
posed, like a Dutch master's painting. The
theme—conundrums and complexities, one man's*

lips to another man's ear—repeats itself twelve times as Carla counts those present in this living tableau of scarlet robes and weathered flesh. All at once, faces turn, pausing for a brief moment as the princes of the Church watch who enters the chamber and then return to their conversation without further acknowledgment.

The pope's bedchamber doors sweep open. A sickroom smell carried on an ill wind of overconditioned air strikes Carla at once. The pontiff's room is empty except for his bed, the medical equipment, and the team of nurses and attendants who hover over him, checking digital displays, making entries into logs, keeping him clean, comfortable.

The bed is long and narrow. In fact, as Carla draws near, she notices that the pope himself must have been an impressive man at full height; Carla reckons well over six feet. The slope of his abdomen describes a man who has taken care of himself with a commitment to exercise. His deeply creased face and white, thinning hair seem to blend in with the all white bed linens. A gurgling, green nasal tube protrudes from his nose, carrying a bile-colored liquid, drop by bubbling drop, into a suction canister that rests on a dolly beside his bed. His ventilator pumps a rhythmic volume of air into his lungs through a coiled tube connected to his trachea. The clear, rose-colored respiratory tubing drapes over his chest and collects tiny droplets of condensation that jiggle with each rush of air. The Holy Father's closed, full lips are gray at the edges. Seated at the pontiff's bedside, a nurse wipes away the mucus residue that has collected at the corners of his mouth. Carla studies the pope's face. His cheeks are gaunt and hollow, his high, regal forehead is furrowed, his skin seems sickly; pallid, yellow. In his eyes she sees bewilderment—and fear.

The old cardinal speaks, interrupting Carla's thoughts with an introduction to Cardinal Verrechio who stands at the far side of the pontiff's bed and greets her with a silent nod. His calm, gray eyes are informed with a studied grace and sophistication. Verrechio motions for her to step closer to the pontiff's bedside and then carefully leans through the maze of tubing and wires, across the bed, and slides the sheet down, exposing the pope's right hand.

Carla looks down at the large, knotted vascular hand, splotched from countless intrusions by intravenous catheters. The neatly manicured fingernails, waxed and buffed, speak well of his care.

"Holy Father, may I present Dr. Carla MacGregor," Verrechio announces quietly into the pontiff's ear.

Carla bows her head deferentially, her eyes drawn to the pope's tremoring hand, which he attempts to lift without success.

"I'm afraid he's having some difficulty," Verrechio explains, snapping the sheet back over the pope's hand with a quick flick of his wrist. He makes a gesture to the medical attendants as he extricates himself from the web of medical paraphernalia and steps out from behind the bed. *"Come, we can talk in the salon,"* he says, motioning back toward the door.

Carla rises to her feet and steps away from the bed. Her eyes linger on the man considered by Catholic Liberationists worldwide to be the world's final pope—the last religious monarch in a line of men that spanned two millennia. An odd feeling of denouement grips her as she turns and leaves the room.

Carla opened her eyes and took another sip of her drink. A faint current of cool air moved over her brow from the nozzle above her head. Dolefully, she drew in a deep breath and looked out the window; down, to the wind scattered canopy of rag-like clouds and, beneath that, to the vast expanse of steely, slate-green ocean that seemed to cover the entire earth below. A wide, sun-dappled swath of sea stretched out before her like a glittering avenue of shattered glass. For a moment she was back in Mexico with Eddie—his smiling face, the soft feel of his skin—but as the plane passed over a low ceiling of clouds and as the water darkened before disappearing from view, the stinging reality of Torrez' call came back to her. A nightmarish image of Eddie passed before her—a death mask, a cadaver. She took another sip and closed her eyes, struggling to keep her anguish in abeyance.

"You should know something, Carla," Verrechio speaks to her before the group of cardinals. His voice is smooth, throaty, a faint trace of Italian evident in his words. "I have been aware of Dr. Balcourt and his . . . revolutionary work for some time." He speaks softly, meeting each man's eyes in turn. "I've already arranged for our agents in Switzerland to make the necessary funds available to this research effort through Dr. Sandy Benson at LMC."

One of the elder cardinals interjects, his liver-spotted hands trembling, "On the surface, there doesn't appear to be any moral difficulty with this technology. We have no more moral interest in advanced artificial limbs than we do in advanced auto-driven wheelchairs."

The others pause a moment as if to reflect. Verrechio draws a deep breath before continuing, the window at his back now highlighting the curve of his high cheekbone, the lean, square shoulder of his finely tailored, crimson robe. "Still, we'll need position papers prepared at once. I'd like you to begin work immediately. And please, be sure to give all sides of this issue a rigorous treatment. There could be some delicate moral issues we'll need to address. I need not remind you all, nothing is ever as simple as it seems." He moves toward the door and raises his hand to the laser sensor, signaling that the meeting has come to an end.

The double doors scrape open loudly. Carla stands as the cardinals file from the room.

"Thank you all. I think I'd like to take a few moments to speak with our young science counsel here." Verrechio nods toward Carla.

The pontiff's appointments secretary, a youthful, heavy-set man with an oval-shaped face, enters the room. He speaks quietly. "Excuse me, Excellency. It is now midday."

"Thank you, just a moment alone—" Verrechio holds out his arm, summoning Carla to remain with him in the salon, then gestures for her to sit.

"So, tell me . . . are you, like our dear friend Torrez . . . a Liberationist?" he asks, standing between two chairs, one hand resting on each ornate chair back.

The question catches her by surprise. "I'm a Christian, if that helps you. A fundamentalist, I suppose you could say. But a Liberationist? No. Politics leave me rather cold, I'm afraid."

The Liberation. *Torrez has become obsessed with it, and even though Carla is not a Catholic herself, it breaks her heart to see her friend so complicate his love for his Church.* My Father's house has many mansions. *To Carla, the Liberation* looked like just another populist movement. *Buzz-word promises. Rebirth! Renewal! Reformation!* True, maybe in some ways it had delivered on its promises. The base communities had certainly prospered. But, then again, it was hard to see that as a purely Catholic phenomenon. No, lately a darker, more radical, militant side had emerged, an ugly side; proud, rebellious. What had started as a humble movement to empower the people by empowering their bishops to act independently in the day-to-day operations of their diocese, had more recently, with the fundamentalist surge within the base communities, turned to a movement to eliminate the office of the Pope altogether, reshaping the ancient church all over the world from one centrally controlled by the pope and his curia in Rome, to a loose confederation of independent Christian communities.

"Maybe that's why I feel so at home in Pachuca—I don't have much of a stomach for power struggles," Carla said.

The cardinal drew in a deep, contemplative breath. "Power," he nodded, his voice deep, this time heavily accented. "A strange paradox. Less . . . is always . . . more."

Chapter

7

Pachuca, Mexico
October 14, 2065

Fear not! Carla could not believe her eyes as she stepped into the terminal. An old man with a short, sparse beard and shoulder-length hair the color of pale ash stood at the jetway holding Eddie in his arms. His manner carried a keen spirituality, a gentleness.

"Eddie!" she cried, taking him from the old man's arms and hugging him tightly. "Are you okay? They told me you were sick."

"Hey . . . Carla," he said, giggling over her hugs and kisses. Then he added haltingly in his best English, "Angel says absolute evil is much more subtle than we know. And he says that you are the woman of the wilderness, that you will make war with the great red dragon, the Antichrist. Fear God, and give glory to Him, for the hour of His judgment is come. And worship Him who made heaven and earth and the sea and the fountains of waters."

Carla's eyes snapped open. She turned to the benevolent old man at her side. Smiling, he seemed peaceful, oblivious to the child's words.

"You mean—" she began, then dismissed the thought. "I'm sorry, sir. It's the language, the Bible study. He gets things a bit confused sometimes. I'm Carla."

"Don't we all," the old man replied, extending his hand. "Your little friend here couldn't wait for you to come back."

"Well, I'm back!" She hugged Eddie tightly. "I'm back. I'm back."

"Here, why don't I take him?" The old man smiled, nodding toward the door. "We're right outside."

"We've got a limousine!" Eddie said enthusiastically, wrapping both arms around the old priest's neck as they walked.

Carla breathed a sigh of relief, "You don't know how happy this makes me. And he seems to have taken to you so quickly."

The old man smiled and brushed Eddie's brow with his lips. "Children are like that. They're quick to reflect the love they receive. And this one—" he said, shaking the boy's belly as the two of them smiled at each other like long lost friends, "this one is special."

"Yes, he is." Carla slid into the back of the limo and held out her arms. "Come here so I can squeeze you, *mi gordito!*" Eddie went eagerly into her arms and giggled. Carla shook her head. "I can't get over it. You look so good!" She turned to the old man, "Of course! The Texas people! The ultrasound!" She hugged

Eddie to her, pressing her cheek to his soft skin. "I can't get over it!"

Carla leaned back against her seat, cradling her baby in her arms. She closed her eyes and smiled. "I'm home, Eddie," she whispered, touching her lips lightly to his cheek. "Home."

The limousine pulled up to the entrance of the two-story, white adobe building. Eddie had fallen fast asleep. Carla laid him gently on the seat, propped his head with a crumpled afghan, and stepped out of the car.

"Come." The old man nudged her elbow. "There's much work to do. The archbishop's waiting to speak with you. You go ahead."

The archbishop's secretary looked up from her desk as Carla rushed into the foyer, maneuvering around the wet terra cotta tiles. "Hello, Carla," she said, peering over the top of her glasses. "I hope the trip wasn't too difficult."

Carla smiled. "I'm just glad to be done with it, thanks."

"And . . . you're feeling okay?" the woman seemed to pry.

"Yes. After seeing Eddie, I'm better than okay. I feel great! Really! Is the archbishop in?"

The woman stood up and opened the double mahogany doors leading to the archbishop's suite, a puzzled look twisted her face. "He's expecting you."

Carla entered the simple office and found Torrez at his desk. He stood up at once. "Carla, I'm so sorry."

His tone was rueful, heavy as he took her into his arms. "Truly sorry."

She stiffened at the archbishop's seemingly incongruous words. "What are you talking about?" she asked.

The archbishop pulled away, gripping her lightly by the shoulders. "Did you receive my transmission before you left?"

"What transmission?"

"Come over here," he said, leading her gently to his couch. "Sit down."

Carla sat on the couch. "Alejandro, what on earth is going on here? Will you kindly tell me?"

"I sent you a transmission late last night. You should have received it before you boarded the shuttle. I'm afraid it's bad, very bad news." He sat down on the couch beside her. "It's Eddie. He passed away yesterday evening."

Carla stared at him for a moment, incredulous as to what was motivating this obscene encroachment, "What are you talking about? I just saw Eddie moments ago. He picked me up at the airport."

The archbishop leaned over and again took her into his arms. "You've had a long trip. A lot of stress. I understand."

"No, Alejandro! You don't understand!" Her voice rose and she pulled away. "What are you talking about? Is this some kind of bizarre joke?"

"Carla, Eddie . . . is dead," he explained, surprised at the acerbity of her words. "I know how painful this must be for you."

"You haven't heard a word I've said, have you?" She was vehement as she stormed toward the door. "I'm telling you, they're right out here." She threw open the door, startling the archbishop's secretary as Carla nearly leaped into the reception area. "Where did they go, Margaret?"

The same queer expression on the secretary's face as before, "I'm sorry?"

"The people I came in with. Where's the limousine? Where did they go?"

"You came in alone, dear," she replied with a baffled backward glance toward the archbishop.

Carla stood in the reception room, staring reticently at her two friends, a feeling of deep, deep malaise brewing within her.

"Come back into my office," the archbishop murmured, gently leading her back inside. "I'll get something for your nerves," he said, nodding to his secretary.

They went back into his office and sat on the couch. For some reason, the office smelled unfamiliar, sweet, like fresh fruit, vanilla, roses. "Can I get you something to drink?" he asked, the light from the window forming a faint corona at his back.

"I don't understand, Alejandro. I was just talking to him. He met me at the airport. He was with the old man."

The archbishop walked over to the wall bar and selected a small bottle of chilled water from the icebox. He poured the water into a tall glass and added several ice cubes. "Did you take anything for your flight?" he asked, handing her the glass.

Carla accepted the glass into her hands, took a sip, and shook her head.

The archbishop stood there staring down at her, a look of grave paternal concern etched on his face. "I'll just have Margaret give the limo company a call, then." He stepped over to his desk and buzzed Margaret. "Find out who accompanied her in the limousine." The archbishop looked up to comfort her, "We'll get to the bottom of this."

A look of stunned amazement took Carla's face. "Alejandro . . . I am really frightened." She placed her glass down on the mahogany butler.

Margaret rapped at the door and then entered carrying a tray with a glass of water and two red capsules. "Oh, you've already got your water," she said, placing the tray on the butler beside Carla's drink. "Here, honey, take these. They'll help you relax."

Carla looked up at the archbishop, who nodded his approval.

The archbishop glanced at his secretary, "Any word?" he asked quietly.

Margaret turned her back to Carla and silently mouthed her response, "No one." Then she whispered as she passed, "The driver said she never showed up at the terminal. They were just getting ready to call us to see if we wanted to reschedule—said they figured she changed her flight at the last minute."

"I see. That'll be all for now. Thank you, Margaret."

Carla cradled her head between the heels of her palms and rocked back and forth. The doors closed.

"Am I losing my mind?" She looked up at the archbishop. "I'm telling you, Alejandro, I saw him. *I saw them!* He was with—" she stopped mid-sentence and looked away. Her expression puzzled suddenly. "He was with. . ." She paused a long moment then turned back to the archbishop. A tear broke loose and ran down her cheek.

Chapter

8

Montreal, Quebec
October 20, 2065

Masako seemed to rise like ether, higher and higher
into the lambent mist. For a long time, she felt she
lingered there, cloud-hidden, teased, and dazzled
by the spidery play of electrified atmospheric
effects. Then came a distant, almost tidal rumbling
as low and rhythmic as the sea. Abruptly, the
lightning stopped. A tongue of fire emerged from the
roil. No, not fire—a man, his countenance afire, as
bright and shimmering white as if the entire cosmos
were in collapse, as if all the celestial light in all
creation were suddenly reduced to one blinding
singularity: *Light! Light! O Light!*

"Masako!" The abrupt sound of her own name
startled her.

Again, "Masako!"

Now her father's voice was unmistakable.
Masako came awake with the sharp tone of his third
and final call.

"Yes?" she rasped.

"We've got a problem out here. Pull your blinds. *Ima! Ima!*"

Now! Now! Always "ima," he says . . . Masako lifted herself on an elbow and opened her eyes. Her ecru paper shades were drawn, the bamboo-pattern watermark print aglow in the morning light. Below the window shades, through the sun-streaked glass, she could see a large crowd milling about on the lawn.

"What?" she croaked. Staring out she dropped the shades all the way, then pulled one panel askew to get a clear view. Squinting, she gazed into the dappled morning sunlight at the mob that had collected. Yellow police barricading tape stretched from tree to tree and across the driveway, cordoning off a riot perimeter around the town house. Police cars and mobile news vans spilled out into the boulevard from the obscure cul-de-sac. The normally quiet street now resembled a sprawling Arab bazaar.

Reporters, holovision camera crews—hundreds of people, Masako thought. A muffled noise rose from a vocal group of protestors at the back of the crowd. Bystanders seemed to form a human fence at the curb.

Chilled, Masako moved away from the window. "Dad!" her voice was nervous, husky, as she threw on a flowered silk robe and headed for the kitchen.

"Daddy . . . what's going on?"

Silence.

She looked for Henri in each room she passed, closing open blinds as she found them.

Guest room.

Living room.

Breakfast room.

Kitchen.

Dining room.

Den.

Finally, she found her father in his study, still dressed in his robe and pajamas, talking quietly on the phone. Sandy Benson's hologram hung in the air like a diaphanous ghost between Henri's black lacquered desk and the collection of fine porcelain geisha dolls Masako had inherited from her mother. The geishas' traditional silk kimonos and graceful powder-white features had always seemed so exquisite, so elegant and demure, more feminine, more human than mannequin to Masako, almost as if they were about to step lithely out of their sealed glass caskets and into the holographic fashion pages of *Vogue* magazine. An ornamental raw-silk screen formed a partition between Sandy and the wall.

Masako leaned against the door jam and listened.

"Most unwanted. I thought we agreed—no press." Henri was irritated, his voice clipped.

"One of our staffers evidently leaked the story, Henri. I'm trying to find out who, as we speak." Sandy's tone was incredulous. "I told you, I spoke to Cardinal Verrechio at the Vatican and no one else. You've got my word on that, Henri."

Henri felt a sudden intrusion on his sense of well-being. "I wouldn't be surprised if someone trying to subvert the Vatican leaked the story," he murmured. "Roman politics . . ." He shook his head.

Sandy kept silent.

"I feel so . . . so *invaded!*" Henri lifted the study blinds and looked out across the lawn to the milling crowd. He turned back to the phone. "These people have no dignity. Crazy people—slinking around my home! I've got to get to work. Masako's got to get to her classes, the zoo—"

"Henri," Sandy broke in, "listen, you just completely changed medical history. You can't expect to do that in a vacuum. Sooner or later the world's going to hear about it. You can't engineer the single most radical surgical procedure in history and expect to keep it a secret."

Henri muttered under his breath in Japanese.

Again, Sandy kept quiet and waited.

He drew in a deep breath. "The Vatican is not the only one with its hands full; we've all got more than we could ever have dreamed from this particular project."

Sandy folded her arms. Her thoughts went to the political turmoil surrounding the Vatican and its Liberation. The potential for financial instability loomed ever more as a threat to her. The earliest and largest investor in their humanitarian good works was the Roman Church itself. The large concentration of capital having come from one main investor now made the WEDGE vulnerable; Sandy was nervous.

"I'll tell you what this press coverage has accomplished," Henri said, "I've heard the morning news. The freeways are backed up from the city to the WEDGE, twelve miles in every direction!"

"It's not what you think, Henri. I mean it's a mixed bag. Sure, some of these people are part of the radical fringe, protestors and what not, but many—most in fact—are here to show support for Lane, for the work. Try and look at it like this, word had to get out sooner or later."

"Maybe so, but at least *later* would have given us time to prepare. This—they're estimating fifty thousand people already gathering on the lawns around the WEDGE. Lane isn't even out of bed yet!" Henri's voice rose. Abhorring a show of emotion, he tried a softer, flatter tone. "How are we going to get around after this?"

"Why don't you and Masako pack your bags and plan to stay at the WEDGE until the novelty of this whole thing blows over? People need to get used to it, that's all."

Henri's glance went to his daughter in the doorway. "What about security?"

Sandy unfolded her arms. "We've beefed up our security. I've personally gone over the entire procedure. Safety for you, for me, for Lane, the entire team—we're all concerned with the same thing, Henri." Sandy added, "We simply have to deal with the press. We aren't working in a darkened lab anymore. You need to play ball on this one."

▼

Lane stirred in bed and opened his eyes. Azeem stood before him, nervously fingering his beard; his black, shoulder length hair, pulled tight against his skull in his usual ponytail, seemed to exaggerate the expression of wonder on his face. Sandy appeared over Azeem's shoulder, her short blonde hair and pale features a stark contrast to Azeem's olive complexion. "Is this the visitation of the two wise men? Uh, excuse me, wise *persons!*" Lane gave Sandy a wink.

"I can't . . ." Azeem shook his head. "Sir, you look as if you've never been sick, never been . . . How do you feel, sir?"

"Watch," Lane replied, smiling. He threw back his sheets and inched his way to the edge of the bed, biting his bottom lip, the overhead lights glaring on his bald head as he shifted his weight.

Sandy moved to help him.

"No. Just watch." Then, using the side of his bed as a balance, he slowly placed one foot on the floor, then the other.

Azeem gasped. Lane's smile widened; he straightened his back, and stood to his full six-foot height. Lithe, muscular, his skin seemed flushed, almost bronze against the pastel blue tint of his hospital gown. His blue-gray eyes seemed to glow with the reflected light from the window.

"Now, there's a thought . . ." Azeem rocked up and down on the balls of his feet, smiling. " Finally a man like myself could add a few extra inches to my height!" He cleared his throat and nodded enthusiastically at Sandy, his face etched with all the wonder and excitement of a child beholding Santa Claus.

"Now, watch." Lane began to take halting steps, this time without balancing himself on the bed.

Slowly, he stepped out into the center of the room. He held Sandy's gaze and smiled as he passed. "This . . . feels . . . really . . . good," Lane said, his hospital gown showing his bare back and buttocks as he made his way to the observation room window.

"Lane, that's fantastic! No pain, no coordination dysfunction?" Sandy asked.

"You mean," Lane spoke in a jocular tone as he turned and headed back toward the bed, "I try to move my arm and my leg moves instead?" He caught his balance as he reached the bedside. "No, I'm a little clumsy, but not dysfunctional." He sat on the edge of the bed, swung his legs up onto the mattress, and pulled his sheets up around his waist, "So . . . where's Henri?"

▼

Henri took his daughter's elbow as two escorts carried their bags into the top-floor apartment of the WEDGE. Masako waited, then followed the men into the living room.

"Dad," she called out, "they want to know where to put these things." She smiled at the large arrangement of silk flowers at the center of the coffee table. A gift for her father, the flowers gave the austere white-on-white room a pleasant multicolor focus in crimson, amber, amethyst, sapphire, and jade. She was happy to see how willingly he had accepted her feminine touch.

Henri left the door ajar and stepped into the kitchen. "Right there would be fine," he said, speaking over the breakfast counter that divided the kitchen from the living area. He put his shoulder bag down on the butcher's block and opened the refrigerator.

"There's plenty to eat," he called out, shutting the refrigerator door and taking a quick inventory of the pantry. "Very good."

Masako thanked her escorts for their help and accompanied them to the door. When the men had gone, she slipped her shoes off, collected them in her hands, and padded through the deep pile carpet back to the living room. She slung her two bags over her shoulders with a grunt and hauled them into her room, dropping her shoes by the closet door as she entered.

Opening the closet, she unrolled and hung on the wall her favorite poster—an enlarged holograph taken in the south of France showing two opposing teams of beaming teenage faces. The picture was taken during a break in the action of a memorable game of volleyball played out on the beach of Le Voile Rouge near St. Tropez. She had chosen her team's name, *Shinjinrui.* The Japanese word came back to her now as she turned and laid her bags out on her bed: the young people.

She stepped over to the curtains strung at an angle along the glass wall of her temporary bedroom, the gossamer fabric barely concealing a flock of pudgy clouds that had scattered and smudged the sky. She pulled back the curtain. *Shinjinrui.* Her gaze dropped from the morning sky to the sprawling human sea covering the lawns. *Not really "young people" ... that's colloquial. What is the literal... shinjin... Ah! That's it,* "*new human species.*"

"I've got to get going," Henri said from her doorway.

Masako turned, "When will I get to see him?"

"Later this afternoon, maybe. We've got a lot of tests to do," Henri glanced over her shoulder out the window at the crowds.

"It'll be okay, Dad, really," she lied, reading more danger in her father than he had read in the crowd. "I can feel it."

▼

Lane followed Sandy's gaze to the door. The sound of Henri and Azeem in lively conversation lingered just outside. The doors swept open: no one.

Sandy shook her head, waiting in silence for the accolades to come to an end. Finally, Azeem disappeared down the hall. She rose from Lane's bedside and spoke apologetically as Henri entered the room at last. "Report is . . . more than a hundred thousand people now," she said, as the doors hissed shut behind him. "They're setting up camp. Looks like they're planning to stay a while."

"That is only half the story," Henri said, the sound of the crowds outside his home and now gathering on the LMC lawn still echoing in his ears. "You should see the roads on the way in." Henri bowed smartly before Sandy. He moved toward Lane sitting cross-legged on the bed.

"Ohyto gozai imasu, Lane'san." Good morning, Lane.

"Henri." Lane held out his arms and pulled Henri to his chest. After a long embrace his voice cracked, *"Yattas, Henri'san. Yattas . . .* I did it, Henri."

Henri patted Lane's back then stepped away from the bed. "Yes, you did it." He turned toward Sandy and cleared his throat, his eyes wet. "We must learn to control ourselves. How can we expect anyone else to get used to this man if every time we think about what he has done *we* become blubbering fools?"

Sandy grinned. "I don't think I'm as worried about that as you are, Henri. But don't feel all alone. We've all got some adjustments to make." Her eyes returned to Lane.

Henri nodded imperceptibly to Lane. "How do you feel today?"

"Fatigue's gone. I feel good, really good."

"No problems?" Henri held out his hand for Lane's chart.

Lane shook his head. There was an odd, preoccupied expression on his face.

"What is it?" Sandy asked, handing Henri the medical folio.

Lane seemed embarrassed. "This may sound, I don't know, a bit silly, but—"

"What?" Henri cut in, after he'd finished leafing through the pages.

"My body, the old . . . the *other* body . . . what happened to it?"

"You mean after the transfer?" Sandy asked.

Lane nodded.

"Incinerated," Henri answered for her and then snapped the charts shut. He watched the smile, gracious and genuine, disappear abruptly from Lane's face; a strange twitch knitted his brow.

"The oven," Lane muttered.

"Waste is all it is," Sandy consoled, with a reprehensive glance Henri's way. "Don't give it another thought."

Lane nodded. "Adjustments," he said slowly, his smile returning.

Henri noted the speed with which Lane seemed to shift emotional gears. He continued, paying closer attention to his friend's affect and demeanor, "The question is how do we proceed now? Circumstances have brought this deluge of publicity. We can't have distractions if we're going to get anything further accomplished. You heard what she said. One hundred thousand camped out on the lawns, scores more on the highways."

"Distractions or not, the press is here to stay," Sandy said, lifting the holovision control wand from Lane's bedside. "Look at this." Abruptly the wall opposite the foot of Lane's bed disappeared behind a brightly colored hologram. "Just watch."

Across the bottom of the holovision's image scrolled the continuous news flash she had wanted Henri to see:

*Stay tuned to CNN for the latest news . . .
from the rash of global earthquakes to the WEDGE
in Montreal . . . Stay tuned to CNN for the latest*

> *news from the rash of global earthquakes to the*
> WEDGE *in Montreal...*

"Ah," Lane said softly, as Sandy switched off the screen. "It's already started." He paused a long moment.

"Let's not get caught up in all the press hype. We need to take this very slowly," Henri continued. "Very carefully." He took a seat on the mattress opposite Sandy, then fixed his gaze directly on Lane. "We need to run more tests. A lot more. Physically, you're fine. And that alone is a miracle. But we have yet to run a comprehensive psychological battery." He turned to Sandy. "Our minds are a precarious balance of ambiguities. I want to know if this man before us now is all he was before the procedure. Has he suffered any psychological deterioration?"

"Makes sense," Lane said quietly. "I'm curious about that myself."

"That is the beginning." Henri said. He looked at Lane. "Let's say everything checks out fine. Then what? Is this a one-time operation? Do we make it available to others? How? On a limited basis? An experimental basis?"

Sandy leaned forward. "You know I've kept the Vatican's secretariat apprised of our work. I spoke with Verrechio." She looked steadily at Henri. Carefully she dropped the next words into the silence. "It seems ... there *is* someone who wants to be next. It seems ..." She looked at both men. "It's the pope."

Henri turned on her angrily. "What? What do you mean, *next?*"

"The pope wants this same procedure—the transfer. He . . . demands it, Henri." Sandy took a breath.

"Out of the question!" Henri stood abruptly. "You can't be serious!"

There was a long silence. At last, Sandy spoke. "Look around, Henri. You know how much this facility cost to build—computers, personnel, medical research equipment." She paused briefly, then continued, "The computer alone cost two billion . . . How many billions are we talking in capital invested here? A *lot* of money," she shook her head, "and we all know it came from the Vatican." Her voice was even.

Henri shoved his hands into his jacket pockets. "So what are you telling me, that we're bought and sold?"

"No."

"I just think, especially now," Henri's tone was cool, deliberate, "that it would be a good deal wiser to distance ourselves from all these ecclesiastical groups . . . tampering with religious figures is too dangerous. Do you want to be accused of killing the pope?"

Lane cut in. "I don't see a problem here. He is the chief executive officer of the largest multinational corporation on earth. The largest and most successful organization in the history of the world, for that matter. As for the pope himself . . . we wouldn't kill him. Quite the opposite." Lane looked calmly at his two colleagues.

"So you propose to make the man immortal." Henri's look was incredulous. There was another long silence.

"You want to keep this procedure from the one group that made it possible?" Sandy paused a moment. "Or better yet," her voice grew sharp, "let's not let anyone have it! We'll keep it to ourselves! Is that what you want?"

"I . . . am concerned . . . about . . . the risks." Henri looked at Lane without blinking. "*All* the risks. Even those that aren't so obvious."

Lane leaned forward. "All right. Bring in your shrinks, Henri. I want you as happy as I am. We're all on the same team here. We're all family."

▼

The purring sound of automatic doors disturbed the silence. A small man in a fraying lab coat bounded into Lane's room. Ginger-haired and gap-toothed, the bespectacled psychiatrist spoke. "Dr. Balcourt, I'm Dr. Jalal Kazaz." He reached out his hand amiably.

"Our Babylonian psychiatrist," Lane said with a bemused smile, leaning forward to shake the man's hand. His eyes went to the dense hair sprouting from the psychiatrist's ears.

"Yes . . ." Kazaz managed a clumsy smile, then looked around and found a chair in the corner of the room. "We're going to get to know each other very well over the coming weeks. I want you to feel you can talk openly with me. Hold nothing back." He drew the chair up close to Lane's bed. "Ah, a student of the

Bible?" he asked, nodding toward the black leather-bound volume Lane had closed on his lap.

"No, not really." Lane moved his coffee cup aside and dropped the book on the nightstand. "One of the nurses gave this to me. I find it interesting. A fantasy, really."

Kazaz felt around over his jacket pockets and thought of Dr. Nakasone's words. *Possible delusional disorder.* He pulled out a miniature recorder from his breast pocket and checked the batteries. "Do you mind?"

"Not at all. Beats taking notes." Lane leaned back serenely.

"All right, then," Kazaz fumbled with the switch and placed it upon the bed, "The Bible. You said—"

"I said: I'm not a student," Lane repeated, watching as Kazaz scribbled something into his note pad.

"But you're reading it." Kazaz sat back in his chair.

"The Bible deals with the ascent of mankind in very naive terms. In a primitive way. Have you read it?"

"I'm familiar with it, of course. It's amazing how many religious themes surface in my work with schizophrenics."

"I'm not surprised. Brain chemistry's a funny thing." Lane threw back his sheets and got out of his bed. He walked to the window and leaned his shoulder against the casement, staring out at the crowd.

Kazaz leaned forward. The setting sun highlighted Lane's shaved head with a dim golden luster. His large blue eyes were keen and attentive. He seemed oddly tranquil, yet coiled and alert. Lane turned and faced Kazaz. *"Et ego si exaltatus fuero a terra omnia traham ad meipsum,"* he said, without blinking.

"Latin?"

Lane smiled.

"I'm a little rusty on my Latin." Kazaz chuckled, intrigued with the sudden shift in language. *"Et ego . . . et . . .* uh—" he muttered, scratching vigorously his scalp before giving up. "I'm afraid you'll have to help me out."

Lane returned his gaze to the crowd, "And I, when I am lifted up on the earth, will draw all men to myself."

"A scriptural quote?" Kazaz asked, still scribbling.

"Yes . . . scriptural. It's in the Gospel of John, I believe." Lane turned. He looked into Kazaz' eyes. "Prophetic, don't you think?"

"I suppose that depends . . . on what one believes."

Lane returned to his bed. "There I disagree, Doctor. Nothing in this world depends on what one *believes,"* he said with conviction, "Because . . . what one believes *does* nothing. Belief is empty."

Kazaz sat quietly, almost as if to force the long pause that followed Lane's remark. Again, he jotted something in his notes, then fixed his gaze on the window. "Dr. Nakasone mentioned several times during our meeting, something he called the Methuselean effect. What is your understanding of this . . . effect? I assume you're familiar with the term?"

Lane sat down and elevated the back of his bed. He crossed his legs in the lotus position, the white linen sheets gathered around his waist. "He's speaking about the life-expectancy maximum," he replied nonchalantly. "Through the transfer procedure, we've extended our life expectancy for an indefinite period."

"We?"

"Humankind."

Kazaz leaned forward. "Immortality?"

"Given repeated transfers, yes, it is certainly possible. Probable in fact."

Kazaz shifted in his seat. "Probable immortality," he mused, chuckling at his notes. "Sounds like a . . . mental disease."

"There are those who will think so. And they will come. They will come to oppose the proliferation of my work, to oppose *me.*"

Again, Kazaz lowered his eyes and hurriedly scribbled something into his notes. "Why is that, do you think?" He put down his pen and turned his attention to Lane. "Why would anyone want to oppose you personally?"

Lane kept silent. A faint smile touched his lips.

"I could see where some might—"

"If," Lane interrupted, his eyes growing wide, "If you can see, as you say, then *you* are a blind man,

Doctor." He paused, taking the psychiatrist's measure. "Why do you hunger so for death?"

Kazaz seemed to force the silence.

Lane answered for him. "Because you are small and weak, too weak to live. Gird up your loins like a man, Doctor. They will come. And they will oppose me. No matter that I have come for them; no matter that I have come to glorify their condition with pride. They will oppose me. And in their opposition," his voice dropped to just above a whisper, "I will be made *great!*"

Again, Kazaz persisted in silence.

"Nietzsche was a prophet. I know this. Who you see before you now is the *Ubermensch*—the superman . . . I am 'above' you. Yes, Doctor, they will oppose me. They will oppose me, and they will fail. I can afford to be patient. God isn't built in a day." Lane smiled.

Kazaz nodded, picked up his pen, and returned to his scribbling. "What are you saying? God is man?"

"I believe that through this procedure man becomes God."

Kazaz rested his pen on his notebook. "Are you . . . God, Lane?"

A long moment passed before Lane spoke. "I am the resurrection," he said finally, his voice calm and even.

Lane's words seemed to transfigure his expression. Suddenly, he looked inspired, almost radiant. It was as if he had become very large; Kazaz felt as if he were losing his balance, falling in toward Lane.

"What about death?" Kazaz asked, struggling to regain his composure. "Naturally, not everyone can or will avail themselves of your procedure."

"That will change. That *must* change. I think we all agree that death is the enemy. This is biblical as well as humanist. We've fought death since the beginning of time. Now," suddenly, his eyes opened wide, "we have won. It begins again—in me."

Kazaz said nothing, quietly slipping his pen into his jacket pocket.

"Through this procedure, we may truly say that we have become resurrected." Lane leaned back gently against the mattress.

Kazaz sat in silence for a moment while he watched Lane. "You say *we* have become resurrected. Actually, though, only *you* have become resurrected."

"I am the Alpha." Lane's gaze went to the window. "But I am not alone. What I have I will not keep to myself." He met Kazaz' gaze. "I am simply one anointed to deliver life everlasting. What I do, I do for all humankind."

Kazaz leaned forward slightly. "Your choice of words is interesting. You say *anointed.* 'Anointed' in the Hebrew tongue is *Mashiah.* You come very close to calling yourself the Messiah."

▼

Later, dreaming, Lane felt he was enveloped in something—the night itself, liquid thick and dark as carbon. There was a pin-prick of white light. Slowly, as he focused on the white dot, it began to pulse.

Somehow, he fought the urge to blink, to breathe. Instantly, the light grew larger, growing, expanding, more brilliant than a star, a thousand stars. It drew him in. He studied the light, amazed, thrilled. At its center, there appeared an even more brilliant white dot, more luminous, more faceted, gradually growing larger and larger until it too seemed to consume him, as if he had been cast into the sun—and yet, somehow, he continued to exist. He felt exhilarated; all that he was pulsed in harmony with his luminous surroundings. And then, he was not alone.

The figure of a solitary man approached him. The man seemed afire, clothed in a burning robe—white light, within white light, within white light. The bearded figure, now upon Lane, looked at him joyfully, laughing. Lane felt oddly comforted by the man's laughter, which seemed as luminous as his form. He felt he somehow shared the laughing man's mind, his boundlessness, his clear and uncluttered sense of absolute *being*. Lane, too, wanted to laugh. For countless moments, he lost his own boundaries. Transcendent, limitless, he drifted above all language, all puny human categories, until there was only the laughter, endless laughter.

Abruptly, Lane awoke, the laughter persisting like a tingling whisper in his ears. The seam between the world of his subconscious and reality had torn, he felt both tickled and empowered, like a cup continually overfilled, dumping its contents into outstretched and thirsty hands. *What role for me now? Have I become merely the giver of gifts?*

▼

Masako hurried into the recovery room. She turned, surprised to see Lane fully dressed, standing at the window in black slacks, black collarless silk shirt, a galaxy of campfires flickering at his back. "You look great!" she announced as she entered.

Lane moved away from the window and reached out to embrace her, "Masako!"

"Oh, Lane," she said, pulling away, making quick use of her jacket sleeve to dry her eyes. "I told myself *not* to get—"

Lane gently stroked her face. "Hey . . . I'm okay. I'm okay." He stepped back and held his arms out to prove his point, then he gestured toward the door. "I was just going to have dinner. Would you join me?"

Masako let out a sigh and nodded.

"I hear you moved in," Lane said, ignoring the glances and murmuring that suddenly filled the hall as he and Masako passed through the medical unit on their way to the elevator.

"We had to," Masako replied. "The crowds were getting pretty big around the house. Dad's afraid of a riot."

Lane held the elevator door open. "I don't think that will happen."

"I don't either," Masako agreed, stepping inside, mildly excited that he shared her views. "Fact is, I'm more concerned about my father than I am about the crowd." Abruptly, she put her hand over the control panel, "Hey! Why not come up to our apartment? I can put something together, sandwiches, fruit, whatever you'd like."

"How could I refuse an offer like that?"

Masako smiled, then ran her fingers around the collar of her turtleneck sweater. She draped her hair forward over one shoulder. "I hear more than half a million people will be camped out here by late tomorrow evening."

Lane smiled and picked a loose string from her wool sport coat and let it fall to the floor. "I know."

As the elevator doors opened, Masako stepped out and moved toward her door. "I think—" She turned and smiled at Lane as she held her hand up to the laser scanner. The door clicked open, "How can I put this . . . the crowds—"

Lane followed her into the apartment. The lights came on as Masako made her way to the kitchen. Lane went directly to the living room, over to the window, and opened the shades.

Masako raised her voice over the breakfast bar. "There's something . . . I don't know, it has the feel of a . . . what? A medieval fair out there. Don't you think? Medieval, I mean."

Lane stared out at the crowd, the grounds pocked by craters of amber firelight as far as he could see, the lawn twinkled like a city viewed from the air.

"There's something more primitive about it," he said, his eyes on the window, "Atavistic . . . they almost look like beasts of the field," he murmured, lingering for a moment, looking out. The sound of a cupboard slamming shut made him turn.

"Masako," he said, moving toward the kitchen, his voice suddenly bright, "Put that stuff down. Let's go out there."

Masako shut the refrigerator door and looked at him. "Let's see for ourselves." He turned toward the window again. "Up close."

"Are you well enough?"

"Of course."

She paused for a moment, then smiled. "Okay then. Dad will—"

"Uh," Lane's hand went up, "let's just keep this little excursion to ourselves. Your dad has enough to worry about."

"Let me get my coat," she said without a second thought, turning to the bedroom. She stopped at the doorway and smiled as she spoke, "I'll get you a parka. It's cold. You should cover your head."

Lane felt the stubble atop his skull bristle against his palm and went to the door. Masako came around the corner, her ankle-length beige cashmere overcoat lifted gently behind her as she moved.

"Very striking." Lane reached out for the black parka, noticing for the first time her classic ensemble—red brushed corduroy pants, black turtleneck sweater, beige and cream geometric print sport coat. "You have really grown up, Masako," he said appreciatively, slipping into his parka. "To think . . . you were just ten years old—"

Masako opened the door and gave him a dubious look, "Lane, that was *fifteen years ago*. I've grown up twice since then."

"So you have," Lane laughed, following her into the elevator, eyeing her as she moved. "So you have."

They stepped out through the side door. A crisp, clean fragrance of night-damp grass and wood smoke lingered in the chill night air. Like sudden, strange flares campfires had sprung up all over the lawn. The air crackled with the static of police radios and shouted commands. Rising from the mob came a high, sharp chant, growing louder, staccato, filling the air with nervous energy. "Satan! Satan! Satan!"

The sound of a distant explosion ignited a frenzy of screaming at the front of the building. A squad of men outfitted in riot gear scrambled toward the flash of light. Someone hurled stones and obscenities from the shadows as the police ran past. Lane grabbed Masako by the hand and dashed through a sudden break in the police barricade, disappearing undetected into the crowd.

Winded, they turned and watched a phalanx of police encircle a group of stone-throwing rioters. The violence was sporadic, isolated among several small, vocal groups at the front of the WEDGE near the fountain. A tangle of crimson light crisscrossed through the smoke filled air as the police launched their first assault with tear-gas and then moved into the crowd, swinging their lasers like clubs. Tear-gas canisters littered the scene like toppled smokestacks, billowing ashen smoke into the night. Several protestors were knocked to the ground and dragged off into waiting paddy wagons. Most escaped to hurl stones from the cover of nearby trees.

Lane turned and shook his head. "What is wrong with these people?"

Masako squeezed his hand and followed him deeper into the crowd, "They don't understand, that's all. They're afraid."

Lane looked at the countless faces surrounding the campfires, all strangely similar in the flickering golden light. The pungent aroma of burning hemp wafted across the field. After a bit, he felt the dew soaking through his shoes. Smiling, he stopped near a large bonfire and wiggled his toes in ecstasy.

"What are you doing?" Masako asked under her breath, nervously canvassing the crowd.

"Being *here*," Lane looked up from his feet and grinned. Suddenly then, all eyes lifted. Lane followed their gaze. "Meteor shower," he said in response to Masako's gentle nudge. His tone was reverent.

She was silent for a moment, her eyes on the sudden fusillade of shooting stars. "I don't like this, Lane," she said, leaning closer. "What if someone recognizes you?"

Lane lifted a finger and pointed to a shimmering light nearly overhead. "Betelgeuse," he said, matter-of-factly. "Supernova."

A woman's voice lifted in a quiet song of lamentation, drew them nearer to the bonfire. The mood was pained, desperate. They searched the faces for the source of the dirge. Dozens of people had gathered around the flame, men and women, old and young, alone and in couples, some on stretchers, some blind. Finally, they located the voice. The woman held her sick child in her arms and rocked back and forth, singing *sotto voce.*

Lane released Masako's hand and stepped into the firelight. He read the anguish in the woman's eyes. "Why are you here?" he asked.

The woman brushed her lips against her son's cheek and kept singing.

Lane's gaze went to the boy, a severely retarded hydrocephalic. His lips were chapped, his face reddened by wind and drool. Lane stepped toward the woman and knelt on one knee. He asked again, "Why? Why are you here?"

The woman stopped her song and looked at him. Even in the firelight, he could see anger and bitterness etched in her eyes. "I came," she said sullenly, "I came . . . for my boy." She raised her chin and drew in a haltingly dignified breath.

A police bullhorn rang out in the distance. The metallic, amplified voice rose in yet another angry attempt at crowd dispersal. Lane turned his ear to the sound of their chanting lingering in the air. "Satan! Satan! Satan!"

A moment passed before the chanting died down; Lane returned his gaze to the woman and her child. Tears now glistened on her cheeks. She wiped both sides of her face against the boy's hair and looked at Lane. "Those people are stupid," she said, bitterly. "I don't care if Dr. Balcourt is Satan, as long as he can heal my boy," her voice caught. "What kind of God would do *this* to a child anyway?" She started to cry and gathered her son into her arms.

Lane stood up and looked across the fire at Masako. *The flame fires her features like gold,* he thought before turning his gaze over the rest of the huddled crowd. A moment later, he raised his voice. "I *know* Lanning Balcourt. I know him well. What would you have me tell him?"

"Tell him to heal *us!*" someone called out.

"Heal us!" another voice added.

And another, "Heal us!"

"Tell him to heal us!"

Abruptly Lane felt a surge of people pressing around him. Grabbing at him, tugging at his coat sleeve. "Heal us! Heal us! Heal us!"

Alarmed, Masako watched the crowd surround Lane. She stepped into the firelight and grabbed him by the hand. "Come on, let's go."

Lane couldn't move. An old woman clung to his knees, pleading, "Heal my child! Heal my child!"

Someone shouted, "Nakasone's daughter! Nakasone!"

"It's him!" someone else chimed in. "It is! It's him! It's Balcourt!"

Suddenly Lane felt himself being carried away by the crowd. He reached out over the people for Masako's hand, but he could only touch her fingertips for a split second.

"Heal us! Heal us! Heal us!" the crowd shouted.

Masako listened, mortified, as the tumult moved through the crowd like a wave. A blind man appeared at her side. "What are they saying—is that Balcourt?"

"No, it's an argument, I think," she lied, holding back for a moment, until the stranger passed. When he had gone, she moved closer to the crowd, her attention divided between Lane and the bellicose mob at the front of the WEDGE.

"All right!" Lane finally raised his voice. "Enough!" he boomed, extending his arms.

Moses and the Red Sea, Masako thought, watching in wonder as the crowd sat before him and gradually became still. As the murmuring subsided, Lane stood alone in their midst. Slowly he met their gaze, his eyes aglow in the firelight.

"Look at yourselves," he said, finally, his words sharp, admonitory. "Here you are . . . here *we* are . . . look at yourselves. Blindly spinning about the universe on this dim cinder, completely unaware that the dawn of the second millennium is upon you . . . now! Have you learned nothing? No better than the apes from which you evolved?"

He raised his hand over his head, waiting for the assembly to look up. A moment later his gaze moved from his pointed finger to the crowd, "You look at the stars in the sky, and in your wonder and confusion you fall on your faces crying, 'God! God!' " Lane dropped his arm by his side. "I tell you, you know nothing!"

Masako tried to step forward.

Lane waved her off, then continued, "Those of you who can, listen to me! Do you really think by grabbing after me, touching my sleeve, falling at my feet—through some foolish mystery or miracle of blind faith—that God will heal you? That I will heal you? I tell you now, ignorance makes fools of you all!"

He stepped through those seated in the audience, refusing to grasp their outreached hands. "Because you have heard that I have conquered death, you say, 'God!' Listen carefully, I say . . . yes, *I* am God . . . but you poor sleeping fools . . . so are you! I and you—*we*—are one. We are *all* God, but not through magical notions nor mindless faith. We are God only because we have aspired to *be* gods! We have beaten the enemy—death!

"Look at yourselves! Your hearts are so full of hope and fear that you cannot see! I say, slay your hearts; slay your hearts this moment! Slay them and think! Use your minds! Fill yourselves with pride! Henceforth, let your reason guide you! Truly, I say to you now, not one among you will reach his or her potential . . . not one will be truly healed . . . not one will live long enough to rebuild this dying old earth as the paradise it once was and will be again, except through me . . . I am the new covenant, the covenant of the everlasting body. Go home. Wait. I will be here always. Soon, we will make this procedure available to each one of you. Go home. There is no magic here for you. Not here. Not in this world."

"How long must we wait?" someone cried out.

"Only a little while longer," Lane answered, then passing through to the edge of the crowd, he clasped Masako's hand and headed back to the WEDGE, leaving them to murmur among themselves.

Another explosion sounded. There was a mad scrambling of police and protestors at their backs. "Let's go," Masako said, running ahead of him. As she ran, she kept looking over her shoulder at the illumined fountain at the front of the building. "You shouldn't have told them that, Lane," she panted, falling quickly out of breath.

"It's time somebody told them the truth." He slowed to a walk as they reached the building. Masako raised her palm to the laser scanner. The door clicked open and they stepped inside.

She rattled the door behind him as he passed by her, then they moved into the darkened boiler room.

"That's not what I meant. I mean, you could've been hurt," she raised her voice over the syncopated mechanical clamor.

Lane watched her closely, her face and hair tinted red by the night-light. The boilers droned the lusty beat of an ancient steam engine. He stepped toward her. "What?" he shouted, his mouth practically on her face.

There was a long, awkward moment before she tried to speak, then, "I said—"

Abruptly, Lane took her into his arms and kissed her hungrily. For a long time he lingered on her lips, his tongue exploring her mouth. Startled, she returned his kiss with a groan, pressing her body into his.

Chapter

9

Montreal, Quebec
October 28, 2065

Lane got up from his desk and answered his door. *"Co nichi wa,"* he bowed his head in afternoon greeting, stepping graciously aside for Henri to enter.

"So . . . " Henri offered a smart bow in reply, "you're all moved in?" He entered Lane's apartment and went to the computer console that stood in place of a couch at the center of the otherwise empty living room. "Very *Nihonjin,*" he teased, looking around.

"Has it ever been otherwise?"

Henri nodded and pulled up a side chair, his eyes drawn to the miniature hologram of human neural anatomy, limbs asprawl like a five-point star, hovering over the projection ring at the desk. He tilted his head back, studying the tangled, brachial form through his bifocals.

Lane plopped down behind his desk and abruptly switched off the computer. "I prefer it minimal like this," he said, as the hologram vanished. "Sort of a techy, ski-lodge feel, don't you think? High ceilings, fireplace, and all . . ."

Henri glanced over at the hearth. A monolithic slab of polished black marble rose through the ceiling like an Egyptian obelisk against the far wall. At its base a natural-gas flame silently tongued the air, throwing shadows on the walls and across the Persian carpets scattered around the floor.

It was a long moment before Henri blinked. Returning his gaze to Lane, he asked, "Have you spoken with Sandy? Masako's just about got dinner on the table."

"She's in her office. I just got off the COM with her. Said she's on her way up."

"Good."

Lane crossed his hands at his chin. "You know, Henri, I can't help noticing that you seem tense, upset . . . I don't know, with me, everything, everyone. What is it? What's eating you?"

"I've spoken my mind quite clearly—"

"That's what you say, but I don't believe you."

Henri draped his leg across his knee and checked his watch.

"Is it Kazaz? Did he say something?" Lane pressed.

"No," Henri replied, watching carefully Lane's manner of speech, how his eyes sparkled and seemed to punctuate every word.

"You say you're concerned about the crowds, afraid they'll riot. I was out there, Henri. I was with those people."

Henri folded his arms across his chest. "That was ill-advised."

Lane unfolded his hands and leaned forward slightly. "Not in my judgment, it wasn't. Henri, I hate to be the one to break it to you, but those people are not going to riot." A faint smile creased the corners of his mouth. "Think of it! There's more than a half million people out there right this minute. All they want to do is see me." His eyes widened. "See . . . *me;* that's it." Lane seemed impassioned and aloof at the same time. Exultant.

"And what does that mean to you?" Henri asked.

Lane leaned forward. "I should *go* to them." His voice was urgent. "I have to—I should give them the good news."

"Crowds this size, you've got potential for real trouble. We know for a fact there are zealots, professional agitators . . ."

"You haven't listened to a word I've said, have you?—I was *out* there. I *spoke* to them."

"You spoke to a *handful* of those people. What about the fanatics? The militant extremists who—you know just as well as I do—will stop at nothing to keep our work from moving ahead. And I'm not talking about the transfer."

"There are more than five hundred thousand people out there. And more on the way! Really, Henri, how many do *you* think are out to get us? Who's delusional here?"

Exasperated, Henri stood up and went to the window. "How long, Lane? How long, without fresh water, food, sanitary facilities, emergency medical facil—"

The sound of the COM line cut Henri short.

He turned away from the window in time to see Sandy's hologram appear in front of Lane's desk. "Sorry, guys." She frowned. "I'm still in my office. Just a few minutes more. I'm—well—I'll tell you about it when I get up there. Just a few minutes more, okay?"

"We'll be here," Lane said, signing off with a casual salute. Sandy's hologram vanished. "Where were we?"

Henri returned to his chair and sat down. His voice betrayed his fatigue. "I was asking you to think about what you're saying. How long do you think this crowd will stay manageable without—"

"Right, right." Lane nodded. "Look, according to Sandy, the promoters, the local business people, they're taking care of it. Smart to do it, I might add. Positive brand association, Henri! That's what it's all about, right? Everybody wants a piece of our action."

"Lane," Henri's voice rose, "it's out of hand! We are really hanging out here. We need to make contingency plans. What happens if things turn ugly?"

"Then we chopper out—"

"And what about all the people who depend on our work? What about the equipment? The computer? This isn't some holiday carnival we're in the middle of here."

"Oh, but it *is* a carnival." Lane's brows lifted as he smiled. "Exactly that! *Carnelevare.*" He got up and went to the kitchen. "These people are coming from the four corners of the earth, Henri," he called out. "Unannounced, unexpected, like the wind!"

Henri went to the counter, pulled up a barstool, and watched as Lane rummaged through the refrigerator.

Abruptly the noisy clatter of bottles and glassware stopped. Lane looked back over his shoulder. "Want a soft drink?"

"*Hai, dozo,*" Henri answered quietly.

"Make it two!" Sandy called out as she entered the living room.

"Two it is," Lane echoed merrily, stepping out of the kitchen with bottles in hand. He gave her a hug. Henri stood, bowed slightly, then pulled a barstool away from the counter. "What took you so long?" he asked, gesturing for her to sit down.

Lane placed her drink in front of her. "Thanks," she said with a nod. She took a long sip, then set the bottle aside. "I spent over an hour with the city and state police. The government's claiming emminent domain on all property surrounding the WEDGE."

"Good." Henri took a sip of cola. "Maybe that'll put an end to the violence."

"Wait, it gets better. They don't want this thing to turn ugly, believe me. So they got some business types to put up some money—a lot of money, Henri." She touched his arm reassuringly. "They're going to set up tents, facilities, everything. They're sending film crews in here. They want to treat it like an open-air festival."

"Carnival," Lane smiled.

"Festival, carnival, call it what you want. Truth is, there are too many people here, too many more on the way, and they don't have a clue what to do about it. You should have heard the mayor. 'We've got a second city here almost overnight,'" Sandy's voice went *basso profundo,* "'with absolutely no infrastructure to support it. We'd by gosh better get those people some supplies, and we'd better get it done fast!'"

"So what do they want from us?" Henri asked.

Sandy smiled at Lane, and her voice returned to her usual register. "They want Lane to make an appearance. If all these people want to see him, why not let them?" She looked straight at Lane and picked up her drink. "You think you're up to it?"

"I'm ready." Lane smiled.

Henri shook his head. "I am *totally* opposed to this."

"Why, Henri?" Sandy put her drink down. "He has to talk to them sooner or later . . . remember. So it turns out sooner. We've got the entire city government working to keep the lid on this thing. We've got business people, security people, what could go wrong?"

"He's going to talk to them?" Henri asked.

"Of course. Why not?"

Henri got up and began to pace the room, he stopped at the window and turned. "What are you going to say, Lane?" Lane gave Sandy a confused look.

"What's going on with you, Henri? You saved my life, and now you want to control what I say, is that it?"

"Henri—" Sandy broke in.

Henri cut her words short. "I want to know what it is you want to tell these people. I don't want to control you, Lane. I just want to know what it is you have in mind. Tell us, why don't you."

Lane met Henri's gaze evenly. "I'll tell them the truth."

Henri raised his eyebrows and approached the bar. "The truth! And just what might that be?" he echoed sarcastically.

Again, Sandy broke in, "I'm afraid I'm as confused as he is, Henri. What's gotten into you lately? You're so . . . so hostile."

"Why don't you just listen to him? Tell us, Lane, what is the truth?"

Lane held up his hand before Sandy had a chance to speak in his defense. "The truth . . . the *truth* is that we have conquered death. The truth, Henri, is that we have consciously evolved humankind to become like gods."

"Is that what you are, Lane? Have you become God?"

"Henri!" Sandy cut in.

"Let him finish," Henri said forcefully. "Tell me, I want to know. Are you God?"

Lane smiled. "He's getting metaphysical on us, Sandy. You can't see, can you, my friend?" He turned and gave Sandy an apologetic glance, "'The kingdom is spread out before them but they do not see.'" He waited for Henri to return to his barstool. "Maybe it is I who should be questioning you, Henri. What do *you* think? Maybe your view of God is too limited. That's right, I almost forgot, you think God is *out there.* A person. The Absolute Other. How do you relate to that?" he asked, directing his query to Sandy. "No, Henri, I say, God is *within us all,*" he tapped his breast. "Within, Henri, within."

Henri turned to Sandy and spoke as if Lane wasn't present. "He's hedging."

"No, I'm not hedging. Listen. I no longer share your reference frame."

"Reference frame?" Henri left the last swallow in his cola bottle and gently pushed it away on the counter.

Lane continued, his tone now controlled, pedagogical. "Every thought, every impulse you have is shaded by the inevitability of your own death. That is your moment. You cannot escape it. It is your reference frame. From that vantage, you attempt to see the world, but you behold it 'as through a glass, darkly.' You are blinded by the ever-present shadow of your own demise. I have already died. Yet, I stand before you now, re-created. Raised by my own *boundless* pride."

Henri and Sandy exchanged glances. "It seems to me you had a little help from your friends," Henri said.

"As it was meant to be." Lane glared. He took a sip from his drink. "Before you go around judging people as to whether or not they call themselves God, maybe you should know what God is. You want a metaphysical explanation, I'll give you one. God is dead! He destroyed himself long ago to give men life, knowing full well *that* which He creates, He creates in His own image. He knew the day would come when humankind in His image would overcome darkness and ignorance and superstition and hatred and every other perversity of the pygmy human spirit and would claim its rightful place in the cosmos as children of the stars, children of *chaos!* He gave His life so that you and I might live and know *being* as separate and unique individuals, so that the One might become many. So you can pass judgment, you ask me, 'Are you God?' And I must answer you truly, I am the resurrection. As He was in the beginning, I am."

Henri got up and shook his head. "Pardon me for saying so, but if that isn't delusional, I don't know what is."

Sandy kept quiet, her gaze fixed on Lane. "I disagree, Henri. I mean, I'm no philosopher, and certainly no theologian, but given his context, I find nothing fragmentary or delusional about it. He's right about one thing, you know." She turned and read the disdain in Henri's eyes. "His reference *is* different from ours. He *has* become immortal, and he knows it. We don't share his perspective. Because his perspective is unique, I don't think you can evaluate him using existing standards. Clearly, he's outside of *our* point of reference."

"So you're willing to say that this man is divine?" Henri split a disbelieving gaze between the two of them.

"I don't think he said that he was divine." She turned and gave Lane an inquiring glance. "Did you?"

"We are *all* divine," Lane replied matter-of-factly.

Sandy nodded, "I've got no problem with that. That seems to me to be a widely held—"

"I do," Henri said abruptly. "I have a number of problems with that. He is not just saying that we are all divine in some mystical way. He is saying that he is divine *through this procedure,* that we, too, are divine if we elect to undergo this procedure. Am I right?" he glared at Lane.

"Exactly," Lane replied.

"*That* is a perilous concept! During the Second World War, my ancestors almost annihilated themselves with this notion of humans as God. They went to war under the banner of the *Tenno Heika,* the 'God-king.' And we all know how much suffering and misery they brought down upon themselves and upon the world for that delusion!"

"Their delusion, as you say, was in mixing their emperor's divinity, or so-called celestial authority, with the military's jingoism," Lane responded.

"And what are we doing? You said it yourself, Lane. We are consciously evolving ourselves. Just using the word *evolution* connotes a biological imperative. Where is the walk with God? Where is the Creation? How long, after your speech, will it take for the scoundrels of the world to manipulate the masses into yet another phylogenetic delirium? How long will one group sit idly by and wait while another avails itself of your so-called everlasting life? Even if you weren't suffering from a delusional disorder, which I am not yet ready to concede, the prospect of introducing this procedure into the body politic without giving it a great deal of thought would lead to the total collapse of the—"

Lane cut in, "Collapse of the established order."

"Exactly." Henri locked his jaw.

Sandy looked uncomfortable. "Look, you two, I shouldn't have to remind you that Henri did what he had to do to save a friend. Nobody started a revolution."

"I'm not so sure," Henri said. "Tell me, how soon before we bring back the ovens? I mean, we'll have to incinerate the carcasses. You can't bury them. The Nazis lived that logistical nightmare."

"I am not a Nazi, Henri." Lane raised his voice.

Henri glanced at Sandy. "I'm not so sure."

Sandy broke in. "Hey-hey-hey! Come on, let's, uh ... let's take it easy here. We've got plenty of time to work out our differences," she said with a nod Henri's way. "Now it seems to me that Masako is expecting us for dinner, isn't she? Did I hear that right? I mean, are we arguing and missing out on your daughter's gourmet cooking?"

Henri's shoulders seemed to sag. "You're right. Dinner's . . ." He checked his watch. "We're already late."

▼

Henri stood aside and allowed Sandy and Lane to enter his apartment before him. The limpid dissonance of an enigmatic scale from a synthesized Japanese string concerto played softly in the background. The sweet fragrance of oriental spices and tempura permeated the apartment. Masako stepped out of the kitchen, quietly closing the door behind her. Her wide-sleeved, tight-fitting floral silk kimono gathered at her waist with a broad scarlet sash that restricted her gait. She smiled and then led her guests into the living room, scurrying with short rapid steps that brought attention to her ankle-high fluorescent white stockings, her *tabi.*

Lane followed her with his eyes. Her long, dark hair was pulled up, off her neck, twisted into a traditional knot and fixed with chopsticks and tiny baby's breath flowers at the back of her head. He watched her move with a fluid grace that called to mind falling water, trailing a faint scent of lemon blossoms in the air.

"Henri," Sandy said, "Your daughter is beautiful."

Henri drew in a deep breath, the burden of his work left at the door. "I am afraid she is no longer *jogakusei.* Her mother would be very proud."

Sandy looked to Masako for a translation.

"No longer *a schoolgirl,*" Masako blushed.

Lane nodded in agreement. "No, Masako, you are certainly *not* a schoolgirl. You look . . . stunning. Very, very beautiful."

Again, Masako blushed. "Come." She reached out for Lane's arm, leading him to the thick, rectangular straw mat at the center of the living room floor. Smiling, she bowed reverently toward her father and Sandy. "We'll begin with *chado.* Japanese tea."

Sandy looked down at the straw mat. A tea setting for four was neatly arranged around a single white chrysanthemum afloat in a shallow ceramic bowl. "Ah." She turned to Henri and smiled. "The tea ceremony?"

"*A* tea ceremony." Henri corrected her use of the definite article, as he slipped out of his shoes. "Each is unique unto itself."

Masako stepped away from Lane and gestured for her guests to make themselves comfortable on the floor along facing sides of the straw mat. Then, gracefully, she adjusted her kimono, spreading it slightly at her ankles, and knelt at the server's place at the head of the worn straw mat, the worn *tatami.*

Lane sat down and crossed his legs, his gaze moving over the elaborate, stippelated bamboo pattern cast into the surface of the iron kettle at Masako's knees. Directly in front of her, meticulously arranged like surgical instruments, lay an ornate lacquered wooden tea container, a slender bamboo ladle, and a stubby, slit, tentacular bamboo whisk. A large ceramic bowl and four tea cups sat empty by her side. At each place, a glistening sugar candy lay on a delicately folded, rose-colored tissue. A small freshly cut twig fork lay beside each one.

Masako paused. Then, speaking no words, she lowered her eyes. She leaned forward in a deep, reverent bow, then sat back on her heels, rinsing each cup one by one with hot water drawn from the kettle.

Lane noticed the graceful, dream-like quality of her movements mirroring the swirl of the piping hot water in each cup, her gestures deft, sensual, as she emptied the sluice into the large ceramic bowl without making a splash. An eddy of steam lifted off the surface of the water and clung to her hand like a ghost from the bowl back to her knees.

Masako finished rinsing the cups, bowed low, then opened the lacquered tea container. Placing the container's lid gently on the *tatami,* she leaned forward again and lifted the slender bamboo ladle. Holding her sleeve back out of her way, she carefully ladled a small amount of powdered green tea into each cup. With another graceful bow, she leaned forward and returned the ladle to its proper place. Then, sitting upright, and with great reverence, she closed the wooden tea container. Her slender fingers were reflected on its shiny lacquered surface as she held it in place against the *tatami.*

Lane studied her movements with heightened interest as she dipped into the kettle with a long-handled bamboo ladle and added hot water to each cup. He watched as traces of the *o-cha* powder swirled to the surface, changing the contents of each cup to a pale shade of yellow-green.

Masako leaned forward, picked up the bamboo whisk, and deftly frothed the liquid suspension one cup at a time.

Lane smiled at Sandy. They watched while Masako worked. Again, his gaze rested on her slender hand as she returned the bamboo whisk to its place. After another reverent bow, and using both hands, Masako presented the tea cups, left to right, until each guest held his own.

Lane accepted his cup with both hands, enjoying the warm feel of the delicate ceramic in his palms. He drew in the musty fragrance of the aromatic tea. His eyes drifted to the snug folds of Masako's kimono just below her neck. The ceramic's smooth, rounded surface seemed to pulse. His mouth began to water.

Lane turned his gaze to Henri as Henri, in solemn ritual, three times rotated his cup. After the third quarter-turn, he raised the cup to his lips and then, sucking loudly, drank its contents in one swallow.

Lane finished his tea in the same way, following along as father and daughter inverted their cups inches above the *tatami*. Each intently studying the hand-painted *kanji* characters representing the name of the cup's maker, the cup's shape, the delicacy of the ceramic glaze. That done, they returned their cups to the mat and then used the small, cut twig as a fork to lift the sweet to their mouths.

Lane felt his senses expand as the sweet taste of sugar dissolved on his tongue. Suddenly the dissonant music seemed a perfect balance to the harmony of the moment. The fragrance of the tea rose subtly over the aroma from the kitchen.

Again, Masako's kimono drew his eye; the fine down along her cheek and neck seemed to glow like the moistened petals of the white chrysanthemum. Again, he felt the warmth of the tea.

Masako averted her gaze. Her eyes seemed to shine. It wasn't until she blushed again that he realized he had been staring. He smiled, watching appreciatively as she gathered the utensils on a tray, and then in one fluid motion rocked back on her feet and stood up.

Lane glanced over at Henri. His eyes lowered before him, he seemed to be lost in the moment.

"I'll make the salads. Please, seat yourselves at the table," Masako said in a hushed voice, and then disappeared beyond the kitchen door.

The abrupt tone from the COM disturbed the quiet. Masako answered it in the kitchen. She opened the shutters over the counter. "Daddy . . . it's for you," she announced, then pulled the shutters shut.

Henri got up and took the COM in the living room. His expression went blank, then surprised. "We'll be right there," he said abruptly, and then hung up.

Henri moved toward the table, his face reddening as he moved. A long moment passed before he posed his question to Sandy, "Did you know the pope was on his way here?"

"What?" Sandy blurted, standing up.

"That was security," he said, slipping into his shoes. "They just received word that . . . the pope . . . is on his way from the airport. They were asked to prepare the helipad for his arrival."

Sandy stepped away from the table. "Henri, we've worked together for fifteen years. I've never lied to you, and I'm not about to start now." She fixed her gaze on his. "I'm telling you . . . I knew *nothing* about it."

Henri looked at Lane. "Wait here," he said, heading for the kitchen. Masako appeared at the door. "*Sumimasen,* Masako. I'm so sorry," he said, with a slight bow. "Something's come up. I don't know how long we'll be. Why don't you and Lane just go ahead and start without us. We'll get back as soon as we can."

"Dad . . ." Her voice dropped.

"Hai. You two go ahead and eat. We'll get back as soon as we can."

Lane stood. "Are you sure you don't want me—"

"Please," Henri said with a gesture that insisted Lane stay put. "We'll be right back."

Sandy followed Henri out the door. When the door closed, Masako returned to the kitchen.

Lane found her at the butcher block, slicing watercress. He stepped up behind her and brushed his lips against her neck, lingering in the sweet, heated scent of her perfume.

"I wanted to do that for you," she said quietly. "I wanted to give you a Japanese tea." She tried to turn, but Lane pressed against her. With both arms, he reached around her and pulled a pomegranate from the osier fruit basket. She watched, nervously aroused, as Lane cut a wedge from the fruit and then held it to her mouth.

"Do you . . . have any idea . . . what it's like for a man to be trapped . . . in a wheelchair . . . for *fifteen* years?" He touched her neck, then the lobe of her ear with his tongue. She bit into the fruit, scooping the tart, red berries into her mouth. Lane took a berry from her lips to his, pressing himself against the silk back of her kimono. He brushed his mouth against her throat, but this time the slight pressure of his bite made her chill. She smiled, anxiously. His mouth moved over her shoulders, nibbling through the padded silk fabric. He returned to her neck, his tongue this time tickled the back of her ear like a viper.

Masako moved her head aside and lifted the uncut pomegranate to his mouth. She held it steady as he bit into the fruit, the crimson juice soon drenched his chin, dripping down his neck, staining his shirt. The drift of oriental music from the living room now seemed a dizzying backdrop to his seductive whispers. Like her own conscience he kept at her, and at her, and at her, and at her, *whisperingwhisperingwhispering.* She turned and slipped away, knocking the fruit basket from the butcher block, sending oranges and pomegranates scattering across the floor and into the shadows.

Startled, Masako lifted her gaze. For the first time Lane seemed strangely appealing to her, dangerous, exciting. His energy coiled tight, ready to strike—his wide unblinking eyes seductively hypnotic, penetrating, snake-like.

▼

The whirling buzz from the approaching helicopter gradually drowned out the crowd noise coming from the grounds below and in the distance. Its ten thousand candle floodlight instantly washed Sandy and Henri in bluish white. They stood with their backs tight against the wall as the hovering aircraft twisted into place just above the red cross on the roof and sat down on a cushion of air in front of them, hurling dust and debris all around.

Sandy turned and watched as the gusting blast from the rotary blades pressed Henri's clothing tight against his body. Jaw set, eyes like dark slits, his face took on a fixed countenance like stone. He took a halting step forward and leaned into the wind, shielding his eyes with his hand, his hair thrown back slick against his head.

What have I brought down upon us, Lord? Is there to be no guidance for me now? Where is Your voice? Henri turned and nodded as the chopper's doors swung open.

Sandy followed him in a crouched jog. They reached the aircraft just as the medical team dislodged the pope's gurney.

"Dr. Nakasone?" The thin, bearded man called out, his voice barely audible over the slow, dying drone coming from the helicopter's disengaged engines. "Dr. Ralph Peterson." He extended his hand across the gurney as the three technologists dropped the gurney wheels into place.

Henri refused to shake his hand. "Let's get him inside," he said instead, gesturing toward the door.

"Hi, I'm Dr. Benson," Sandy said, reaching for Peterson's hand in an awkward compromise as they moved inside. She looked down at the unconscious man on the gurney.

"Who authorized this?" Henri snapped, following the gurney into the elevator.

"Cardinal Verrechio," Peterson answered as the doors shut. "Look, Doctor, it's been a long day for me. I'm a little jet-lagged; I'd appreciate it if you'd drop the combative tone. I'm not your lackey."

"Of course not, Doctor," Sandy soothed. "It's just there's been some confusion at this end."

"Is that what this is?" Henri asked. "Confusion?"

Sandy gave Henri an incredulous look. "He never mentioned it. I just talked to him—"

Henri cut her off. He turned back to Peterson, "And just what were your instructions?"

"Is he always like this?" Peterson furrowed his brows at Sandy.

"I'm sorry. It's nothing personal," Sandy explained. "We didn't expect your arrival, Doctor."

"This is an uninvited *intrusion*, Doctor," Henri said flatly. "An intrusion. Do you have his medical discs?"

Peterson lifted his satchel.

The elevator doors opened in the medical unit and Henri stepped out. "This way," he said, starting down the hall.

"Observation?" Sandy asked.

"*Hal.* We'll run some tests. Maybe there's something we can do short of the—" his eyes went back to Peterson. The observation room doors swept open. Henri gently tugged the doctor's elbow and continued, "—instructions."

"Right over there," Sandy interrupted, directing the three medical technologists to the bank of monitors along the far wall. "Go ahead and put him on that bed."

Henri waited for Peterson's reply. "I think we should discuss that privately." The Catholic doctor spoke quietly, his eyes following the technologists as they lifted the pontiff into bed.

"Very well . . . Sandy," Henri called, heading toward the nurses' station.

Sandy nodded. "Let me get these hooked up." She connected the leads that draped across the bed.

Dr. Peterson stepped into the nurses' station and dropped his satchel on the counter. Henri stood by the door and waited for Sandy to finish. She flipped several switches on the instrument wall, then went to the nurses' station. "He's all right for the moment," she said, taking a seat at the counter next to Peterson.

Henri shut the door, leaned back against the counter, and crossed his arms. "Go ahead, Doctor."

"I was told . . . all about your breakthrough," Peterson began slowly. His gaze went to Sandy. "I know that Dr. Balcourt . . . well, that there was an accident. You folks were able to save him—I know about your radical surgical procedure . . . I don't know *how* you did it . . . some variation on your work involving nerve and tissue synthesis, I presume."

"And . . ." Henri peered over the top rim of his spectacles.

"Well, I spoke to a woman here . . ."

Henri glared at Sandy.

"No, wait a minute . . . wait a minute. I told you, I'm a bit jet-lagged." He smiled apologetically. "I spoke to a woman in *Mexico* . . . Carla MacGregor. Is she here?"

"No," Henri answered.

"Well, she will be. It's my understanding that she will brief you on the Vatican's position."

"The Vatican's position," Henri repeated incredulously.

"Look," Peterson leaned forward in his chair, "I was told to see to it that the Holy Father received the very best care you can provide until he can undergo the same procedure you used to save Dr. Balcourt. That's it."

Henri uncrossed his arms. "I will tell you right now, Doctor, that I will not perform another procedure. Not on the pope, not on *anyone* else, for that matter, until we have fully studied the data from the first procedure." He stood and paced to the door, looking out through the glass. "And that," he said, without taking his eyes from the pope, "is going to take a long, long time."

Peterson leaned back in his chair. "I certainly understand your feelings, Doctor. I'd probably feel the same way if I were in your position." He looked at Sandy briefly for any help, and then continued, "But, you may want to reconsider in light of Dr. Carla MacGregor's arrival, which I presume," he checked his watch, "will be within the next few hours."

Henri turned. "What are you talking about?"

"The Vatican secretariat was very specific. The Holy Father *must* undergo this procedure. Verrechio had anticipated that you might object. I believe his representative coming from Mexico is prepared to ask for your resignation should you decide to oppose his wishes."

Henri looked at Sandy. "Well the good cardinal had better be prepared to *take* my resignation . . . because that's exactly what he'll get. Mine *and* my entire staff's!" Henri's voice tightened. "I absolutely refuse to be dictated to in this high-handed manner!

The Vatican may own the buildings around here, but they don't own this team."

"You'd better rethink that, Doctor. To the extent that your expertise has been encoded in computer software, they own it. You should know, you signed off on the international patent applications. Your team's work, your inventions, all met the standard criteria—novel, nonobvious to someone in the relevant field, useful—"

"I don't need," Henri voice grew louder as he spoke, "a lecture on the patent process."

"Of course you don't, Henri," Sandy interjected. "I don't think Dr. Peterson is—"

"All I'm trying to say," Peterson broke in, "is that the Vatican owns the rights to all the work that has come from this lab. All of it, Doctor. Believe me when I say I understand your . . . your resentment. No doubt I would feel precisely the same way that you feel now. What I'm asking you to do is to be reasonable. Try to avoid elevating this to some moral, ethical level. We're talking about one man. One very sick man."

"I refuse," Henri said flatly. "I will look at the pope's medical discs. Perhaps there is something short of the transfer that we can do to help him. But my answer to you, to the cardinal, to Carla MacGregor, to anyone who asks, is an unqualified *no!* Period. Absolutely not!"

Sandy stood up. "Doctor, would you excuse us for—say . . . a half hour? I'd like to talk to Dr. Nakasone in private, if you don't mind." She extended her hand to Peterson.

"I think that would be wise." Peterson shook her hand then stepped past Henri with a nod. He reached the door and turned. "Is there someplace I can freshen up, maybe get a cup of coffee?"

"Lounge is down the hall and to the left. You can't miss it," Sandy said, drawing a map in the air as she spoke. She waited for the doors to close before she turned and spoke to Henri. "He's right, you know."

Henri paced the room. "This is all about political expediency, Sandy. There's nothing humane or virtuous going on here. Why don't they dress up a mannequin? No one would ever know the difference."

"I don't think they see it like that. Verrechio looks at this as a Godsend."

"God?" Henri shook his head.

"I believe him, Henri," she plopped back in her chair, "I believe they will force you out."

Henri stared at her, exhausted. The overhead light washed out his features; he seemed very old.

"I don't share your view on this one, Henri," she said.

"You too, Sandy?"

"It's not like that, and you know it. How many years have we worked together? You've always respected my opinion, even when we've disagreed."

Henri stopped his pacing. "You're not thinking this through. I'm not just arguing some abstract point on science policy. We've got the largest religious institution on earth telling us what it is we should do, when we should do it. Sandy, this is *not* about saving one sick man. This man, this pope—he's the incarnation of everything these people believe. The first among equals. And we're going to make him immortal?"

Sandy turned away and looked at Henri's reflection in the side glass. "Are you really willing to give up everything?"

"If you leave with me, I won't have to give up anything. They will reconsider. I know a little something about human nature. I have faith that economics will prevail over issues of political expediency."

"I can't do that."

"You mean you won't do it."

"All right, then . . . I won't. I've worked too hard. So have you. Henri, can't you see? We've done it! Why are you so eager to destroy so much over so little?"

PART THREE

Chapter

10

"Get me Dr. Stephens." Carla took a sip of hot tea and leaned back in her chair. She looked sullenly across her small studio apartment, her hermit's cell. Off to the side, pressed against the spartan calcimine wall, partially obscured by a small hand-painted cross, was a drying palm frond the color of withered grass. One of the children had twisted it into a Möbius strip; a figure eight, sideways. *Infinity*, Carla thought.

A blank, timeless moment passed. Her gaze fell to the small bed in the corner. Drawing a deep, mournful breath, her eyes returned to the cluttered desktop, to the lucite triptych frame that held the holograph of Eddie standing in the hall of the children's hospital in his crumpled flannel pajamas; his hand gripping the slender chrome neck of the IV rack that had shadowed him through the hospital like a steely guardian angel. Something like Mozart's

Requiem stirred in her heart. *Sleep well, little man. Sleep well.*

A familiar, gravelly voice finally answered her call. "Hello."

"Reb!" She smiled half-heartedly, her voice slightly raised for the intercom. "You sound about as chipper as I feel."

"Yes?" came his response, probing.

She leaned forward in her chair and cleared her throat. "Reb, this is Carla."

"Carla!" His voice seemed to smile back through the wire. "Carla! Where are you?"

"Mexico. Can we go to image?" She wanted to look him in the eye when she spoke. She hoped his end of the COM line would facilitate a clean transmission.

At once the psychologist's hologram blinked into focus at the center of the room in front of her desk. He pushed the wire-frame glasses back on his nose and smiled warmly. "I got to where I thought I'd lost my sparring partner," he said in a reassuring, friendly voice. "How many days? I was beginning to worry. I thought you gave up on me, Carla, and just when I was about to drop everything and move to Pachuca!" He laughed.

Despite his mirth, the yellow hue of his office lighting seemed to exacerbate the poor quality of the transmission. His skin seemed sick, sallow. Sweat filmed his bald head; his mottled salt-and-pepper beard appeared to wander down his neck partially obscuring his blue cable-knit collar. He looked older than his forty-four years.

"I'm sorry. It's been hectic here. Something's come up. A very, very dear friend passed on. It's been . . . difficult," she said.

"I'm sorry. Is there anything I can do?"

Carla hesitated, then nodded. "Actually, yes, there is something. That's why I called, really. I need some . . . well, it's a little awkward . . ." She struggled to come out with it. "I've uh—well, I need to talk to someone, Reb. It's a . . . it's a *personal* matter. You being a psychologist and all, well, naturally—"

"You do me an honor even to have considered me, Carla. How can I help?"

She paused for a moment, hesitating. "Reb, I think maybe I'm coming undone," she said with a nervous chuckle. Her expression was searching, as if he alone might be able to confirm her own dark suspicions on the matter of her mental health.

"I doubt that, Carla. If *you're* coming undone, then I guess we're all in trouble. Me included."

Carla shifted uncomfortably in her chair. "No, I'm serious." She gazed momentarily at her hands, collecting her thoughts, pacing herself. She tried another approach. "Have you . . . in your practice . . . do you . . . I mean, is there—"

"Hey, come on, Carla, it's me you're talking to. Just lay it out. What is it? What's eating you?"

"Okay—all right." She drew in a deliberate breath and then said, "I guess . . . I would like to know if there's anything in the recent psych literature on—this is going to sound funny, Reb, I know—but, is there anything on . . . on ghosts?"

"Ghosts? As in spirits?"

"Yes. Spirits."

"Carla, I'm a clinical psychotherapist, not a parapsychologist." Under different circumstances, her question might have prompted an affectionately prankish, almost brotherly response. Not this time. Carla's disturbed expression spoke clearly the deep anxiety she felt at this moment. He read the strain and tension on her face. There was an odd formality between them, a somber unfamiliar tone that had not been there before.

"What exactly are you after? Could you be a little more specific?" he asked.

Carla leaned forward, her arms folded on her desk. "I was visited by the child, at least, I think I was—I was very close to him. The little boy, I mean. Reb, I held him in my arms and hugged him. I felt his breath; I kissed him—"

"And you think he may have been a spirit?"

"I don't know. All I know is that he is dead, was dead, or—I found out he died the night before I arrived here."

The psychotherapist responded deferentially. His voice took on a subtle, professional edge. "That sort of thing is not that uncommon when we grieve for those we have loved and lost—"

"This wasn't grief, Reb. Besides, I didn't know he was dead."

"So you say, but you may have been with others who did know. It's a painful thing. You may have blocked it out without realizing it."

Carla leaned back in her chair and crossed her arms. "Reb, I was on an air shuttle, ten miles above the Atlantic. *I* didn't know and no one else knew either."

"Who were you travel—"

"I was traveling alone."

With slow finger strokes the doctor ruffled three times the underside of his beard, his moustache, then added reluctantly, "Let me look into it. But I have to say that I'm not all that familiar with the appearance of heavenly bodies." He smiled warmly.

"Look," Carla let out a sigh, "I'm just trying to figure out what's happening to me. I don't know what's going on, only that something's not right. Something is definitely happening. Like there's something odd in the wind."

His expression turned empathetic. "Let me suggest another possibility, Carla. Everything need not be so black and white. You've been living in a very *spiritual* community for a long time now. You lose your husband and adopt a totally new way of life there in Pachuca. You have no time for a charming guy like me . . ." He paused and smiled. "Listen, Carla, from what you've described to me, you've been so immersed in your work, there hasn't really been time for the necessary self-reflection."

"Self-reflection," Carla repeated flatly.

"Exactly."

"What does that mean? Self-reflection?"

"You're living out a highly ascetic life down there, Carla. You've withdrawn from the world around you. You've practically turned yourself into an anchorite. I mean, just look at yourself. You're a nun almost."

"There is a great deal of *joy* in what I do, Reb."

"I know that. All I'm trying to say is that the more we focus—and by the way, this is quite common among the devoutly religious—the more *sensitive* we become, the more *perceptive* we are, the more we open ourselves up to the unseen world around us . . . sort of like a *counterposition* sets up in the unconscious. Look, there's ample evidence for this throughout Christianity, in fact, even in the Bible, we see evidence of it breaking through. A prime example, and one that Jung cites in his essay 'Answer to Job,' is what we see happening to the author of the epistles of John. Jung explains it like this. He says since the apostle preaches the message of love so ardently—*God himself is love. There is no fear in love, but perfect love casteth out fear*— that it should come as no surprise to anyone how next we see John moved to warn us, in seemingly contradictory language, of the false prophets and teachers of false doctrines, and it is he who announces the coming of Antichrist with all the apocalyptic terrors—"

Carla jumped from her chair, the feeling of an icy lancet at her heart shivered her with fear and angst. "Why did you just say that?"

Her sudden change of tone startled him like lightning falling from heaven. A look of profound confusion appeared on the psychotherapist's face. "Say what?"

"The Antichrist? Why did you just use the Antichrist as an example for me when we were talking about whether or not I had actually seen a little boy's ghost?"

"Carla, relax, I was simply trying to make the point that things we dismiss at the conscious level can sometimes erupt from the collective unconscious. Hey, don't get me wrong; I'm not contradicting your faith. Not at all. Quite the opposite, in fact. There is no contradiction in the symbols we see emerging in the Apocalypse of John. The dark images of vengeance and destruction only *seem* to contradict the gospel of love preached in John's earlier epistles. The fact is his devotion made him extremely sensitive. 'There is no fear in love, but perfect love casteth out fear.' His visions probably came to him—"

"In the form of a violent revelation." She knew his words before he spoke them.

He gave her a small smile, an odd concern apparent in his eyes.

"One can love God but must fear Him," she muttered, distracted, preoccupied with her own growing sense of fear.

▼

It had been hours since her disturbing conversation with Reb; Carla rested her chin on her knuckles and surveyed the modest room that had been her home for the last ten years. Her eyes moved from the papers beneath her elbows across the austere oak desk to the open oak armoire one of the villagers had carved for her and stained lightly with oil. A knock sounded at her door. "It's unlocked," she called.

The door opened. The old archbishop poked his head in, "How are you feeling?" His voice was soft as his eyes scanned her face.

"I'm okay." The corners of her mouth turned up at the sudden flash of white that came from his understanding smile. His wizened face was ruddy, like hide tanned in the sun. "Come in, Alejandro, please." She got up and hugged him.

He held her in his arms and patted her on the back. "Are you packed?"

She pulled away gently and motioned toward her open suitcase on the bed. "Nearly."

The archbishop went to the bed and sat down with some difficulty. Carla took a seat at her desk. "Did I detect," he coughed out a bit of a laugh, "a hint of enthusiasm in that response?"

"Now you *know* better than that!" She shook her head. "Archbishop Torrez . . . *you* are incorrigible."

He laughed as if he'd been caught with the goods. "I only thought—"

Carla cut him off. "I know what you thought, Alejandro," she said with a cynic's grin. "And I know what this Liberation means to you."

"To us," he corrected her with a deferential bow of his head.

Again, she shook her head.

"I fear . . . Verrechio is up to something." Torrez turned and squinted his eyes toward the sudden light from the window. "You don't move a dying man halfway around the world without a very good reason. Keep us informed, Carla. That's all we've ever asked—just keep us informed." Abruptly, he turned and met her gaze. "Did you reach your friend?"

"Yes. Just now."

"And?"

Carla picked up a pencil and studied it as she rolled both ends between her two hands. "He was . . . *Reb*." She smiled an awkward smile.

Torrez leaned forward and rested his elbows on his knees. "Did you tell him why—"

"No." She looked straight at him and let the pencil drop to the desktop. "Alejandro . . . if I *am* losing my mind . . . it will just have to remain *our* little secret."

"Ha!" Torrez laughed. "And so it will. So it will! One hand washes the other."

Carla got up from the desk and went to the oak armoire. Reaching in, she pulled out a stack of folded blouses. "You know," she said, tucking the clothes away in her suitcase, "I suppose this is . . . I don't know—kind of ironic, in a way. I mean, my luck. I come to this community to get away from the sciences . . . now I'm being pulled back."

Torrez nodded his head. "Your place is with the children here; we all know that. And you *will* come back to them. Meanwhile . . ." He shrugged. "You go where you are needed."

Carla looked puzzled. "Is this a calling?" She turned back to her packing. "I guess I figured I'd had myself pretty well fooled, wrapped up nice and cozy in my faith like a blanket."

"That's understandable."

She returned to the armoire and reached for more clothes. "Comfortable is a better word I think . . . or maybe numb. Yeah, numb. Comfortably numb—I guess I found a safe place to hide." She dropped some sweaters into the suitcase, folding them in place where they lay. She looked up, "Now, this . . . this vision or whatever it is." She looked him straight in the eye. "He was *real.*"

"I don't doubt you believe that, Carla."

"You know me, Alejandro." Her voice was even, controlled. "I wasn't feverish. And I'm not prone to emotional tangents."

Torrez' silence spoke his acquiescence.

"So why me?"

"Why not?"

She flipped the lamp on, slid it off to the side of her desk and leaned back in her chair, "I don't know what all this means . . . Does it mean I'm supposed to *do* something?"

There was a pause. Finally, then, the archbishop nodded.

"What? How will I know?"

Torrez rose slowly and opened his arms to her. For a moment, she clung to him as a child would to her father. "You will know," he said.

Chapter

11

Montreal, Quebec
November 1, 2065

Carla stood alone in the conference room at the WEDGE. She leaned against the glass wall and looked out over the sprawling LMC grounds. In the foreground, a fountain sent twisting acrobatic jets of water high into the air. These tubular coils took the form of a sparkling liquid double helix, illuminated from below by lasers—ruby, sapphire, amethyst. Like shattered glass the spirals disintegrated at apogee, dropping back into the gold- and lapis-tiled reflector pool like rainfall.

Carla stared uncomfortably past the waterworks as a surging mob of protestors pushed against a serpentine line of police decked out in riot gear. Bullet-proof police shields bobbed up and down as they fought back the mob, many using their lasers as cudgels to keep the disorderly crowd at bay. The distant, desperate sound of their cries still rang in her ears from her rooftop arrival. "Satan! Satan! Satan!"

Many had come to show their respect for the miracles of Dr. Lanning Balcourt, others to protest the further advances of genetic medicine, and, as always, there were those who had come to witness the spectacle.

Beyond the picketers, smoldering rings of fire sent plumes of smoke against the sky. The late evening haze, a pale bluish-gray, hung like angora over the horizon, merging with the marbleized patina of the sunset.

I have seen this all before—she thought, drifting. Carla jerked back away from the glass with a start. She felt abruptly cold; her breath moved over the cup of tea she cradled in her palms. In her mind, she heard again the music from the Vatican, the rise and fall of a Gregorian chant—then, a long-forgotten trip to New York, the Metropolitan Museum of Art, flashed before her eyes.

> *She is standing before a fifteenth-century oil on canvas panel.* The Last Judgment . . . Hubert, or is it . . . Jan . . . Van Eyck? *A palpable sense of anxiety washes over her. She feels submerged, unable to come awake as she studies the artist's depiction of an earth in flames; the dead rising frantically from their graves like flowering stalks of smoke toward an airy paradise juxtaposed with a shadowed, teeming hell; the damned being ripped apart by spiny bat-like demons in Satan's subterranean realm . . .*

"Excuse me, Dr. MacGregor," said a voice at her back.

Carla turned abruptly. "Yes?"

Sandy held out her hand. "It's good to see you again."

Carla smiled wanly.

"Why don't we sit over here," Sandy suggested with a gesture toward the large etched chrome and glass conference table. She waited for Carla to take a seat on one of the high-backed, black, tear-drop leather chairs, then pulled out a chair of her own and sat down next to her. "Has Cardinal Verrechio briefed you?" Sandy sat back in the plush, cushioned seat and folded her hands in her lap.

"I know the pope has been moved here; I understand there's been . . . a breakthrough." Carla spoke haltingly, searching Sandy's eyes for confirmation.

Sandy cleared her throat. "There has." She reached into her breast pocket and pulled out a small envelope sealed with wax and handed it to her.

Carla recognized the exquisite monarch paper as Vatican stock. Turning the gilded envelope in her hands, she let her fingers move across the gold satin ribbon and the plump dollop of scarlet wax. She opened the letter and read:

Dear Carla:

I have been advised that there may be some there within the community of scientists at the WEDGE who may wish to thwart our attempts to help the Holy Father in his hour of need. I am asking you as our consultant on scientific affairs, by your presence there, to reaffirm the Vatican's substantial interests in this enterprise to those who may wish to exploit controversy for their own ends. Please contact me at once, should the need arise. We are praying for the Holy Father's health and speedy return.

Yours in faith,
Massimo Cardinal Verrechio

Carla refolded the note and set it down on the conference table. "Seems straightforward," she said, her voice neutral.

"I wish it were. Straightforward, that is."

Carla waited for her to elaborate.

Sandy studied her hands, then met Carla's gaze, her eyes narrowing momentarily as if she were staring into the sun. "Dr. Nakasone will not perform the surgery."

"I don't understand." Carla looked at her. "He's changed his mind?"

Sandy paused. "Henri never agreed to do the surgery in the first place. The truth is we didn't even know the pope was being moved here."

"That's strange. Has he explained *why* he objects?"

"Well, now there we get a mixed bag. On the one hand he says he's not convinced the procedure works."

"And you agree?"

"No." Her response was clipped.

Carla's eyebrows rose. "And on the other hand . . ."

"He's against making a religious leader . . . immortal. That's it. His words."

"Immortal," Carla repeated, slowly digesting the word.

"Yes."

"Are you saying that Dr. Balcourt has now become *immortal?*"

Sandy hesitated.

Suddenly a voice from the door cut through the silence. "There you are!" A lean man with short, fuzzy dark hair and a rich blue, balloon-sleeved, textured shirt entered the room. He smiled at the two women.

Sandy tried to stand.

"Don't bother." Lane gestured for her to keep her seat and went to Carla with both hands outstretched. "Welcome, Dr. MacGregor. I hope your trip was pleasant."

She stood, and he kissed her on both cheeks in the manner of the old world. "Thank you . . . and yes, we had some minor delays in Mexico City, but the flight itself was very pleasant."

"Good, good." He pulled out a chair and sat down with her.

Carla marveled at his appearance, his vigor. "I was in Stockholm when you accepted the Nobel," she said, unable to blink.

Lane nodded and smiled, his eyes translucent, gelid.

"Needless to say—but you've made *quite* a recovery, Doctor."

"Lane, please." He smiled as if he had just let her in on a secret. His eyes went to Sandy. "We hope . . ."

he said with a nod and somewhat of a sigh, "to do the very same for the pope." His eyes returned to Carla.

"Dr. Benson has just informed me that there could be a problem—"

Lane laughed. "Oh, I don't know. Henri's being a bit *difficult.* Very regimented, you understand. He just wants to be careful. I'm sure he'll come around."

"I'm not so sure," Sandy added.

Carla looked straight at Sandy. "Is there a schedule?"

"Not yet."

Carla turned back to Lane. "What exactly *is* Dr. Nakasone's objection to performing this procedure? You seem fine to me. How could he think—what did you say?" She turned to Sandy. "On the one hand he's—"

"He's not convinced the procedure has worked."

Carla looked back at Lane and shook her head. "That *seems* preposterous. I mean, just one look at him—"

"He thinks I'm delusional," Lane said calmly.

"Delusional," she repeated. She paused a moment then turned back to Sandy. "That's easy enough to check, isn't it?"

She nodded.

"Well? Certainly there must be tests or something?"

Sandy leaned forward and crossed her hands on the table. "He's already undergone a comprehensive psychological battery."

"You mean exhaustive," Lane corrected.

Sandy rolled her eyes.

"And?" Carla looked impatient.

"He's fine. According to Dr. Kazaz—and I interviewed him extensively when he finished his testing—Lane's probably better adjusted than the rest of us."

"Kazaz is the psychologist?"

"Psychiatrist," Lane answered.

Carla let out a sigh. "Well, pardon me for saying, but it sounds to me like Dr. Nakasone has *other* reasons for his opposition. Perhaps a . . . hidden agenda?"

"No. Henri's not that guileful." Sandy chuckled. "He'll tell you flat out what's eating him."

"Then I'll talk to him. Maybe I can get him to tell me what the real problem is." She thought about it for a moment, her gaze fixed on Lane's. "I don't want to sound subversive here, but, can this procedure . . . be done *without* Dr. Nakasone?"

"Yes," Lane said flatly.

"By you, I presume?"

"No, no!" He laughed. "I'm a research scientist, not a surgeon. Dr. Benson assisted during my transfer. I'm fairly certain she could lead the team."

"*Would* she lead the team?" Carla turned to Sandy.

Sandy sat back in her chair. "This places me in a very awkward position. But . . . yes, if need be, I will lead the team."

"Really?" Carla was suddenly conscious of a need to mask her growing sense of intrigue.

"Look, Dr. MacGregor, it wouldn't be telling you secrets to say that this whole thing has caused a bit of a rift among the senior members of the team," Sandy said, with a glance Lane's way. "I think Henri is having a crisis of faith. His Christian *ethos* doesn't leave him a lot of room to operate, if you know what I mean."

Lane nodded.

"Is there a problem with his having a Christian *ethos*?" Carla asked. When there came no answer, she vented a dismissive breath and continued. "I'd like to speak to Dr. Nakasone before I confer with Cardinal Verrechio. I take it you've not spoken with the cardinal?" She waited for Sandy's reply.

"My understanding was that liaison was your responsibility."

"And the pope? I take it he's—"

"Henri has him in for a pre-op MRI survey." She checked her watch, "In fact, I've got to run right now." She pushed her chair back away from the conference table and stood.

Carla stood with her. "I'd like to see that. Can you arrange it?"

"Of course," Lane said, pushing his chair back abruptly to join them. "Come. You can watch it with me—bring your tea with you. We've got an observation room overhead." He turned and smiled at Sandy. "I can't vouch for the entertainment value however; I'm afraid it's a little like watching a haircut." He moved aside so Carla and Sandy could pass through the door ahead of him.

"Where I come from, haircuts are considered prime Saturday night entertainment!" Carla smiled and stepped out into the hall.

The double doors swept open to the darkened observation room. Masako sat at the center of the first row of seats, completely engrossed in the procedure taking place in the surgical theater one floor below her. Unaware of anyone's arrival, she leaned forward, crossed her arms on the polished wooden railing that encircled the illuminated glass bubble at the center of the room, and rested her chin on her knuckles.

"Have they started yet?" Lane asked in a hushed voice, as they sidled their way into adjacent seats.

Masako turned, a smile of welcome on her face. "No. I think they're getting ready now." She craned her neck to smile at Carla. "Hello. I'm Masako, Dr. Nakasone's daughter," she said, standing to shake Carla's hand.

"Carla MacGregor," Carla replied, turning to spot her seat before she sat down.

"You should've been here," Masako spoke aside to Lane as they all took their seats. The uncomfortable look on her face contradicted her words. "They just stopped arguing a minute ago."

Carla leaned forward.

"I'm sorry." Masako met her gaze. "My father and Sandy—uh, Dr. Benson." She looked straight at Lane. "Something about a . . . what was it? Oh yes, a global map, I guess."

Lane sat back in his chair and spoke over his shoulder. "Sandy's pushing to pre-op for the transfer." He chuckled. "Evidently, Henri's having no part of *that.*"

Carla nodded despite her lack of understanding. She lifted her gaze over the railing and watched the team of doctors work below her. The pope's disrobed body was suspended between the gimbal rings of the operating table, his pallid skin a stark contrast to the mint green scrubs and gauzy paper hats worn by the surrounding staff. His body still appeared lean, slightly muscled—no sign of atrophy.

Carla watched as Henri ripped open a plastic bag and pulled out a long, coiled cardiac catheter. He waited as Sandy leaned over the pope's body and carefully jabbed a six-inch needle into his neck near his clavicle. Sandy detached something from the syringe and stepped back, holding the empty glass cylinder in place against the pope's iodine-scrubbed flesh. Henri leaned down and slowly fed the catheter into the syringe until only a small tail was left in his hand. Once the catheter was in place, he pulled on the blunted end and withdrew what appeared to be a piano-wire core; a rhythmic pulse of arterial blood spurted in heartbeat fashion across the Holy Father's chest and spattered Henri's mask and scrubs as Sandy quickly connected the end of the catheter to the central IV line that draped down from a full plastic bag of fluid.

"I think they're ready," Lane said.

Carla swallowed dryly and sat back in her seat, dividing her attention between Lane and the operating room. "What's going on exactly? I'm not much on medical procedure."

Lane turned his head toward Carla to explain. "They just put in a central line. That way they can introduce a concentrated drug feed directly into the aorta. Because of the size of that particular blood vessel and the massive volume of blood at that site, the gadolinium needed for the MRI can be introduced with less likelihood of causing damage to his circulatory system."

"The drugs are caustic?" Carla asked, cradling her teacup with both hands.

Lane answered with a nod and a strange grin.

The observation room doors swept open at their backs.

Lane turned to look. Carla followed his gaze to the door. A petite woman stood in the shadows, the light from the hall uncomfortably bright at her back. "Excuse me. Is there a Carla MacGregor here?" She squinted into the darkness.

"Yes." Carla stood up and began sidling carefully back across the row toward the aisle, balancing her cup in front of her.

The woman stepped back into the hall and held the door open as Carla approached. She smiled pleasantly as Carla stepped into the light, "You've got a fax coming in. I tried to see where it's from, but the transmission is pretty choppy. Solar flares, they tell me. Again!"

Carla followed the woman to an unused office down the hall, thanked her, and quietly closed the door. She flipped on the desk lamp and tapped the COM as she sat down behind the desk. "This is Carla," she said, making herself comfortable in the overstuffed leather chair.

A hushed rapid pulsing tone sounded from the desk-top computer, like ringing in her ears. She tapped the control panel again and read the message that scrolled across the screen:

WEDGEFAX . . . MESSAGE TRANSMISSION . . .
WEDGEFAX . . . MESSAGE TRANSMISSION . . .
WEDGEFAX . . . MESSAGE TRANSMISSION . . .

Following the instructions scrolling across the bottom of her screen, she pressed her thumb on the corner of the CRT highlighted for an ID scan. The electronic signature took a moment to process.

Frowning, she tilted her head to read further, tapped the "print document" panel, and watched as the sheets of paper dropped from beneath the screen in rapid succession.

Carla lifted several sheets and glanced over the unfamiliar handwritten lettering that covered the first page:

May grace and peace be multiplied unto you,
I bring to you a warning in the name of
the Mystery: The Father, the Son and the Holy
Spirit, the Three which are but One; the Holy.

Lord, what have I gotten myself into? Carla studied the text. Each word seemed pronounced by an inner voice, soft and strange, familiar, dimly recognizable, like that of a long-forgotten friend. No, not forgotten at all. This was Eddie's voice: *A warning, Carla, in the name of the Mystery.*

She spoke those words aloud as she read. Still, the child's voice was there, as soft and clear as her own conscience. Gathering the papers, she got up, stepped over to the window, and returned to her reading, startled tears coming to her eyes. In the stillness, she felt an odd wind rise and stir about her. She looked around the room.

Nothing.

Again, she returned to her reading. Again, the same queer, crawling draft, icy on the back of her neck, radiating a chill down the backs of her arms, her legs. She raised her head, thinking she saw in the corner of her eye the gauzy outline of a child . . . a solitary figure . . . veiled in the shadows, just behind the bookcase at the door.

Carla tried to clear her throat. She stepped cautiously back to the desk and slowly reached for the gooseneck desk lamp, lifting it off the desk and out in front of her. The lamp scattered strange angular shadows on the wall as she swept the light back and forth.

No one.

As she returned the lamp to the desktop, she sensed a bizarre distortion of time, as if she were falling asleep and waking up at once. She felt hyperalert, aware of the gradual loss of warmth in her teacup . . . aware of the books on the shelves . . . aware of the tone and aural frequency of the pale yellow light . . . the close nap of the carpet . . . the turpentine smell of the paint on the walls . . . the neat stack of papers on the desk in front of her . . . her own body, her held breath. She recalled the last time she had felt like this—at the airport, with Eddie. She recalled his strange quotation from Scripture, innocent, childlike:

Woman of the wilderness. She returned to the document, her skin tingling in waves:

> We are commanded to keep holy His way! It
> is written *Scientia inflat*: Knowledge puffeth up.
>   "Or do you not know that your body is the
> temple of the Holy Spirit who is in you, whom
> you have from God, and you are not your own?
> For you were bought at a price; therefore
> glorify God in your body and in your spirit,
> which are God's."

Holy Scripture. She thought of what it was her Bible had taught her over the years. Not in sequence, but all at once. In a flash it was upon her, *agape*; as it is—the miracle of conception, the tenderness of birth, the sanctity and dignity of life, the mystery of death, the glory and fulfillment of the Spirit, the blessedness of selfless surrender to the divine will of Him who created and sustains all that is, the unspeakable bliss of the meek—the poor of spirit—who live to see the face of God.

The face of God. How long Lord? How long before we stand at the face of Your unfathomable mercy? For an instant, she felt the need to cry. Quickly she closed her eyes. When she opened her eyes again, the voice continued,

> So it is we must die, die to the flesh,
> perish the empty idolatry of the senses if we
> are to gain the eternal joy prepared for us by
> our Father from the very foundation of the
> earth. Take heart, be brave, live boldly in

Christ for we are the Spirit awakening, and
there is a far, far higher place than this.

Carla looked down at the text on the receding
page in front of her. Feeling herself rise, she read the
last words of the paragraph.

Through the mystery of death and by the
grace of Almighty God, I am resurrected in the
image of the incorruptible Spirit.

The text continued to retreat. For an instant
Carla felt buoyant, as if she too was receding with the
page. The boundaries between first and last, great
and small, real and unreal, above and below, inside
and outside, all seemed to blur and then dissolve.
Something like eternity obliterated her moment. She
felt a flicker of panic, like a burning wind move
through her; the canticle from Luke's Gospel seemed
to sparkle like a cut jewel inside her mind as she
snapped back into focus.

"*Nunc Dimittis!* Now, therefore, let thou
thy servant depart in peace."

It was moments before she could collect herself.
She understood. Her faith was telling her simply: We
must die in this life so that we might find eternal life
with Him who created us for Himself in paradise.

Returning to the page, she leafed through to the
middle of the document.

Fear God, and give glory to Him, for the
hour of His judgment is come. And worship
Him that made heaven and earth and the sea
and the fountains of waters . . . And I heard as
it were the voice of a great multitude, and as
the voice of many waters, and as the voice of
mighty thunderings, saying, Alleluia: for the
Lord God omnipotent reigneth.

Carla stepped back behind the desk and
collapsed into the chair. She switched off the light
and sat alone in the comfort of darkness. She dropped
her head into her hands. An uncharacteristic
trembling like that of profound unworthiness
overtook her as she began to realize what it was that
she was being called to do.

"Lord, help me to see," Carla muttered under her
breath. Fatigued, she felt puzzled, as if remembering
something she'd never consciously known or
accepted. An odd heaviness tugged at her, pulling her
down like a drug. She crossed her arms against a
sudden chill, closed her eyes, and wept.

▼

"Dr. MacGregor," Henri said, remaining at the
door after a slight bow.

Carla blushed. "I'm sorry. I was—"

"You've had a long trip, I understand." He waited
for her to stand, before continuing. "Come," he said,
stepping aside for her to pass. "I'll take you to your
room."

212

She accompanied him down the hall to the elevator. Its doors swept open, and Carla stepped timidly inside. "At least I can splash some cold water on my face. Something . . . I feel like I've been drugged," she said, with a faint-hearted chuckle.

Henri held his peace as the doors closed. The elevator headed toward the top floor.

"You'll have to excuse me, Doctor, but I'm afraid I'm puzzled. I'm told that you oppose—"

"I am completely *against* performing another transfer on anyone." He spoke without meeting her gaze.

The elevator doors opened. "That was my understanding," Carla said, feeling a bit awkward as she stepped out of the elevator. She waited, then followed him down the hall. "I'm surprised. How can you be so set against the very operation you used to save your friend's life? I don't understand?"

Henri stepped aside and guided her into place in front of the closed door, gesturing for her to raise her palm. Instantly, the door clicked open. "This procedure . . ." He motioned for her to go ahead of him into the small studio apartment. The door clicked shut. He turned and looked directly at her. "This procedure was a serious mistake."

Carla sat down on the oxblood leather couch and looked at him.

"I refuse to perform this operation on anyone else until we've completely studied the results of the first procedure."

"But I thought tests had been done—"

"It's too early," he said, seating himself in the stuffed wingback chair. His face seemed drawn, his eyes tired. It was apparent to Carla that the good doctor wasn't telling her everything.

"We just don't know enough. I've known Lane a long time—longer and better than anyone else—and I have to tell you I am very concerned about him. He sounds delusional, dissociative. I'm concerned because, while the part of his mind that controls his physical body certainly seems functional at this point, I'm not sure his higher brain functions have survived the ordeal."

"You think he's psychotic, delusional . . . insane?"

"I'm just not sure."

Carla waited a long time before she spoke again. "What do you propose? What about the pope?"

"We'll do what we can, *short* of the transfer. We'll do everything we can . . . to help him," Henri leaned forward. "Look, I'm a realist. I have to be. I understand the realities in which we live here. I am well aware of the vast amount of capital the Vatican has put into our research efforts."

"I had no idea they were so involved."

Henri continued, "Everything we have accomplished here has been made possible by men and women of good faith and good will. And I also appreciate the political dynamics of the moment, believe me—the need to preserve this one man as titular head of an age-old organization—"

"You're talking Liberation politics?" She looked at him, measuring his response.

"As I've explained . . . I'm a realist."

"So I see."

"Are you a Catholic, Doctor?"

"No, I am not."

"So . . . your *sensitivity,*" she waited to see if she'd used the correct word, "to the Liberation movement—"

"Doctor," Henri stood and spoke without apology, "I am a Christian. I am also a surgeon, a scientist. And in the end, in this world at least, we are what we do. The only interest I have in the Roman organization, or, for that matter, in this . . . this political turmoil that now surrounds the Catholic Church, is as the sole venture partner to us here at the WEDGE. That's it—and perhaps it's important for me to add that while I certainly respect the Catholics as brothers in Christ, I do not share the fine points of their faith."

Carla was silent for a moment. She understood his sentiments; they were her own. "Your proposal . . ." she finally said, holding his gaze. "What is it you propose?"

Chapter

12

Henri stopped Carla just in front of the security scanner at the exit to her guest residence in the WEDGE. He raised his palm to the laser sentry and nodded for her to do the same. They passed through the enormous cut-glass double doors etched with the LMC logo—an unraveling double helix of DNA—and into the quarantined workspace. Henri kept silent as they walked briskly through the elliptical marble corridor braced on both sides by a colonnade of colorful, translucent cylinders containing holograms of early pioneers in the sciences.

Carla turned to Henri. "We're lucky we got through. They told me the cardinal will be incommunicado for the next several days," she looked down at her watch, "starting at seven P.M. Roman time."

"This won't take long." Henri picked up his pace. The morning sun cast an amber haze through the metal-foil solar draperies, bathing everything in a soft wash of golden light. In moments, they reached the conference room. Here the high ceilings of the vast waiting room gave an open feeling of majestic space, and across one wall spread a twinkling, mural-sized map of a human brain, rendered in three dimensions by some long-forgotten laser artist.

"Right this way," Henri said, stepping away from the conference room doors as they clicked open. Instantly the lights blinked on.

Carla went in and waited for Henri to shut the doors. A great oval table, polished burly maple, dominated the center of the room.

"We'll be alone here," he said, moving to the large COM console at the head of the table. Henri sat down and gestured for Carla to sit to his right. "Get us Cardinal Verrechio at the Vatican," he spoke calmly to the computer.

Carla watched as the opposite wall rolled back. Moments later the cardinal's familiar scarlet robes materialized in the semi-circular alcove. "Dr. Nakasone!" he said in a rich, Neapolitan accent. "It *is* a great honor."

"Cardinal." Henri, standing briefly, gave a low bow. "I wish this meeting could be under better circumstances."

"That's what we're here to talk about, isn't it?" He gestured graciously for Henri to be seated.

Carla kept silent as Henri took his seat. She looked down for a moment and studied his taciturn expression in the mirror-like shine of the wood. A reverse image, like her own. Here was a man of extraordinary heart, she knew, a brother in Christ. Theirs was an unspoken sympathy. Without saying a word, she knew he had sensed the darkness, the evil just as keenly as she.

Evil—the potentiality that leads man to calamity, a false glorification of the self, beyond reason, beyond love, beyond redemption, a simple turning away from God. She remembered the words she had learned as a child, words that had preceded Satan's fall. *Non serviam,* I will not serve.

"Perhaps Carla has already told you, but at seven my time I'm beginning the first in a series of meetings with the council of bishops and laypeople slated to inherit the papacy." He paused. "Excuse me . . . I mean . . . assume control of the newly liberated church." Verrechio nodded in Carla's direction. "I understand you have some concerns about the Holy Father's . . . well-being, shall we say?"

Henri cleared his throat. "I am afraid I have more than concerns, Cardinal. I am absolutely against this whole suggestion. Our team must *not* perform any more procedures—on the pope or anyone. Not until a great deal is resolved and rethought."

"But you performed the very same operation on your friend." Verrechio looked confused.

"Yes."

"And, from what we hear, it was successful."
Verrechio fixed his eyes on Henri, his accent sweet, melodious.

"Not exactly." Henri took a breath. "Yes, Dr. Balcourt survived the operation physically."

"He's *non compos mentis?*" Verrechio leaned forward in his chair.

"No, I can't say that."

The cardinal leaned back and watched Henri. "Then I'm afraid I don't understand."

Henri unfolded his hands and rested his palms flat on the table. "It is too soon. We aren't completely convinced." He glanced back at Carla. "*I* am not completely convinced that it was successful. Physically, yes. But mentally, emotionally, I am still not sure. It is very strange. Lane has become completely preoccupied with a . . . a messianic perception of himself and his life. He is obsessed with the notion that he's become . . . *immortal*—that he represents the salvation of humankind."

Verrechio was silent, thoughtful.

"That is just one problem," Henri continued. "We are getting into a nasty situation—press hype, religious fanatics going berserk on our grounds—what do you think would happen if the pope himself has the next transfer?"

"Is it possible that the doctor suffered a delusional personality disorder prior to the surgery? And you're only beginning to see it now?" Verrechio leaned forward again.

"I have known Lanning Balcourt for more than fifteen years, worked closely with him, and I have never before seen any evidence of this. And believe me, we have spent enough time together."

The cardinal paused for a moment.

Carla unfolded her arms. "You say he's *obsessed* with immortality," she said, directing her gaze at Henri. "I'm interested in this obsession. What are we talking about, really? I mean *is* Dr. Balcourt immortal, as he seems to assume?"

Henri shifted in his seat. "I really don't know how to answer that. Technically speaking, I suppose . . . yes, he has become immortal."

Verrechio leaned forward, his furrowed expression evidence of the keenness of his attention.

"Let me explain," Henri clasped his hands together. "We are all biological machines, really. The programs that run these machines of ours—our bodies on the large scale and the cells within our bodies on a smaller scale—these genetic codes, have been set in such a way as to limit the number of cell divisions possible within this living system. At some point, when we have reached the finite boundary of our cells' program, our bodies begin to shut down. They fail, one system at a time, until the body finally dies. Biological entropy," he added with a glance Carla's direction. "It is almost as if the whole reason for our existence were to give us an understanding of death. Our bodies reach a point, the biological life expectancy maximum within each individual, where they begin to destroy themselves by design."

"And that does not happen after the transfer?" Verrechio asked.

"No. It does not. No cell division—no preprogrammed boundaries. No finite limits. No death, *per se*."

"Why the qualifier, Doctor?" Carla asked.

Henri glanced at Verrechio. "This whole notion of immortality makes me very uncomfortable. Yes, it *is* theoretically possible that Dr. Balcourt will never die. Still, the fact remains that almost anything could happen to terminate his consciousness prior to his being able to repair or replace a physically atrophied body."

"Such as?" Verrechio asked.

"Such as any traumatic accident. An accident in which his body was destroyed, rendered unable to hold his consciousness." Henri met the cardinal's gaze. "So you see, this immortality question, well . . . it's hyperbole, really."

Verrechio thought about it for a moment in silence. "Hyperbole—that is my thought exactly, Doctor. This transfer calls to mind the story of Jonah, who tries to escape from God—the very God who *created* the oceans—fleeing by sea, hiding in the hold of a wooden boat. Imagine Jonah's naive state of mind, to think he could escape the Lord God Almighty! Hiding from the One who spins the cosmos with a mere turn of His wrist; from Him for whom all the waters of the sea are but a particle, Jonah hides in a boat—made from sticks, no less." The cardinal chuckled. "No, I tend to side with George Bernard Shaw on this matter. I say the notion of physical immortality is nothing less than comical. Let's get back to your medical concerns, Dr. Nakasone. Your specialty is obviously not psychiatry. Have you had him tested, evaluated in any way?"

"Of course. We had a comprehensive psychological battery done on him immediately following his vivification."

Verrechio glanced at Carla and then back to Henri. "And the results?"

"He . . . does not seem to have any diagnosable mental disorders of any kind," Henri looked unconvinced. *"Ostensibly,* those were the results."

"And yet you continue to be concerned?" Verrechio probed.

"Yes, and I have tried to explain why."

Verrechio drew a deep breath and pushed himself back in his chair. "Dr. Nakasone, I am not a scientist. You know better than I." He paused briefly. "As far as I am concerned, your procedure is a true miracle."

Henri said nothing.

Verrechio stood, his face suddenly aglow in sunlight as he glanced off to the side. "I am a man of the Church. As such, I have a sacred trust, a duty." He turned and appeared to pace. "I have been entrusted to see that the pope receives the very best care possible. It is a responsibility that I take very seriously. Especially in light of the recent moves to reform this Church." He nodded Carla's way, and then continued. "You are probably aware that this is the last pope."

"I am aware of that."

Verrechio nodded. "Carla tells me that you are not a Catholic . . ."

"Hai."

"Then perhaps you are not aware that according to our faith, the pope is considered first among equals. Catholics consider him protected by the Holy Spirit."

A confused look appeared on Henri's face. "I am not sure what you mean."

"I am trying to allay your fears, Dr. Nakasone, to mitigate what you have said is your primary concern." Verrechio sat back down, the light from an unshuttered window outlining his lean frame. "The Church's situation is precarious. You, your team—you have brought forth something just when this ancient community of ours faces its most difficult challenge." His gaze went to Carla, then drifted away. "Difficult challenge," he repeated abstractedly. *"That is a euphemism."*

The Cardinal's face turned back to Henri, his voice grave. "I fear this . . . *Liberation* . . . is tearing this Church apart—we are tearing ourselves apart! As far as your fear about performing a transfer on the Holy Father, that somehow he could survive physically and yet be scarred mentally . . . emerge psychotic, somehow . . . well . . . that is simply not possible. This is a fact: The Holy Father *is* protected. By faith, I know that he will die during the operation, or live with all his faculties, as is the will of God."

Verrechio saw the disbelief on Henri's face and continued. "Try to remember it was our money that built your lab and enabled you to staff that facility with the men, women, and equipment that helped make your dream a reality. The way I see it, we have a stake in . . . *whatever* comes from your labor."

Henri stirred in his seat. He opened his mouth as if to speak.

Verrechio interrupted him with a benign gesture of his hand, "And, if I am not misinformed, you are alone in your opposition to this procedure. I am told your organization is completely behind the transfer."

"Cardinal, with all due respect, I do not believe you are looking at this thing clearly." Henri rose from his seat. He drew in a deep breath and began to pace, his face now full of foreboding. "We are not talking about saving the life of one human being any longer. What we are talking about," his voice suddenly grew unsteady, "is the . . . total annihilation, and extinction . . . of humanity in the extreme, since this would sterilize each and every individual transferred. Project it out yourself. At the extreme, we succeed in sterilizing the entire human race. No more children. No more hope. Period."

Henri paused briefly and glanced at Carla. He continued, "Perhaps we can do something short of the transfer itself that could help the pope—buy some time to thoroughly check this procedure out . . . to look at this from the medical ethics angle. I am telling you, it is—"

Verrechio interrupted excitedly: "Doctor, who better to fashion a rational medical ethic than the Church?" The cardinal smiled, his tone inadvertently condescending. "That, after all, is our business, Dr. Nakasone. Man's salvation has been our concern for more than two thousand years." He nodded at Carla with a look that made her wince. "But I agree. We should exhaust all other possibilities before going ahead with so radical a procedure. You mentioned that you may be able to do something short of a transfer. Such as?"

"I don't know. We're looking at his test results now."

Verrechio stood up. "There it is," he said, signaling in his accustomed parliamentary manner that the meeting had come to an end. "That I think we can do. I'll wait to hear from you. Other than that, we'll have to see. You've certainly given me something to think about. I'll include you in my prayers."

Carla waited until the cardinal's hologram vanished before she spoke. "Dr. Nakasone," Her voice was low and tight, "is there a recording made of Lane's psychiatric interview?"

"Yes." Henri frowned. "I have the discs in my office. Why do you ask?"

"There may be a great deal more to this procedure of yours than you realize. I need those discs."

"Cardinal Verrechio—" Henri began.

Carla interrupted him, "The cardinal sees your procedure as a way to preserve the papacy and with it, I wouldn't be at all surprised, his own exalted station. He knows that as long as this pope lives, there will be no liberation. The Roman Church will remain intact—*and* in Rome."

Henri stared at her, taking in her anxiety, measuring her.

Carla went on, "You heard what he said. He truly believes that the transfer procedure is the work of

God, part of the divine plan. And if the procedure makes this pope 'immortal,' all the better."

Carla looked out through the window. Three rows of police cars formed a shark-tooth barricade. A ring of armed police in riot gear formed an arc just beyond the reflector pool that wrapped around both sides of the building. "We don't have much time, Doctor." She turned to Henri. "If the Church backs this operation—and it will if this pope survives . . ." She stopped mid-sentence. Her face was strained, her tone edged with desperation. "We've got to stop this, that's all I know. This procedure is blasphemy."

Henri eyed Carla uneasily.

"Look here, let me show you something," she looked up at the clock, reached into her briefcase, and pulled out a stack of photocopied pages. "Recognize this?"

"Scripture, I suspect," Henri said, leafing through the pages. *"Hai,* the book of Revelation, I believe. I recognize a few of these passages."

"Look again!" She spoke urgently. "Do you see anything familiar?" She reached for the papers. "I ask," she seemed to struggle with her composure, then continued, her voice under tight control, "because *I* see something very disturbing here." She looked pointedly into his eyes.

"What are you telling me?"

Carla sat down beside him. His face seemed stern, implacable, his jaw locked. *I can trust this man.* Holding his gaze, she knew.

"May I?" Henri held out his hand for the documents.

Carla reached back into her case and again handed him the stack of papers. "I see a prophecy of Lane's transfer."

Henri studied the papers. For a long moment he was quiet, then, *"Hai,"* he muttered, his head moving almost imperceptibly. *"Hai."*

"And that document is almost two thousand years old."

▼

"Why do you insist on making a circus of this?" Henri demanded.

At the window, Lane ignored him. He kept his eyes on the crowds.

Henri looked from Lane to Sandy, then exploded. *"Hype* is *not* the solution. It is just *one more* problem. Every time I turn around, someone is talking to the press. Where is the finesse?"

Lane raised his voice and said, "Henri, we've gone over this enough already."

"He's right," Sandy cut in, her tone deliberate, businesslike. "He's got to speak to these people. They're going to stay here until he makes an appearance. We've got to do *something.*"

"Your opinion." Henri's voice was clipped.

Sandy leaned over the table, her weight on her palms, and glanced away. "No . . . not *my* opinion, Henri. That's the way it's got to be."

"What? Are you in charge now?" Henri's eyes grew dark, defiant.

"Yes." Sandy stood and drew in a deep breath. "And I've been *in charge* for a long time now, Henri.

I've been running this place, paying the bills, scheduling the surgeries, hiring, firing. Yes, Henri. I *am* in charge. And, if you'll remember, it was you who first put me in charge." Sandy looked straight at him. "He's going to speak to them."

Henri's face flushed. He felt suddenly old and embarrassed.

Lane stepped away from the window. "People should be able to choose for themselves."

"Choose what?" Henri glared through moistened eyes. "I transferred you to save your life—it was your procedure. Your life's work. You had made your choice already. What choice do you propose to give them?"

"They are like children. They need me." Lane met his gaze. "I am giving them the opportunity to raise themselves."

Henri stared at him. "Lane, what are you talking about? Elective surgery?"

"There's no way to know how long they have before it's too late." Lane's voice had a strange new resonance, cello-like, deep.

"There is no way we can put healthy people through a transfer like yours—it is too much of a gamble."

"It's no gamble, Henri," Lane looked inspired. "No more than life itself."

Henri clenched his jaw, "No, not in theory, maybe. But you stand there in the operating room, ankle deep in blood and excrement, and do one of these procedures yourself. *Then* you tell me!" Henri turned, and walked out.

▼

Henri returned to his apartment with a splitting headache. "I don't know, Masako," he said, pouring himself a strong cup of coffee, "They're not listening to me. I can't seem to get through to them."

Masako folded her book onto the coffee table. "What?"

Henri sank onto the couch and took a sip of black coffee from his cup. "It's Lane," he said, finally.

"What about Lane?"

"He and Sandy want to take the transfer and sell it to perfectly healthy individuals. Lord, what have I done?"

"Daddy, you saved his life!" Masako looked up; her eyes seemed green in the light, enchanted, bewitched.

"We build greater than we know," Henri muttered. "This is all moving too fast. The Church, Sandy, Lane—they actually want to make this an elective surgery!"

Masako watched her father.

Henri looked away. "Most unwanted," he muttered again. He took another long pull from his cup then returned it to the saucer. "This is dangerous. Lane scares me."

Masako leaned forward and folded her hands on her knees. "Maybe he's right, Dad."

Henri's eyes snapped to his daughter's face.

"Maybe it's good to . . . I don't know . . . *evangelize* this procedure. I like Lane—and, I mean, after all, he *is* immortal."

Henri got up and returned to the kitchen to pour himself another cup. "In the strict technical sense, *hai,* I suppose he is." He put the coffeepot back and with his head down, pushed himself back, letting his fingers spread slowly on the surface of the counter. "What have I done?"

"Daddy . . . you made a decision to save a friend's life. You did it." The green highlights shifted in his daughter's eyes. "You're a part of something that will truly save the world."

"I made a decision, all right." Henri stared at the steaming cup of coffee he held in his hands. "I just may not have made the right one."

Masako went to the counter and touched her father's hand. "Why shouldn't we seek immortality?"

Henri looked at her, a diffusion of light at her back from the white shades. Her face glowed darkly. "It's not that easy. . . ." He lifted his cup and took another sip. "Think. Say we make this *immortality* available, how do we allocate it? It's expensive. Who gets it? Who pays?"

▼

Lane switched off his COM and stretched. *I'm going to tell her,* he thought, reflecting on his dream. *Sandy will understand.* He threw back the covers and shuffled to the bathroom to shower and brush his teeth. He stared into the mirror, fascinated at the lean, muscular body reflected in the glass before he reached for the shower faucet.

Minutes later, the doorbell brought him from a steamy reverie. He turned off the water, stepped out of the shower, wrapped a towel around his waist, and went to the door. "Thought I'd get cleaned up before you came."

Sandy stepped into his apartment wearing an old pair of faded blue jeans and a baggy, paint-spattered Harvard sweatshirt with *VE . . . RI . . . TAS* emblazoned in gold on the burgundy fabric. She smiled at his towel.

Lane stepped back out of the way and greeted her with a kiss. "What's up?" he asked, moving toward the fireplace in the living room.

Sandy went to the kitchen. "Got anything cold to drink?"

Lane returned to the bath and quickly threw on a robe. "Check the fridge," he called out from the other room.

Sandy grabbed a moist can and shut the door. "I think Henri's going to be a problem," she said. The soft drink belched quietly open. "I don't know, Lane . . ." She returned to the living room. "We do need to work a few things out. This Christian thing of his."

Lane moved near, taking the soft drink can from her hand and then his mouth was on hers.

Sandy pulled away with a nervous, mildly embarrassed laugh, "Uh, Lane . . ." She blushed, and her voice seemed to crack. "Let's keep our . . . ," she took her drink back, "relationship . . . professional. Please."

Lane pulled away and sat in front of the fire, aloof for a long awkward moment before he finally gestured for her to join him. "I was having another one of my dreams when you called," he said, gathering the folds of his robe between his legs.

"You're still having those?"

"Same dream." He stared at the crackling flames. It seemed a long time before he spoke. "You know, Sandy, throughout time—in myth, in legend, in our religions," he said, lifting his fingers gently to his own lips, "the human saga tells the same recurring tale: creation, death and re-creation." Abruptly, he dropped his hand and smiled. "The poets, the prophets, the mystics, the saints, all tell us this. *That's* what my dream is telling me. My surgery is far more than just a physical transfer. It's re-creation. It's the . . . the transfiguration."

Sandy fidgeted a bit. "I'm afraid I don't understand the distinction."

"Think of it . . . centuries of dreams, prophecies, voices, visions, pouring forth from the collective unconscious, weaving together until our time. This time." His voice was quiet and steady. "One of my favorite passages in the Bible is 'The kingdom of heaven is spread out upon the earth, but men do not see it.'"

Sandy raised her eyebrows. "You're saying immortality will enable people to see the kingdom of God?"

"Absolutely, because the only way to see God's kingdom is to become God." Slowly, he showed his face. For a fleeting moment, a proud, self-satisfied smile twisted his lips.

Sandy watched the firelight shift in Lane's eyes. There was a glimmer of white gold. His face was serene. "And what about you, Lane? What do your dreams say? What's your role in the unfolding of God's mystery?"

"In me there is a fusing of two worlds; the temporal and the spiritual. I *am* the union, the path between parallels."

Chapter

13

Montreal, Quebec
November 3, 2065

"The chopper's on the roof," Sandy called into Henri's office. "You are coming, aren't you? Masako's already there."

Slowly, reluctantly, Henri took his eyes from Lane and nodded. He pushed his chair in behind his desk and stared at the computer screen he had yet to switch off. His mood darkened at the thought of Lane's upcoming speech to the crowd now anxiously waiting to see the world's first immortal, to hear his wisdom. *Perish the day on which I was born.*

Sandy stepped into the room and split her attention between Lane and Henri. "Look at it this way, Henri, Lane will make his appearance, say a few words, and ask them to go home. If this works we'll all be back in our own homes, sleeping in our own beds before you know it. We've got to do *something.*

These people are going to get ugly if we don't at least make an appearance."

"I'm ready," Lane said, moving eagerly toward the door.

Sandy let the two of them pass. The elevator opened to a small utility hall that provided access to the roof through double automatic security doors. She stepped up to the laser scanner and raised her right hand. The doors opened. Instantly the shouts of an angry crowd growing more and more violent rose from below. There was a sudden concussion from a nearby explosion, then a woman's shrill scream, a scattering of voices, urgent commands barked over police radios and bullhorns. Then everything seemed to fade beneath a whine of sirens.

The trio stepped into the chill night air and peered over the side of the waist-high wall that encircled the roof like a battlement. A faint updraft of smoke lifted Lane's eyes to a clear sky deepening to the color of slate, and then to the setting sun's amber light that struck and swept the stark line of the horizon.

"Crowd control's done an outstanding job." Sandy's voice rose above the whirling beat from the aircraft coming to life at the center of the helipad. "They've made a festival out this thing. Smart, I think. The stage is over there." She pointed to the arabesque dome of white light in the distance. A tangle of red and green and blue lasers swept the smokey air around the dome.

Lane looked out over the crowd aglow in the shifting light. "We will build a paradise on earth," Lane smiled. "And travel to the stars."

Henri was silent, carefully studying his colleague's exuberant expressions. Lane's messianic remarks grated on him. Henri's thoughts turned to the words of the apostle Paul: *"Oh! Who will deliver me from this body under the power of death? Who will permit me this good that I might die and go to see my Lord Jesus Christ! I do not desire death in order to be delivered from the labors that I endure . . . only so that I might see Him."*

Sandy leaned into the wind from the helicopter's rotors and started for the aircraft's open door. Lane and Henri followed behind her. The door slammed shut and locked. The chopper lifted into the air, turned, and banked slightly as it lifted up over the edge of the building. Lane looked out the window at the hundreds of people in the firelight below. A mosaic of laser light swept the crowd, which pressed tight against the elevated stage for handouts of food and water.

Suddenly Lane shouted, startling everyone with his excited gesticulations, "Circle back. Look at that, right there!"

The helicopter circled around a massive inflated display. They all looked down on a three-story balloon figure of a man in a white laboratory coat, fixed to the ground with ropes.

The helicopter came around the front of the balloon. Henri watched the odd expressions on Lane's face as Lane marveled at his own image on the face of the balloon. His own face, his short stubbly hair, his every personal detail wafting there below him on a forty-foot inflated balloon.

Lane shook his head. "I like the lab coat!" he shouted. He met Henri's cold gaze and laughed. "Don't think I've ever worn a lab coat!"

▼

Carla stood next to Masako at the side of the great stage that rose over seventy feet above the anxious crowd. "Here they come," Masako said. Her words came in steamy breaths as she nodded in the direction of the helicopter approaching the grassy knoll at the rear of the enormous tube steel and canvas structure.

Carla turned to face the roar of wind from the aircraft's blades. She watched with a growing sense of dread as the chopper touched down on the grass, where it was immediately surrounded by a ring of armed guards. Lifting her hand above her head to shield the glare of light from the spotlights, she stared out at the scene. Three familiar figures climbed out of the chopper, crouched, and ran toward the stage. Sandy and Lane arrived at the stairs in laughter. Henri and Carla exchanged knowing glances. Henri bowed slightly.

"Big night tonight!" Masako shivered and smiled at her father, her hands in her pockets, her collar drawn up snug around her chin.

"We certainly have the audience for it." Lane's proud expression spoke clearly his deep sense of satisfaction. His gaze traveled from the crowd to the camera crews hanging from the scaffolding towers that jutted one hundred feet into the air at the two forward corners of the stage.

"Well, here we are," Sandy said, stepping forward. "What say we get started." Smiling broadly she went to center stage and took up the microphone.

"Ladies and gentlemen . . . please . . . may I have your attention," she said, her voice thundering across the acres and acres of uplifted human faces. Gradually, the crowd settled into an uneven silence. "On behalf of the men and women of Lucien Machine Corporation, I welcome you."

Cheers rose and seemed to explode like fireworks. Sandy raised her hand over her head in a victory salute. She smiled back at Lane and Henri, then went on, "Allow me to introduce to you *the man of the millennium!*"

Again, the crowd erupted into applause. "Ladies and gentlemen," Sandy spoke over the cheers, "you've all read about him. You've followed his remarkable achievements—and his miracle. Please welcome . . . Dr. Lanning Balcourt!"

Henri felt his stomach tighten as Lane took center stage. Sandy gave him a warm embrace. A cacophonous roar hung in the air as individual cheers combined and were lost in an eerie, rumbling thunder.

Lane stood alone on the enormous stage. He lowered his head in silence before beginning.

"Thank you, everyone, thank you," he said, raising his hands to quiet the crowd. A hush, one million strong, played anxiously throughout the crowd, and then . . . silence.

Lane glanced back at Henri, at Masako, at Carla, at Sandy; he turned back to the crowd and then began again, "The miracle," he said, his voice, low and rich, washed over the crowd like the sound of a great church bell, "the miracle is upon you . . . *this* is your judgment."

▼

Henri sat down hard on the bed. "Really!"

Masako laughed. "Lane's speech . . . what he said—it's still ringing in my ears."

Henri looked at her. Masako shook her damp hair out over her shoulder. Her eyes seemed to stare into a distant place her father could not see. "Especially the part about the radicals trying to block people from choosing."

Henri interrupted. "Opposition will come—and from more than just the radical elements."

"Yes. Like Lane said, social groups, church groups, any group that attempts to think for the individual, to usurp our free will."

"He went on an attack." Henri shook his head.

"I didn't hear it that way. No, I rather thought he was . . . gentle." Again, her eyes looked out at some far point. "Every one of us must now choose. What will it be: life or death? Lane's right, you know. Organizations derive their power from people's fear of dying, so naturally he expects them to resist the procedure. He warned us about that—he just wants people to open their eyes and accept this breakthrough as a blessing, as an opportunity to build a new paradise here on earth." She turned serenely. "I think he's right."

Henri stirred uneasily, "Masako, please. Lane may not be well, he—"

"Dad, that's ridiculous! He's probably the greatest human being ever created—er . . . re-created."

"I am telling you, daughter, I am seriously concerned that something is terribly wrong with Lane. Listen to me."

"Dad, you know I believe in you. But . . . you're wrong on this . . . you're wrong." Slowly, with an odd new dignity, she left the room.

▼

Masako realized she was dreaming. Her dreams always began the same way. She was floating somewhere, hidden, then the visions would start. But this dream was different somehow. Different, almost as though she were locked inside someone else's head.

She looked down on a barren desert that stretched as far as she could see in every direction. The sky seemed haunted. Unearthly shades of violet and indigo flashed before her eyes; a canopy of lightning streaked around her like the white-hot capillary roots from some uprooted cosmic tree. In the middle of the storm stood a solitary figure, a man. His silhouette cast a long, stretched shadow across the desert floor—*Lane's dream,* she thought. *And his landscape.*

Here he is. She smiled. *Lane.* His familiar form drew her. She now stood before him, watching in silence, for somehow she knew he could not see her there. Suddenly tears streamed down his cheeks. She put out her hand, but his image was only mist before her, his face she could not touch. Lane stood alone and unreachable, a tortured phantom before her eyes.

A stranger draped in a pauper's robes appeared from nowhere. The man's voice spoke—a tormented voice—and then slowly, the man began to wither and die, vanishing into dust, collapsing before Lane's feet. Lane looked down at the dust and raised his arms heavenward. Fingers extended as if he were clawing the sky. He drew every muscle tight, and, filling his lungs full, he screamed, *"I am!"*

Under the force of his voice, Masako fell to the ground. She lay on the desert floor, stunned. A brilliant white gash transformed the night sky to vivid daylight. She looked up and saw Lane standing above her. His body was now draped in the stranger's robe.

Lane's back arched; his arms spread, as air streamed past him, and again came his strong, unearthly cry, *"I am!"*

His body formed a human cross against the flashing sky; his voice seemed to command the elements.

He's the one, she thought. *The one foreordained.* A silence came upon Masako so suddenly that it startled her out of her sleep. She opened her eyes. "Lane," she said aloud and swiftly rose from her bed.

▼

Lane rolled out of bed and slipped into a pair of black linen slacks. He moved sleepily into the kitchen and fixed himself some toast and coffee, switching on the morning news. News anchor Tom Argus recapped the hot story. "Everyone is describing yesterday's bombshell announcement at the WEDGE in Montreal as extraordinary. For more on the promise of life everlasting, we go live to Brian Sawyer at the WEDGE."

A ruddy-complexioned Brian Sawyer faced the camera, the WEDGE, like a toppled obelisk, jutted from the velvety green lawn directly behind him. "Just when you think you've heard all the news there is from Dr. Lanning Balcourt, he shocks you with yet another breathtaking announcement."

Sawyer turned toward the WEDGE. The broadcast continued in voice-over as the camera zoomed in for a close-up, then slowly panned across the shiny black facade, lingering on the fountain at the front of the building. "This time, Tom, Balcourt and Nakasone have truly outdone themselves. A crowd over one million strong has assembled on the lawns here to get a glimpse of the man credited with conquering death—the world's first truly immortal human being."

Lane poured his coffee as the door's laser light flashed. "I'll be right there," he said, looking at the image of Masako that had appeared in a small corner window of his screen. As he opened the door, she just stood there, wordless.

Lane led her inside and closed the door. Masako gripped his hands. "Lane. Your dream. It's our dream. I was there with you, inside the dream, last night. I've been with you in the desert. I've seen the man in the robe."

Lane leaned toward her.

"I know who you are." Her voice was low. "Do you?"

Slowly, he nodded.

"I've been in your dream with you. I know what it means."

He held her face in his hands. "Then you also know what you must do."

Chapter

14

Vatican City
November 3, 2065

Carla reached for the control wand and reset the microdisc for the third time. This interview between the psychiatrist and Dr. Balcourt was disturbing. She shook her head. Lifting the wand from her mattress, she fast-forwarded to the end of the interview. Lane now sat on the edge of his bed. His eyes were wide, his expression radiant.

"I am the true light of the world. Through me, through pride, reason, intellect, we will finally slay man's blind hope, finally slay man's vain heart. What else is it to imagine life beyond the grave if not ignorance and vanity? We are men. *This* is our paradise. God is dead! I *am!*"

Carla stopped the disc and reached for the COM panel at her bedside. "Get me Archbishop Alejandro

Torrez." After a moment Torrez appeared before her on the screen.

"I've finished the microdisc of Lane's psych battery. You need to get out here right away, Alejandro."

"Then it is as you had feared?" His face wrinkled in weariness and concern.

"Worse. I assure you, the issue is not medical or ethical or even moral. The issue *is* spiritual—and serious. I believe . . . the *Beast* . . . is among us." Carla looked lamentably at Lane's image on the screen of the disc player, the tiny hairs of her skin standing slowly under a macabre, crawling chill. Kazaz pressed on. "And if they oppose you?"

Lane's voice continued in the background. "Then I will leave behind me a shining path."

"I'll leave now," Torrez said. "I'll speak to Verrechio as soon as we're finished here. When I get there, I want you to bring your documents and this case before the curia."

"I'll be ready."

▼

The microdisc had haunted Carla throughout the night. She twisted in the covers, waking several times to the sound of her own beating heart and the persistent memory of her darkest thoughts regarding Dr. Lanning Balcourt. Does the Beast *know* he's the Beast?

Finally, toward morning, she slept, and the nightmare began.

Before her eyes she beholds an ancient, knotted tree. She watches, unnerved, as the tangled branches begin to move, writhing in slow, seductive motion like a gloomy coral hand against the tide. Overhead, appearing and then disappearing behind the wispy clouds, cycles of a lightless moon begin to shift in rapid succession across its face, rendering it a faint flickering beacon as it shines down upon the shimmering leaves.

Light without illumination.

Carla can see Lane clearly, leaning against the tree's twisted trunk. Slowly, deliberately, he peels off his own dead skin down around his neck like a snake, pridefully careful to keep his molt in one continuous sheet. She moves closer, compelled by something deep within her own nature.

Three faces hang loose at his chest like a discarded carnival mask, revealing glistening new facial tissue. Lane just sits there, alert, alone, intent on picking himself, peeling the old skin now beneath his collarbones. Looking up, he sees Carla and chortles through an ugly smile. Gripping the discarded flesh like a furtive three-headed dog between his jagged yellow teeth, he tears it loose with one violent jerk of his head and offers it to her with twisted fingers.

"Hey! . . . Carla! . . . Carla!" She turns and sees another figure, a child kneeling in prayer. Eddie! She feels the sudden sting of tears; her face is wet. She leans down toward the child as Lane's shrill laughter fades behind the child's melodic canticles from the first epistle of John. "I write unto you . . . and ye have overcome the wicked one. Love not the world, neither the things that are in the world. If any man love the world, the love of the Father is not in him."

Chapter

15

Montreal, Quebec
November 5, 2065

Henri leaned despairingly against the kitchen counter, his arms across his chest. In his fatherhood he had sometimes felt omnipotence, sometimes futility. This was definitely one of those futile moments. He wanted to grab his daughter by the scruff of her neck and shake some sense into her. Carla had said that he couldn't stop it, that it was too late. But by all that is holy in this world, he *would* stop it. *I got us into this mess—I will get us out!*

"There's nothing to say." Masako stood regal and still, the outline of her white lace camisole showing faintly through her silky white gauze t-shirt.

"You'll stand here and tell me what is going on!" It was not what he wanted to say. He didn't know how to say anything. Henri just clenched his teeth. His face suddenly felt hot.

Masako took her hands out of the back pockets of her jeans. She held his gaze as she lifted her hair off her neck and twisted it into a knot. She had suspected all along that her father wouldn't understand. They had never thought the same way, not really. Goals, aspirations—how could he see the world the way she did? She didn't need his blessing. But she would not be called a fool. Hers was a loftier plane than her father had even thought possible. Here she was, in love with the holiest man who'd ever lived—a man greater than any leader, anyone who had gone before. She understood. She had her craft. Her own life was now a part of this new life, and she would nurture it.

"Just wait—right here." She finished with her hair and pointed her finger at her father.

Moments later, she returned, carrying a dog-eared copy of the *Nag-Hamadi* scrolls, the *Gnostic Gospels*. "Listen," she commanded. Still standing, she began to read: "'Jesus saw infants being suckled. He said to his disciples, "These infants being suckled are like those who enter the kingdom." They said to him, "Shall we, then, as children, enter the kingdom?" Jesus said to them, "When you make the two one, and when you make the inside like the outside and the outside like the inside, and the above like the below, and when you make the male and the female one and the same . . . then you will enter the kingdom." '

She closed the book and looked emphatically at her father. "Don't you see? The kingdom has come—*now*, because of you and Lane and . . . *this*." She shook mildly before him. "This isn't about children. Don't you see? It's a metaphor—above, below, inside, outside, the two as one—it's a *metaphor for eternity*. This is our *moment!* Thanks to you, we can now do this!"

Henri looked at his daughter in disbelief and sadness. "What has he done to you?"

Masako quoted Lane's favorite biblical passage, "'The kingdom is spread out upon the earth and men do not see it.'"

"I didn't raise you like this."

"No, you raised me to think for myself. And I love you for that. This is what I think; it's what I know."

"Masako," his voice rose, "you have placed your soul in mortal danger!"

"It's *not* in mortal danger. I'm building a new world . . . a better world. Try to understand."

"Masako," he growled. Suddenly, unexpectedly, his eyes filled with tears. He wanted to control his voice, to make her understand, but the words seemed to ignite in his throat and explode. "I *forbid* you to see him!" he screamed. "Do you understand?"

Henri left the kitchen; in the den, he paced.

Masako burst into tears; she followed right behind him. "I don't understand you. There's nothing wrong with what you've done—you've just got to do more!"

"Enough!"

"Do you mean to tell me that if you were walking along a street and you saw someone choking to death, you wouldn't even stop and try to save him?"

"Masako, just what is it you think I've been doing my entire life?" Henri's voice trembled.

"I know, Dad. That's why Lane is . . . is *evangelizing* your work."

Henri rose, still shaking. "Stay away from that man! He has changed you, poisoned you—you've become part of his sickness. He's not even a . . . a human being."

"He's the future, Dad." She wiped her face and tried to collect herself. "And I'm part of that. I'm going to have the same procedure."

"Enough, I said!" Henri shouted, his face now flushed. "That's it! Do you hear me? There will be no more procedures! I will not do them!"

Masako watched her father in disbelief. She stood against his rage as if it were a gale-force wind. When he finished, she looked at him in pain and bewilderment. "You're so wrong." Her voice trembled as she held back her tears. "Sandy's going to train an entire surgical team to perform the transfers without you."

"What?" He stepped back; her words slapped him in the face.

"You can't stop this."

▼

Henri raised his hand to the laser scanner and stormed into Lane's apartment unannounced. Lane, sitting at his computer, raised his head, startled. "Henri'san!" He laughed in relief.

Henri reached across Lane's desk and grabbed him by the collar. "What is going on? We have been through too much! Too many years!"

Lane looked at Henri's hands, then met his gaze incredulously. "What are you talking about?" Slowly he pried Henri's hands off his collar and stepped out from behind his desk.

"I want to know," Henri struggled to get his voice under control, "I want to know about this other surgical team. And I want to know what you've done to my daughter."

"Henri, settle down," Lane said, totally baffled by his friend. "First of all, Henri'san, we simply *must* train another team. You know that as well as I do."

"But what that team will be doing seems to vary depending on who you're talking to. There seem to be three separate versions here; yours, mine, and Sandy's," Henri said.

"Henri—"

"Or, for that matter, my twenty-five-year-old daughter's." Henri stepped toward Lane.

"Look, I'll level with you. Sandy's contacts in Rome aren't happy delaying the pope's transfer. They want the procedure done, and they want it done soon. They don't think you can be trusted."

"And what do you think?" Henri's eyes narrowed.

"I think we need to resolve our differences."

"That is no longer possible."

"I'm serious. I think we all need to sit down and air this thing out. It serves no one's interest for us to be at each other's throats."

"Live and let live." Henri's tone was sarcastic.

"We both know that I wouldn't be alive if it weren't for you. I can never repay you, I realize that. But I can't sacrifice who I am—not to you, not to anyone. We've been working on this project for fifteen years."

Henri leaned into Lane's face. "I *know* that. And I also know deception when I see it."

"What are you talking about?" Lane stepped back.

"Your meetings behind my back, your insistence on making inflammatory public announcements, your plans—your delusions. This most unsubtle subterfuge of yours."

"*Delusions,* Henri?"

Henri stepped closer. "Yes. Your sick, messianic delusions."

"That's what they said to Jesus."

"You are *obsessed.*" Henri removed his glasses and wiped his brow with the back of his hand. Something in Lane's passive expression seemed to ignite his rage. "Why do you have to *push?*" He shoved Lane hard at the center of his chest.

Lane reeled and then caught his balance. "Obsessed? We've conquered death. I won't stand by and watch political hacks turn this into a luxury for the privileged few. Yes, I'm obsessed—and maybe that's a blessing." Lane grabbed Henri's shoulders and squeezed him, looking him dead in the eye.

"Henri—the world *must* change! There is no ethical high ground in death. None, Henri." Lane's eyes implored as he continued: *"Think!*—you, a surgeon, of all people, should know that."

"Get your hands *off* me!" Henri jerked his arms away and glared at his colleague. "Lane, listen. Listen to me very carefully. *Leave my daughter alone!*" He emphasized each word pointedly.

Lane shook his head. "Look at yourself. You're a pathetic old man. I'm the one with the transfer, and you're the one with the personality change. It's as if I don't know you."

Henri squeezed his hands into fists. "Stay away from her, Lane." His voice, low and tight, was a constricted growl.

Lane paused, then smiled. "I have a great deal to offer her."

"You would consider performing a transfer on my daughter against my wishes?" He swung his fist hard at Lane's face.

Lane jerked back, but not far enough. Henri's blow glanced off Lane's jaw, tearing his bottom lip. A trickle of blood appeared in the corner of his mouth. Lane lunged forward and gripped his hands tight around Henri's neck. Lane's eyes seemed afire as he overpowered his older friend and shook him violently, growling.

"Is *this* what you want, Henri?" Lane asked breathlessly as he squeezed Henri's throat with both hands. Henri's face turned red, then pale. His knees buckled beneath him.

"What are you thinking about now?" Lane asked, his expression demonic. "Will I kill you? Do you want to die?" Lane asked, licking his lips as if his own words were nectar. He seemed to take a perverse delight in this newfound power. He squeezed sadistically his friend's fleshy neck. Henri started to gurgle. His eyes bulged, bloodshot, teary, the veins in his aged face engorged, his lips blue.

Lane bent down over his friend, choking him with all his might, laughing. "It . . . would . . . be . . . so . . . easy," he said, suddenly releasing his grip.

Henri collapsed to the floor, still choking, gasping for air, coughing. *This is no longer the man I once knew. This . . . this corrupt beast . . . has fallen into vanity.*

"You see, there's nothing glorious about death—or we wouldn't fight it so hard." He stepped back to give Henri room to stand. "Quit trying to be the hero, Henri. You don't want to die any more than the rest of us. Look at me; look on my beauty. *I* will help you ascend; *I* will teach you to be like the Most High!"

Lane watched, darkly energized, as Henri staggered to his feet. The surgeon seemed like an old man as he turned and left the room without a word.

▼

"I don't want you to be sad." Masako folded a heavy sweater into her suitcase. Henri stood watching her pack her bags, his hand self-consciously rubbing his own neck.

"Don't go," Henri said, thickly. "He has become evil."

Masako closed her bags and looked imploringly at her father. For a moment, her eyes filled. Then she lifted the bag and walked toward the door. "Daddy, I love you."

The words stung him. Speechless, hands in pockets, feeling desperately sick inside, he watched his daughter leave the apartment.

▼

Lane stood on the rooftop and inhaled deeply. Chanting, anxiety, chaos, rose from the crowd in a dark wave of crackling primal energy. He closed his eyes for a moment, then turned and went back inside, the smell of wood smoke lingering in his nostrils as he made his way to the elevator and then down to Sandy's office. He thought about Henri. *Just can't see the big picture. . . . Master of detail. . . . Can't seize the full scope.*

Lane paced through the corridors. He held the image of Masako in his mind. *Masako,* something within him seemed to take flight at the sound of her name.

"Evening, Dr. Balcourt," somebody said. Lane nodded.

He reached Sandy's office and went inside. She sat at her desk, engrossed in a conversation with Cardinal Verrechio. She turned to see Lane walk in, greeting him with a smile.

"I heard," she said, when Verrechio's hologram disappeared. "Masako's really upset."

Lane nodded. "She's concerned about her father."

"I don't understand why he's being so difficult," Sandy said.

Lane took a chair. "It's this foolish faith of his—we really shouldn't be surprised. Think about it, Sandy, he's reacting exactly as always."

Sandy looked at him.

"This is Henri. We have had a continuing argument since we first got together." Lane took a stack of documents from Sandy. "You know as well as I do that he's a very methodical guy. He's got his eye on the needle's point, the finest detail. What makes matters worse is he tries to balance his whole life by this spirit-minded superstition of his. He never thought we'd move this fast—it scares him, plain and simple."

Sandy chuckled. "You're right. You're right. I guess I've been ducking him for just that reason. He's lost objectivity. I don't think he can stand outside his own fears on this. And with you two coming to blows—who can deal with that?"

"Someone once said," Lane answered, "it is expedient to lose one man so that many might be saved."

Chapter

16

Vatican City/Montreal, Quebec
November 7, 2065

"Why are you so upset by all this? You should be ecstatic," Masako had said.

In his mind, Henri could still see the pained, bewildered look on his daughter's face. He had not expected her calm. Confused, he returned the microdisc of Lane's transfer surgery to its jacket and looked at Carla. There was an order and constancy about her that he found reassuring, almost peaceful. His gaze settled on her dark clear eyes, for a moment he wished his own daughter had this inexplicable strength, this center in Christ.

"I can't seem to get through to any of these people. The transfer worked, that's all they care about. It doesn't seem to matter to them that you've got to literally kill the patient first."

256

"That seems pretty obvious to me." Carla wiped the sweat that had beaded on her brow. Her dark suit amplified her suddenly ashen expression. "I've got to show this to the members of the curia. I don't think they realize—"

"All right," Henri cut in, his words edged with fear and anger. "So they watch it. And let's say you are right, and they realize that it's just too dangerous to go ahead with." Henri stood and paced the room, his face drawn. "So we successfully prevent the pope's transfer—prevent my *daughter's* transfer . . . But what about the next group? What about somebody else's daughter?"

"We'll go to the media, the government. Someone, somewhere in a position of power will listen."

Henri turned on her. "That is a naïve view. We are not dealing with a renegade scientist in some backwoods laboratory. We are dealing with an *immortal,* maybe the most brilliant man who's ever drawn breath. Believe me, he can be very persuasive—and he has forever to make his case. How long before he has the world's top politicians in his pocket? And what about the next pope? Or the next? I am telling you, if there were any other way, I'd find it."

▼

"My friend."

Carla looked around the table at the unreadable faces—so many cardinals and bishops here, awaiting her report. She had told them it was urgent. She met

Torrez' gaze. His words, whispered to her in the hall, came back to her again. "I have faith in you, my daughter."

The time had come. Her palms were moist, her mouth felt dry. Slowly, she reached for her Bible. For an instant, her hands seemed no longer her own.

▼

This brings back memories, Henri thought as he quietly stepped into the darkened lab. *Three A.M. Work fast.* His pulse quickened as the lights blinked on, one panel at a time, until the entire lab was awash in brilliant white "Naturalight." Henri squinted. The old experiments lab had always been an exciting place for the team, he recalled, as his eyes adjusted to the ersatz lighting. This old lab was where their dreams had first taken wing—it had both teased and tortured them.

Henri removed his glasses and rubbed twice his eyes. How many years had he and Lane dreamed of a lab like this? He placed his glasses low on his nose and moved deliberately to the workbench at the far end of the room. It was strange. What had once seemed so miraculous now almost looked rustic, quaint. *Fragments of the past,* he thought, *another lifetime.* His gaze scanned the polymer litter strewn across the benchtop.

▼

Cardinal Verrechio rapped his gavel against its block and addressed the curia. "I'm afraid Dr. MacGregor has uncovered some disturbing information." He nodded in her direction. "If she's correct, it calls our attention to the coming of the Prince of the Apostasy. This Destroyer, in our time, prophesied over two thousand years ago, seems to be linked . . ." he paused, scanning the faces of those assembled, then let his last words drop into the silence, "to the work being done by the Balcourt/Nakasone research team."

The assembly stirred uncomfortably. The capital invested in the Balcourt/Nakasone project on behalf of the Roman Church by its agents in Geneva had reached staggering proportions. It was incomprehensible how the Church could survive such a loss with its treasury intact. A whirlwind of whispers circled the room, a tangle of low voices, faces turned in shock and surprise. Carla searched Torrez' eyes for understanding. His thoughts were on the Liberation. *Would there be no treasury left to divide?*

▼

Henri thought about Lane. They had once shared the same dream. *Or was it the same dream?* The overhead lights flickered. Shadows played across the wall; the once-familiar lab seemed strange, awash in some harsh new light. Henri drew a breath. Abruptly, he saw his wife's grave, then his daughter, her bag in her hand, leaving . . .

He ran his hand across the workbench and adjusted the light. Situating his glasses again, he stepped over to the refrigerator and took out a covered Pyrex dish. The label was clearly marked: "Polymer Substrate." He forced his hands to be steady. *Hard to let go.* He brought the glass basin back to the far bench and set it down gently, before fumbling with the notes he'd made at the apartment.

▼

Carla held the worn, black leatherbound book in her hands. Before her eyes, the print seemed to smear, then clarify. For a moment, she tried to pray. Instead, strange words from an obscure essay raced through her mind. "Not nature, but the 'genius of mankind,' has knotted the hangman's noose with which it can execute itself at any moment."

Jung again, she remembered now. That little book Reb had told her about: *Answer to Job.*

Cardinal Verrechio nodded to her. She stepped forward, acknowledging him, and, as if from a distance, heard her voice begin to read from Scripture *in benedictio.*

"Before I begin, I'd like to read from Paul's first epistle to the Corinthians, chapter 13:

> Though I speak with the tongues of men and of angels, but have not love, I have become sounding brass or a clanging cymbal. And though I have the gift of prophecy, and understand all mysteries and all knowledge, and though I have all faith, so that I could remove mountains, but have not love, I am nothing. And though I bestow all my goods to feed the poor, and though I give my body to be burned, but have not love, it profits me nothing. Love suffers long and is kind; love does not envy; love does not parade itself, is not puffed up; does not behave

rudely; does not seek its own, is not provoked, thinks no evil; does not rejoice in iniquity, but rejoices in the truth; bears all things, believes all things, hopes all things, endures all things. Love never fails. But whether there are prophecies, they will fail; whether there are tongues, they will cease; whether there is knowledge, it will vanish away. For we know in part and we prophesy in part. But when that which is perfect has come, then that which is in part will be done away. When I was a child, I spoke as a child, I understood as a child, I thought as a child; but when I became a man, I put away childish things. For now we see in a mirror, dimly, but then face to face. Now I know in part, but then I shall know just as I also am known. And now abide faith, hope, love, these three; but the greatest of these is love."

Silence took the room.

"Does not parade itself . . . does not seek its own," Carla repeated under her breath.

"The only way to stop this from moving ahead is to take out the computer system behind it. No more Solar 2000, no more transfers. That blow alone would cause them a very painful, very expensive delay. Maybe it would buy us some time—show the world how dangerous this procedure really is." Henri had watched the young woman for a nod of understanding. There before

him was this woman of uncanny Christian faith, his only ally.

"And show them how vulnerable the system is at the same time," Carla had smiled timidly. "What about Lane? He'd just do it again. Believe me, the Vatican coffers are deep. You said it yourself, he's got all the time in the world."

"He's got to be stopped too."

A look of horror had spread across her face, "You mean . . . kill him?" she had whispered. "We can't do that."

Henri had dodged her question, narrowing his eyes. He answered in the oblique. "That may be a question of semantics. In a way, I suppose that you could say the man is dead already."

"I mean, as Christians we can't do that, Henri. The computer, okay; but Lane—we just can't. Don't you see?"

"Then what do you suggest?"

Carla's answer had come without hesitation. "We pray. It's out of our hands."

▼

Carla cleared her throat and read on. "And from the book of Revelation, chapter 12:

Now a great sign appeared in heaven: a woman clothed with the sun, with the moon under her feet, and on her head a garland of twelve stars. Then being with child, she cried out in her labor and in pain to give birth. And another sign appeared in heaven: behold, a great, fiery red dragon having seven heads and ten horns, and seven diadems on his heads. His tail drew a third of the stars of heaven and threw them to the earth. And the dragon stood before the woman who was ready to give birth, to devour her Child as soon as it was born."

Carla turned a page. The rustling paper seemed unusually loud. Around her, the faces blurred. Again, as if it did not belong to her, she heard her voice read on. "'She bore a male Child who was to rule all nations with a rod of iron. And her Child was caught up to God and His throne.'"

She looked up. Someone was speaking.

Henri's voice had been taut and loud. "They have got to be stopped. This transfer procedure is too dangerous. Lane thinks he's the Second Coming. Add that to the fact that the Church is behind it financially and—frankly, I am frightened, really frightened."

"I'll go to Rome," Carla had told him. "I'll make them see."

Henri snapped back to the present. His hands began to sweat. *Chilled substrate . . . more stable.* He closed his eyes to clear them before he read his notes again. *A cookbook,* he told himself. *Just like a cookbook.* He had told himself this as a student. He'd wanted it to be right then. It had to be right, now.

Akirame . . . this stuff isn't like ordinary plastique. Wouldn't want to use this as sterno. Could be worse . . . could be like nitro. More stable than that. Must rig blasting caps once it reaches plastic stage. It's not going to blow up in my face. Akirame . . . you won't help anyone if you blow yourself up while you're cooking it, Henri'san.

Again, his thoughts went to Martha, then Masako. *The clicks of locks on suitcases, on doors, on the coffin. Silent exits, empty closets.*

Henri nervously adjusted the lamp over the lab counter. Carefully, he measured the proper amount of solvent into a wide-bottomed flask. He swirled it gently, watching the liquid change color from clear to cobalt blue. *Copper,* he confirmed with a nod, returning the flask to the bench top.

▼

"Then the woman fled into the wilderness, where she has a place prepared by God, that they should feed her there one thousand two hundred and sixty days."

Carla paused for a moment. She looked up at the assembly of cardinals and bishops and tried to read their faces, each one different—proud, suspicious, angry, moved, perplexed, knowing, fearful.

Knowledge, she thought as she studied Torrez' disappointed gaze. *The only knowledge worth possessing, that being a union with God.* Her mind flashed briefly back on her friend Reb. *Who was his god? Psychologism?*

She drew in a deep breath. Their most recent debate on the meaning of death lingered abstractly in her mind. She remembered it now as one would be prompted to recall a meal by the lingering presence of the bitter stomach that followed it. *Bitter in the belly.*

Her mind returned to the task at hand. She lowered her head and read further from her Bible, as if reading it had fortified her somehow.

"And war broke out in heaven: Michael and his angels fought with the dragon; and the dragon and his angels fought, but they did not prevail, nor was a place found for them in heaven any longer. So the great dragon was cast out, that serpent of old, called the Devil and Satan, who deceives the whole world; he was cast to the earth, and his angels were cast out with him. Then I heard a loud voice saying in heaven, 'Now salvation, and strength, and the kingdom of our God, and the power of His Christ have come, for the accuser of our brethren, who accused them before our God day and night, has been cast down. And they overcame him by the blood of the Lamb and by the word of their testimony, and they did not love their lives to the death.'"

▼

Lord, I know you command that we should love our neighbor and that included in this commandment is the requirement that we must love also our enemies. Yet, how can I love this Beast who would inflame the entire world with his corruption?

Henri carefully weighed out the proper amount of nitrate. He stepped back from the bench and added the nitrate crystals to the solvent, swirling the solution until it began to thicken. Now all memories were far from him. Only this task, these crystals, his training—only these were in his mind.

He returned the flask to the bench and looked down at his notes. *Sukoshi*—a little bit, he thought as he poured the thickened solution into the basin containing the gelatinous polymer substrate. A thickened blob the color of blood oozed out of the flask.

He placed the mixture into the cooler and set the timer. Twenty minutes and he'd have himself one powerful plastique: Ten times more powerful than TNT for the same weight. This particular batch would take care of things quite nicely. *Take . . . care.* Henri sat down on the floor and drew his feet up underneath him.

I love you, Daddy. He leaned his head back and closed his eyes. Haltingly, he tried to preserve the warm, loving feelings and affections he felt for his daughter, setting aflame these endearments of his heart until they rose like spiritual incense upon which he might set his soul to drift, lifting above his worldly burdens until he felt himself once again in the presence of the Lord.

▼

Verrechio stood and quieted the assembly with a wave of his hands. Carla gathered the papers into a neat pile in front of her and closed her eyes. *Lord, help me.* A tingling sensation started in her stomach as nervous butterflies spread throughout her body. She began to feel light-headed; the room seemed to pulse. The assembly erupted again in argument. Faces turned, bodies leaned forward and recoiled, some punctuated their words with their hands, others jerked and snapped about as if they were catching flies. She listened to the words echo in her mind, unable to make out the individual voices.

▼

The timer bell made Henri start. Instantly, he was on his feet. He leaned over, opened the cooler, and withdrew the basin. *Akirame, Henri'san . . . Akirame.* He swallowed nervously, picked up a thin metal spatula from the benchtop, used it to free the plastic mass from the side of its container, and inverted the basin. The block of newly formed plastique dropped to the benchtop with a thud. He tested it with an uneager finger—slippery, cold, clammy.

About six sticks, he figured, dividing the block in his mind. *This will certainly be enough . . . more than enough.*

Henri leaned over the bench. *This is it,* he thought, walking over to the translucent body parts that hung upon the wall. He sorted through the limbs until he found a forearm mold approximately the size of his own, slightly larger, and then brought it to the workbench.

The procedure of cutting the block and shaping it into a thin cast that fit around his own arm took nearly an hour. The plastique had lost much of its former elasticity. In the end it felt reluctant, like drying sculptor's clay. He marveled at how quickly the compound had changed consistency.

Unpredictable. Henri shook his head. *A warrior must be . . . unpredictable.*

The mold formed a thin cast that would allow him to smuggle the explosives under his clothing past the laser scanners in the computer lab. He slid his arm into the cast and allowed his arm to drop to his side.

Looking up, he caught his own reflection in the mirrored glass that formed the perimeter of the experiments lab. He looked pale, overtired. A thin film of sweat covered his face. He checked his watch: 4:30 A.M.

▼

Carla looked anxiously around the room. Faces, statues, and murals blurred. A low murmuring filled her ears. *It effectively kills the soul! . . . mortal sin!*

She tried to read their faces; their eyes, cold, hard. *The order appointed for the procreation of children has been violated! . . . Perverted!*

"Carla!" Verrechio raised his voice slightly this second time. Carla's mind came to attention. "Now then, I think it's important to remember," he turned and scanned the faces gathered around the table, as his voice took on an admonitory tone, "that Christians have endured many storms, many wars, and spanned two millennia to come to this point. We all know the ultimate sacrifice our Lord demands."

▼

"He's late," Sandy observed, looking up impatiently from her watch. "I want to get this thing wrapped up. I've got a lot on my plate this afternoon." She stood and began to pace.

Sandy had called this meeting in her office. She wanted Henri and Lane to clear the air. "We'll have to see. Maybe I can convince Henri to concentrate on the prosthetics and therapeutics side of the business. Keep him out of the transfer loop." She paused. Her face seemed to tighten with the plaintive edge in her voice. "There's been too much accomplished—too much capital invested in this thing. Too many people have dedicated their hearts and souls to this work for me to just stand by and watch everything we've all sacrificed so much for . . . self-destruct!"

Lane gazed pensively at her.

"We're a team here. Let's start acting like one."

Those were Sandy's words. Lane felt differently. He had tried to explain it to Henri. This wasn't about business anymore. It wasn't about medicine, and it wasn't about petty arguments between the principals at the cutting edge of a new technology. The transfer procedure was the beginning of an entirely new way of life. A new age. This was humankind's destiny. Why couldn't Henri see it?

Lane quietly endured Sandy's nervous pacing. The morning light caught the glass just right, smearing prismatic colors across the floor. "I think you're wrong, Sandy. I don't think he'll change his mind."

She turned from the window. "He's worked his entire professional life on this project. I can't see him walking away from it now."

"I just wish he could drop this walk-with-God nonsense," Lane lamented.

Fatigued, Sandy leaned against the window and looked out over the complex grounds. A clutter of white arabesque tents had popped up amid the throngs. "Nobody's leaving," she muttered. A smile spread across her face. "You remember—"

The sharp tone of Henri's voice cut her words short, "This must stop!" he announced from the door.

▼

Verrechio continued, "Whether the man knows he's the Beast or doesn't know he's the Beast, it seems little matter to me. The fact remains that Dr. Lanning Balcourt, by his own hand, by his own works, has blasphemed the Holy Spirit. Surely, by his acts alone he stands condemned. There seems little doubt to me. He is become *Antichrist.*"

Again, a nervous jittering stirred through the room, a tangle of discontent.

"This," the cardinal continued, "from the book of Revelation, chapter 9: 'In those days men will seek death and will not find it; they will desire to die, and death will flee from them.'

"And from the thirteenth chapter of the same book:

Then I stood on the sand of the sea. And I saw a beast rising up out of the sea, having seven heads and ten horns, and on his horns ten crowns, and on his heads a blasphemous name. Now the beast which I saw was like a leopard, his feet were like the feet of a bear, and his mouth like the mouth of a lion. The dragon gave him his power, his throne, and great authority. I saw one of his heads as if it had been mortally wounded, and his deadly wound was healed. And all the world marveled and followed the beast. So they worshiped the dragon who gave authority to the beast; and they worshiped the beast, saying, 'Who is like the beast? Who is able to make war with him?' And he was given a mouth speaking great things and blasphemies, and he was given authority to continue forty-two months. Then he opened his mouth in blasphemy against God, to blaspheme His name, His tabernacle, and those who dwell in heaven. It was granted to him to make war with the saints and to overcome them. And authority was given him over every tribe, tongue, and nation. All who dwell on the earth will worship him, whose names have not been written in the Book of Life of the Lamb slain from the foundation of the world."

▼

"We were going to start without you." Sandy forced a smile.

Henri solemnly closed the office door behind him; Sandy and Lane exchanged glances. Henri walked to Sandy's desk.

"Henri, are you feeling all right?" Sandy asked, her eyes moving from Henri to Lane and back again.

Lane sensed something wrong. "Henri, why don't you sit down. You don't look well."

"I'm not." He looked at them. "I'm not well," he said again, without moving. His face seemed to flush as he spoke, *"This . . .* is going to stop. *Ima! Now!"*

Sandy looked at him. "What are you talking about?"

Lane squinted through the afternoon sun, searching Henri.

"I am putting an end to this man's perverted vision of the future." Henri pointed at Lane. "I cannot . . . *will not* . . . stand by . . . and allow you to murder *innocents* in the name of vanity." Henri's eyes were fixed on Lane. "You have become wicked! You have changed the truth into a lie!"

▼

Verrechio turned briefly and looked with a new and patient understanding at Carla. A benign smile abruptly vanished from his face.

"And he deceives those who dwell on the earth by those signs which he was granted to do in the sight of the beast, telling those who dwell on the earth to make an image to the beast who was wounded by the sword and lived. He was granted power to give breath to the image of the beast, that the image of the beast should both speak and cause as many as would not worship the image of the beast to be killed."

"We have precious little time," the cardinal said when he had finished reading. His tone was somber.

"What are we to do then?" came the group's fragmented response, again turning their minds to earthly politics. "We must pray intently, with devotion. We must give testimony! We shall lift up our voices as one against all who dare drive this pernicious wedge into the mystical body of Christ!"

The cardinal fixed his eyes on Carla and cast about in his heart for the correct reply. Then came the words, not entirely his own, "With . . . news of these developments, comes this reality. We are highly favored; the end times are upon us. We are soon to be in the glorious presence of our Lord. Let us prepare the way."

Verrechio's first conscious impulse was to read from the Gospel of Luke, chapter 1, and as he did, his skin began to tingle.

> "And having come in, the angel said to her, 'Rejoice, highly favored one, the Lord is with you; blessed are you among women!' But when she saw him, she was troubled at his saying, and considered what manner of greeting this was. Then the angel said to her, 'Do not be afraid, Mary, for you have found favor with God. And behold, you will conceive in your womb and bring forth a Son, and shall call His name JESUS. He will be great, and will be called the Son of the Highest; and the Lord God will give Him the throne of His father David. And He will reign over the house of Jacob forever, and of His kingdom there will be no end.' Then Mary said to the angel, 'How can this be, since I do not know a man?' And the angel answered and said to her, 'The Holy Spirit will come upon you, and the power of the Highest will overshadow you; therefore, also, that Holy One who is to be born will be called the Son of God.'"

Carla raised her voice in prayer at the cardinal's reading of the Gospel. She felt a total abandonment of joy and exaltation overcome her. These words she could not stop: "God is a Spirit, and they that worship Him must worship in spirit and in truth . . . He has revealed Himself in the person of Jesus Christ—the revelation of love on earth . . . How can we love Him unless we know this? . . . And unless we know this, how can we love at all?"

She closed her eyes and tried to imagine drifting in the Lord's mild gaze. His eyes perfect like stars, His face radiant. With wide open arms, He smiled at her. She felt the bliss of His countenance, felt His Light drawing near. Drawing near. Drawing near. He, the Light of light, in which there was no darkness. She wept, fulfilled, kissed, complete, even in the anticipation of His glory.

The mood in the room was suddenly electric, filled with silent anticipation. *"Christ is come."*

Verrechio wanted to speak, but he could not. He felt the tears welling deep inside himself. Again, his body began to tingle. A cool breeze swirled around him, swirled around the room; at the back of his neck he felt his hair rise and stand on end. He tried, but he could not speak. What was the very best of all their faith, all their hope, all their love, seemed to swell; something wondrous began to move and grow outside them all.

Then a voice, clear, almost musical, "The prophecy has been fulfilled."

Carla smiled. For a moment a sublime majesty, warmth—like boundless lovingkindness—radiated through the room. *"He* has slain the Beast."

Somehow, Verrechio knew it was true, but still, something in his nature made him ask, "How?" The word rang flat, like doubt, empty of courage, foul and ugly in the air.

Verrechio looked into Carla's shining eyes and smiled. She raised her eyes worshipfully above her.

Something made her speak, *"Abba, Adonai."* She turned back to Verrechio, her expression inspired. "With . . . *His Breath . . .* "

The last word came from her lips like a great lifting up of heavenly voices, a fragrant, heart-piercing angelic aria, a divine symphony of light and sound and color, like wind and rain and ocean and tears and sunlight, moving, yet still, as if all the celestial music from all the planets and all the stars seemed nothing more than a mere fluttering of wings by comparison. Then there was an ignition of God-like brilliance, an epiphany. It filled the room like great billowing sheets of fire and hung in the air, shimmering like the northern lights—white and rose and blue and indigo . . .

Sandy edged toward Henri as Lane began to speak. "Henri, you're stressed," Lane was saying. "We've all been through a lot."

Henri checked his watch. He jerked his head up and met Lane's gaze. A moment passed. And then the first explosion rocked the office sending a jagged fracture like lightning through the face of the plate glass window.

"First, your *prized* computer," Henri said, answering the horrified expressions that appeared with the concussion of the blast. His eyes narrowed into slits.

Sandy screamed, her eyes wide, "Henri! Do you realize what you've done? That computer is directly beneath the chemical storage tanks!" Panicked, she turned to Lane. "This place could go up like a powder keg!"

"I cannot destroy you, Lane, but I can destroy your work." Henri's expression was strained, his voice cracking and tight. His face was wet, tears dropping suddenly onto his chest. His voice stuttered as he continued, "I know who you are, Lanning Balcourt."

Instantly, a blinding white light shot through the window, bleaching color from everything in the room. Sandy raised her voice over the strange, choirlike noise that seemed to come through the glass, her hands a blur over the COM panel on her desk. "I can't get through! We've got to evacuate!" She came out from behind her desk. "Get him out of here!" she said, running to the door.

Henri continued, unimpeded, "You are a false god. You would destroy the world by drowning all of us in mere consciousness and rationality. And those who worship you will surely lose their souls. I will not worship you, Lane. You I will not follow. My soul belongs to Christ!"

Dropping to his knees, Henri lifted his eyes above, held his hands out open before him, and began to pray aloud, tearfully, "Lord, I am weak! Help me! You have created me for Yourself; let Your will be done unto me now! Nothing I could do of my own account could possibly merit Your grace; I have neither created myself nor can I save myself, but by Your gift, but by Your love, but by Your mercy! You alone are good! You alone are great!"

"What are you doing? You poor, simpering fool!" Lane laughed over Henri's words.

Henri continued, not heeding Lane's words, "Nothing I could know, even if I knew all that is, could move me even a breath beyond the radiance of Your face! Help us, O Lord, that we might be redeemed from our foolish pride! Remove this dark wedge from our hearts that we might be redeemed from our cynicism, that we might be made courageous in our faith, bold in our charity, saved from the living death of our own self-importance. Lord, I am not worthy to oppose so great a foe . . . "

"Henri . . . stop!" Lane moved closer. "You're embarrassing yourself. Think about it," Lane held his arms out wide, "*we* are the perfection of the universe!"

Henri continued to pray. Lane inched closer. Finally, standing before Henri, Lane screamed, "There is no God!"

Lane's hand came fast and hard across Henri's face. Henri fell back, stunned, then dropped to his knees again and prayed.

"You old fool, you've lost your mind!" Lane raised his voice over Henri's prayers. "Open your eyes. There is no God but me!"

Again, Lane slapped Henri's face, this time leaving a bright red imprint on Henri's flesh. Henri wept, refusing to stop.

"*I* am! Do you hear me? *I* am! *Me! Me! Me!*" Lane screamed maniacally over Henri's prayers, slapping Henri again and again, harder and harder as he spat each syllable.

The office door burst open. "Lane—*don't!*" Masako screamed as she ran toward her father.

Bewildered, Henri hesitated, started to get up.

Lane attacked.

Henri caught Lane's full weight chest-high just as his daughter reached him, grabbing him around the waist. All three stumbled backward. Henri struggled to keep his footing, but the weight of the two bodies shoved him hard against the fractured glass. For a moment, each saw it as if under water, slow, so . . . slow—the ice-like splintering of the glass, the oddly beautiful opening, the earth veering toward them and then the light, the light, the light. The last explosion came before they hit the ground, vaporizing their bodies like breath into a clotted blood-red mist.

Then there was a great shimmering in the sky, and all unfulfilled potential dropped like lightning from the heavens and there was potential no more—only a great lifting up of voices filling the air.

▼

Our souls do magnify the Lord. The room filled with a strange interlacing geometry of light. The walls seemed to disappear. Verrechio felt emotionally charged, humbled, as if he were a child beneath the waves, watching the buoyant play of the sun on the surface of the undulant tide.

Gradually, the light shifted, changed from white and blue and indigo, to white and blue, then blue alone—azure. A magenta-white star-like cluster hovered above the head of the table where Carla sat. It seemed to unfold, like a luminous zygote in cell division, a human egg gradually growing larger and larger. A feeling of warmth and joy and communion moved throughout the room. Fulfillment. Perfection.

Slowly, Verrechio regained his sense of himself, and he looked at the faces of those gathered around the table—each purged by tears; each informed by awe and wonder; each childlike, glorified, radiant. He felt connected to them, like brothers, like sisters, something resonated among them all. They were like him; he like they; each like the other; all one in mutual charity. He looked back toward the head of the table and raised his voice, "Praise the coming of the Lord!"

His voice wavered. Then, "*Alleluia Alleluia Alleluia.*"

Carla joined in prayer. "Be it unto us according to Thy Word." Something appeared from the center of the brilliant light. She blinked her eyes and struggled to clear her tears. A fiery star swirled at the back of a glorious human form, more than human, divine—Christ appearing as if on a cloud. And then a veil seemed to lift within her, as if all along she had been blind, but now she saw. And all was clear. And all was calm.

Carla smiled with the boundless joy that now fired her heart, a triumphant smile.

Verrechio choked on his tears. His breath began to stutter, never before had he been filled with so many emotions flooding his heart. Never before had he felt so great and so small at once. He felt meek, as if he were watching his own mother, himself, his wife, his daughter, his son, all the blessed children of the world that ever were or would ever be; ten thousand saints standing before him in a glorious procession of love and unity. He fell on his face and wept, enraptured, impassioned. *My God and my Lord . . . my God . . . my God . . . my God . . .*

SOLI DEO GLORIA

ABOUT THE AUTHOR

Ilow Roque is a full-time writer and a former entrepreneur who studied chemistry at Indiana University / Purdue University at Indianapolis. Prior to his writing career, Roque worked with his own options market-making trading firm on the Chicago Board Options Exchange and on the American Stock Exchange in New York. He also founded and operated as president several high tech enterprises which continue to operate internationally today. Roque now divides his time between Austin and Corpus Christi, Texas, where he lives with his wife Sheri and their four children. He is currently at work on his second novel.